He appeared to be sleeping, with his head bent over and his hands resting palms up on his thighs. His ball cap hid his face. A cloud moved across the moon, and since the streetlamp was behind him, I couldn't see well at all. "Hello? Are you all right? Just to let you know, you can't sleep in the park. The cops in this town are pretty strict about that."

Still no response. The cloud moved and the moon's light came through the trees, shining down on us. "Oh, my God," I whispered. It was the scene from the new psycho snow globe in my shop. I pinched myself to be sure I was really awake and not in the middle of a nightmare. I squeezed enough to make it hurt. Ouch.

I was afraid the man might be drunk and vulnerable to . . . whatever. I braved a step closer and then another. My pounding heart threatened to break through my chest. "Sir." I didn't want to touch him, so I picked up a stick lying by my foot and gently touched his shoulder. Instead of lifting his head, he fell forward and toppled onto the ground, landing facedown. I jumped back and then screamed.

The handle of a knife was sticking out of his back . . .

# Snow
# Way Out

CHRISTINE HUSOM

WITHDRAWN

**BERKLEY PRIME CRIME, NEW YORK**

**THE BERKLEY PUBLISHING GROUP**
**Published by the Penguin Group**
Penguin Group (USA) LLC
375 Hudson Street, New York, New York 10014

USA • Canada • UK • Ireland • Australia • New Zealand • India • South Africa • China

penguin.com

A Penguin Random House Company

SNOW WAY OUT

A Berkley Prime Crime Book / published by arrangement with the author

For information, address: The Berkley Publishing Group,
a division of Penguin Group (USA) LLC,
375 Hudson Street, New York, New York 10014.

ISBN: 978-0-425-27080-6

PUBLISHING HISTORY
Berkley Prime Crime mass-market edition / January 2015

PRINTED IN THE UNITED STATES OF AMERICA

10  9  8  7  6  5  4  3  2  1

Cover illustration by Julia Green.
Cover design by Lesley Worrell.
Interior text design by Laura K. Corless.

*To my husband, Dan,*
*who supports me in my endeavors*
*with understanding and love.*

*And to everyone who enjoys picking up a snow globe,*
*giving it a shake, and watching the snow*
*settle over the scene.*

# ACKNOWLEDGMENTS

Thank you to my agent, John Talbot, for his vision; to Michelle Vega, senior editor at The Berkley Publishing Group, for graciously taking on this new series; to her assistant, Bethany Blair; Stacy Edwards, production editor; Sheila Moody, copyeditor; and all the talented and knowledgeable people at Penguin Random House who put this book together. It was a team effort, and I appreciate and commend each one of you.

1

My friend Pinky Nelson pushed open my Curio Finds shop door with uncustomary gusto. "Jerrell Powers is back in town. I just saw him." The color on her cheeks was as rosy as her nickname, and the brown curls on her head were bouncing.

"Who's that?"

"I can't believe you sometimes, Cami. The guy who broke into Erin's house a couple of years ago and stole her grandmother's antique clock collection. He was—"

"The guy who gave me nightmares for months. Literally." Erin joined us from the coffee shop area that adjoined my shop.

Pinky waved at her. "Erin, sorry. I didn't know you were here."

I met Erin in the brick archway that divided the shops

and gave her shoulder a little squeeze. "And I'm sorry I blanked out his name for a minute. You always referred to him as—"

Erin inclined her head to the right and raised her eyebrows, alerting Pinky and me that there was someone else in the coffee shop.

I had to think fast. "—'Mr. No-Goodnik.'"

The older man standing by the former soda fountain, which now served as the coffee shop counter, lowered his cup and swallowed. "I've had a few nightmares of my own since 'Nam, and I'da come up with a better name than 'no-goodnik' for him." Archie Newberry was what some called eccentric, and others called one can short of a six-pack. I had known him since I was a child, when he moved to Brooks Landing and went to work for the city parks division. The town population thirty years before was around three thousand, and at that time everyone knew—or knew of—almost everyone else.

Especially so if there was something a little different about a person. Like Archie. He mowed the grass in the parks, cut dead branches from the trees, and talked most of the time he worked, whether there were people near enough to hear what he was saying or not. Word was Archie had been diagnosed with post-traumatic stress disorder, or PTSD, and I figured talking was his way of releasing some of that stress.

Not that I'm a psychologist. If I were, I could have set up a quiet practice somewhere. I would not have taken the job as legislative affairs director in Senator Ramona Zimmer's office, and I would not have eventually become part of an embarrassing scandal in Washington, D.C. A scandal that necessitated a hasty return to my hometown. But I did my best to limit the amount of time and energy I spent dwelling on that. And thankfully my friends and family believed and supported me and never brought it up. The truth was the truth and bygones were bygones, as far as they were concerned.

Instead, I told myself again and again that my aunt—my adoptive mother—needed me to step in and take over her business while she went through some cancer recovery treatments. And my uncle—and adoptive father—liked having me nearby. He was a basket case over Mom's illness and stayed by her side almost every waking and sleeping moment. Fifty-some years of togetherness did that to a couple.

"Well, I'm not worried about Jerrell Powers anymore." Erin raised her hands in what she called the "ready position." "My self-defense training has given me a whole new outlook and I'm prepared to take him on."

Erin was not much bigger than a minute. She had been born in Vietnam and adopted as a baby by the Vickermans. They were both medical doctors and unable to have children. Dr. Craig Vickerman was in the army reserves, and when the Vietnam War broke out, his unit was deployed to Da Nang, where he served as a surgeon at a military hospital for two years.

Shortly before he was discharged, he visited an orphanage and fell in love with a three-month-old half-Vietnamese, half-American baby girl named Han. He phoned his wife, who was over the moon with the prospect of becoming a mother. He pulled a lot of strings to get Erin to America, but having an American father meant she would not have been fully accepted in her country of birth. The Vickermans changed her first name, but kept Han as her middle name: Erin Han Vickerman.

"Holy moly, Erin, when you do that you make me feel like I need to defend myself," Pinky complained as she stepped back with her right foot, lifted her left arm as a shield, and raised her right hand like she was about to deliver a karate chop. At five foot ten, she was nearly a foot taller than Erin.

It struck me again how different the three of us looked from one another. If we stood in a lineup according to height, I would be placed in the middle of my two friends.

Pinky's facial features were on the sharp side, mostly because she was rail thin. Her cheekbones were prominent, her nose was narrow and straight, and her chin was a bit pointy. Her round, hazel eyes conveyed a sense of mischief most of the time; in my opinion, they were her best feature. And I admired her full head of unruly curls, which she kept fairly short.

Erin had more classic beauty. She had a high forehead; almond-shaped eyes; smooth, nearly flawless skin; full lips; and straight white teeth. I wondered what her father had looked like, because her Vietnamese side dominated her looks.

I made a T with my hands in a time-out gesture. "Stop it, you two. What if another customer—or someone taking the class—walked in about now? We'd scare them off for sure."

"You're right, Cam. When is the teacher supposed to be here, anyway?" Erin said and relaxed her stance.

I looked up at the pink Betty Boop ("Boop-Oop-a-Doop")

clock hanging on the wall behind the coffee shop counter. "Any minute now, I'm sure. She stopped by about an hour ago to get the supplies ready then left to run some errands." I pointed at the three square tables with gray Formica tops and metal pedestal bases in the back of the room that were decked out in snow globe–making supplies.

"I'da never thought there was such a thing as classes for teachin' a guy how to make snow globes," Archie said.

"There are classes for every kind of craft. When that woman May Gregors stopped in the shop last month and introduced herself, she told me she taught those kind of classes. I thought it would be kind of unique, since Curio Finds has about a million snow globes for sale," Pinky said.

"You've never had a class like this here before, that's for sure," Erin said.

"We've never had a class of any kind before, but it's time we start. I mean, we're all set up for it." Pinky waved in the general direction of the back tables. "We have the space, and a few extra dollars will help the business."

"In theory, anyway. By the time we pay the teacher, we'll be lucky to break even," I said.

Pinky shrugged. "You can't expect to make money the first go-around."

I glanced around the room, once again admiring how Pinky had given the 1950s-era café new life. The name, Brew Ha-Ha, reflected the fun side of her personality more than it fit the shop theme. But it worked anyhow.

My adoptive parents had purchased the café, a business that had closed a few years before. The two shops shared an interior wall and they'd had a section of it removed to create an archway between the spaces. They had planned to expand their own retail space, but when push came to shove, they felt the old soda fountain was better suited for food and drinks than to display snow globes and other collectible items. They'd talked Pinky—who was working at the local bakery at the time—into running the coffee shop instead.

The black-and-white tile floor was in good condition and gave Pinky the inspiration to use retro furniture and integrate her favorite color in the accent pieces. But she wanted men as well as women to be comfortable in the shop, so she didn't overdo the pink. Half the gray metal chairs had black vinyl padded seats, and the other half had pink. She'd even used that combination on the six counter stools. It was my observation that men didn't seem to care whether they took a black seat or a pink seat. They didn't even appear to notice. And everyone enjoyed the Lucy and Ethel character pictures and the other memorabilia from the fifties.

Pinky ordered a wide variety of coffee beans in ten, twenty, and thirty-pound bags, and the first hour of the day was devoted to grinding three or four kinds. Brew Ha-Ha featured a daily special. My personal favorite was Kona mocha latte. Mmm.

Her muffins and scones were proudly displayed on the back counter in a lighted, glass-enclosed, three-tier case that revolved when it was turned on. My parents had found it for her on one of their antique shopping excursions.

The connecting shops turned out to be a win-win situation for both sides. People flocked in for Pinky's freshly ground coffee and prizewinning muffins and scones. Many of her customers would wander into the curio side to admire the enviable collection of snow globes my parents had acquired. Although people bought them year-round, they were particularly popular at Christmas. And our curio shoppers rarely resisted stepping next door for a cup of java. The inviting aromas, wafting through to our side, had become part of the shopping experience. I smelled like a coffee bean within my first fifteen minutes of work, but I didn't care. It was better than perfume, in my opinion.

The coffee shop door swung open and Officer Mark Weston came in. Pinky, Erin, Mark, and I had been in the same class from our elementary school days through the junior and senior high school years. Mark and Erin had dated briefly, and it seemed Mark had not lost his crush on her all these years later.

Mark's eyes fixed on Erin. "I thought you should know, Jerrell Powers is back in town."

Erin nodded. "Thanks, Mark. I only hope the entire town doesn't feel the need to track me down to tell me that."

"Just remember, I got your back. I'll keep an eye on him for you. Make sure he stays in line."

Erin rolled her eyes, but kept her tongue in check.

"Mark, I saw Jerrell Powers, too, and almost didn't recognize him for a minute. He looks . . . different," Pinky said.

"Yeah, he did to me, too. He's skinnier, so his cheekbones stick out more. And his head is shaved," Mark told us.

"He'll probably want to grow his hair out with the nip of fall in the air. It's right around the corner, you know," Archie chimed in.

"It's here. It's almost the middle of October," Erin corrected him.

"With daytime temperatures in the high sixties, it feels more like September," Archie said.

"True enough, and it can stay that way for another month or two as far as I'm concerned," Pinky said.

May Gregors, the teacher for the evening, came through the door looking like she'd seen a ghost. She clutched her hands to her chest and opened her mouth, but no words came out.

Officer Mark took a step toward her. Maybe he thought she was having a heart attack. I know the thought crossed my mind. "Ma'am, can you speak?"

"She's not a dog," Erin mumbled quietly.

"Are you able to talk?" Mark asked again when May remained mute.

Finally, she nodded. "I just had a bit of a shock. I ran into my good-for-nothing ex-husband at your post office when I went to mail some letters. The last I'd heard anything about him was when he sent our daughter a letter from a halfway house about two years ago. He said he would be on probation for five years. I didn't expect to see him back around here."

Erin frowned. "You're not talking about Jerrell Powers, by any chance, are you?"

"You know Jerrell?"

"I'm afraid so."

"They had a close encounter of the criminal kind," Mark explained.

May's right eyebrow lifted. "Oh. So you're the one whose house—"

Erin nodded. "I'm Erin Vickerman."

"Gosh, I was out of state staying at my cousin's place the year that happened, and never asked for the details. Jerrell told our daughter someone had slipped a drug into his drink and that he broke into a house when he was under its influence."

Mark stuck his thumbs into his duty belt. "That would be the defendant's version. He'd had a few minor run-ins with the law. A kleptomaniac, if you ask me. Erin came home to find him taking a load of clocks out of her house. His third load of stuff, as it turned out."

Erin put her hands on her tiny hips. "Let's not go through all the sordid details. I ran back to my car, locked myself in, and called nine-one-one. Officer Weston here and Assistant Chief Clinton Lonsbury were there in minutes."

Mark nodded. "We found the entire stash in a wagon behind the house. And with enough coaxing, Jerrell confessed to other unsolved thefts around town. Lucky for him he hadn't gotten around to selling anything, so he got off easy."

"I'm sorry, I didn't know. Jerrell moved here after our divorce. He had a friend here, but I don't know his name. It could even be a 'her,' as far as that goes." May shrugged.

"It is a 'her.' Pamela Hemley is the name," Mark said.

May frowned slightly. "I'm surprised she'd take him back after all that."

Erin gave a quick wave. "Whatever. I can't worry about the life and times of Jerrell Powers. You guys have a class to get ready for and I have to do a couple of things at home, but I'll be back for the class." She left before any of us responded.

"She's not going to hunt down Jerrell, is she?" Pinky asked.

I chuckled. "Erin is spunky, but I think she's smarter than that."

Mark looked at his watch. "I better get out there to finish my shift. But I'm kind of interested in how you make snow globes, so I might stop back later to observe."

"As long as you stay out of the way of our students who paid for the class," Pinky said.

Mark held up his hand. "Hey, no problem. See you later." And he was gone.

Pamela Hemley's name sounded very familiar and then I remembered why. "Pinky, check the names on our class list."

She retrieved it from the front table, glanced at it, and nodded her head. "Pamela's on the list, all right. I don't know her, so I didn't make the association. If I heard her name back when Jerrell Powers got in trouble with the law, I surely have forgotten it by now."

I looked at May. "Does Pamela know who you are?"

"I'm not sure. I started going by my middle name a couple years ago, and I took back my maiden name when I got divorced," she said.

"I'm a thinkin' she knows," Archie said, then left without saying good-bye.

Pinky stuck her hands on her hips. "You don't suppose she signed up out of curiosity, do you? To check out the former competition, what you're like and all that?"

"Gosh, that seems silly," May said.

I shrugged. "Well, we'll know in about a half hour." I looked at the supplies on the tables. "So what is there left to do? Do you need anything, May?"

She took in a deep breath, then let it go. "Oh, thank you, but no, I should be all set. We have twelve signed up, including the three of you. But I have enough supplies and handouts for twenty, if more want to join us."

"Twenty would about max out our seating capacity, with the snow globe supplies on the extra tables, that is. It's counter seating only after that." Pinky pointed to two covered platters on the back counter. "I baked both fresh rhubarb and blueberry muffins. The rhubarb ones have a cream cheese center, I'll run as many carafes of coffee as we need, and there's plenty of bottled water." Pinky loved making muffins and scones almost as much as we all loved eating them. For many of her customers, a muffin or scone was a necessary staple in their daily diet.

People started trickling into the coffee shop about fifteen minutes before seven. At 6:53 p.m., two women came in together. The red-haired woman was big boned and close to six feet tall, with a husky voice that matched her size. "I'm Pam Hemley, and this is my sister, Lauren Engle, visiting with me for a couple of days. We're signed up for the class."

I realized that I recognized Hemley from seeing her around town a few times. Engle was the same height as her sister, but with more lean muscle. They were somewhere in their late forties or early fifties. I hoped I sounded natural when I said, "Welcome. Please sign in and find a seat." I glanced over to see if May had noticed Hemley's arrival, but she was bent over her table of tools and supplies, with her back to us, and appeared completely absorbed in what she was doing. Maybe she was doing it on purpose to gain composure before facing them.

By seven, everyone who was preregistered had checked

in, along with one of Brooks Landing's finest, Mark Weston, and our old friend Archie Newberry, who were there to observe out of apparent curiosity. Erin slipped in at the last minute and sat at a table with Pam and Lauren, evidently without realizing who they were, and ignored my attempts to head her off at the pass. Pam looked from Erin to Lauren and raised her eyebrows.

May clapped her hands and held them together. "Okay, let's get started. I want to thank all of you for coming tonight. I'm going to teach you the basics of making snow globes, and then it's up to you and your own creativity after that. We'll start with a little history on the globes, then I'd like each of you to introduce yourselves. And if you'd care to, tell why you're here. I'm always interested in finding out what brings people to my classes."

*Why I'm here?* Well, that's a loaded question. Long story short, I'm here because a senator's husband decided he wanted to have more than a professional relationship with me, but I wouldn't go for it. The trouble was, before I'd figured out the best way to tell anyone what was going on behind the facade of their happy marriage, his wife walked into my office as he was making one last attempt to convince me we'd make a great couple.

*But I'm sure May was referring to the snow globe–making class, not my relocation from Washington, D.C., to Brooks Landing, Minnesota.* Okay, so I had to work a little harder at not dwelling on my scandalous past. I could thank Pinky for my attendance tonight. She had talked me into offering theme classes, and the biggest theme we had going in our shop of many collectibles was snow globes. Some had traveled from Spain, Austria, Germany, and other places around the world. When I had a minute here and there, I enjoyed picking one up, shaking it, and watching the scene seemingly come to life as multiple snowflakes fell to the ground.

There were any number of nature or village scenes to mesmerize me. Some were quart size, some pint size, others miniature. One of my favorites held a lighthouse on a rocky crag with a boat sailing on high waves heading toward it. There was a switch on the brown ceramic base to turn the lighthouse on, and even with the snow falling fast and furiously, the light was the beacon that would guide the ship to safety.

". . . No one is really sure who invented snow globes in the first place, but they started to appear in France in the early 1800s. Some think they evolved from glass paperweights, which were common by the end of the eighteenth century.

"Snow globes really caught on after the Paris Universal Expo of 1878. Within a year, there were an estimated six companies in Europe making them. Originally, they had a sealed ceramic base with a heavy glass dome that was filled with water. The snow at that time was made from either pieces of porcelain or sand or bone chips—"

"Bone chips?" Pinky asked.

May smiled. "We won't be using those today." She glanced at a sheet of paper. "Okay, so before we get into our lesson, we'll take a minute to introduce ourselves and break the ice, since we'll be working together for the next hour or two. And if you'd like, as I said earlier, please tell us why you'd like to learn how to make snow globes. Whoever wants to start . . ."

Erin waved her hand slightly. "Erin Vickerman. I'm friends with Cami and Pinky, the two managers here, and I thought it'd be fun. I'm a teacher and I'm thinking of making snow globes with my students at Christmastime."

At the mention of Erin's name, Pam gave her sister a sideways glance. She knew the name of her boyfriend's victim all right.

Erin looked at Lauren. "Next."

"Um, I'm Lauren from St. Cloud. My sister invited me. I'm in town visiting because . . . oh, it's a long story." She looked at her sister to go on.

"My name is Pam, and I like to do crafts, and I'd never thought of making snow globes before I saw your ad for this class."

Pam and Lauren had both conveniently left off their last names. And if Pam knew the connection between Jerrell Powers and May Gregors, she didn't let on. And to her credit, May let it slide by also. But what else could she do? Make a big scene, spoil the class, and have the whole evening implode?

The other seven class attendees were two older ladies from my church; a mother and her teenage daughter; one of Pinky's muffin eaters; one of the Curio Finds customers who loved looking at the snow globes but rarely bought one; and a local crafter who had booths at fairs around the state.

I introduced myself, then Pinky wrapped up the introduction session and remembered to thank everyone for coming—including the two observers, Archie and Mark.

May sucked in a quick breath. "To start off, we'll go over all the materials we're going to be working with. Did any of you bring your own figurines or scenes to use?" She looked around the room, and most of us shook our heads. Apparently no one had gotten that memo.

"Okay, that's fine. Sometimes a grandma or mom has someone special who loves the Disney princesses, for example. No matter, I have plenty to choose from." She pointed to a table behind her, where a large assortment awaited us. Wild and domestic animals, trees, farmhouses, barns, stores that looked like they were made of bricks, horse-driven sleighs, children skating or on sleds, people of all ages. What to choose?

May went on, "There are many materials people use nowadays to make the snow, like glitter or crushed eggshells, but I like using benzoic acid because the crystals look more like real snow. I really enjoyed high school chemistry, and it's fun for me to use this method."

"How does that work?" Mark asked from the cheap seats.

May threw a glance his way. "Actually, the snow is made from crystals of water from which you precipitate the crystals of benzoic acid."

"Precipitate benzoic acid?" a church lady asked.

May smiled. "It's not as complicated as it sounds. You can use a glass measuring cup or a flask—I'll use a pan tonight—and add the acid to the water. Then you heat it to dissolve the benzoic acid. You can do it on your stovetop or use a microwave, even a coffeemaker. You don't need to boil it."

"So how do the snowflakes form?" Pinky asked.

"It's magic. Or so it seems. It's like dissolving sugar in water to make rock candy. After it's boiled and cooled, it forms the hard candy."

I had never thought of how rock candy was made before. Or snow for globes, either, for that matter.

"When the benzoic acid cools and approaches room temperature, the solid substance separates from the water, and voila! Little snowflakes. Slower cooling makes for prettier flakes, just like in the formation of real snowflakes."

It made sense. In Minnesota we had everything from hard, driving pellets of sleet to fluffy flakes the size of a small fist. The wet snow was heavy and more difficult to shovel. Dry snow was light, perfect "powder" for skiing and sledding. But on a warm October evening, real snow was not on the list of things I wished for. Winter would come soon enough.

"Okay, class, let's get going on the flakes." May set a glass pan on a portable cooktop unit she'd brought with her. She had a pitcher of water, which she poured into the pan, followed by a premeasured amount of benzoic acid. "I've got the recipe listed on your handouts."

May heated the solution to nearly boiling, then removed the pan from the burner and set it aside. "All right. So, everyone, take some time to design your scene. And I'll help you as much as you'd like me to."

I debated whether to tell Erin who her tablemates were, but decided to wait until after the class, to avoid any potential dramatic confrontation. If Erin knew who Pamela was, she might tell her where to go, and it would spoil everyone's fun. Pamela may have had no control over Jerrell's behavior, but I knew Erin, and she wouldn't see it that way.

The class members got up and perused the items on the display table. Pinky elbowed my ribs to remind me we shared knowledge we should keep quiet about until the time was right. Erin stepped in beside me. "What kind of scene are you going for?"

I eyed a building that looked like an old country schoolhouse, or a church without a steeple, and picked it up. "This looks a lot like the school my parents went to when they were kids, before they closed the country schools and all the kids were sent to town schools. I think I'll make a snow globe for them."

Erin nodded. "After being in the business all those years, it'd probably be the first time anyone actually made one especially for them."

"I'd say that's true. How about you two? Any ideas?" I asked Pinky and Erin.

"I like this little princess with her pink dress. She'll look good in my house," Pinky said.

Erin smiled. "We should have guessed that, Miss Pinky." She picked up a plastic piece and studied it. "Hmm. I think I'll go with a kids' sledding scene and use it as a display model for when we make them in my class. The children will like that." She selected some trees to complete the scene.

Mark and Archie mingled in with the rest of us, examining the little figures and buildings and checking to see what everyone was picking. May helped the church ladies and we all had something chosen within minutes then sat back down at our workstations for the next step.

May walked around, nodding as she imagined the possibilities. "You've come up with a nice variety, class. We'll design the scenes, then glue the pieces on the base."

I looked around and noticed everyone was concentrating on arranging and rearranging the elements of their respective scenes on the heavy plastic globe bases. I set the schoolhouse, a group of three children holding books, a dog, and some pine trees on my own base. It looked good to me.

"When everyone is satisfied, we'll glue the scenes in place with the hot glue guns."

"I've never used one before," the teenage girl said, and another class member shook her head.

"That's quite all right. All we need to do is make sure you don't burn yourself because the glue is very hot. I can tell you after getting it on my own fingers a time or two. All right. You can secure your figures in two ways. You'll hold the figure you're gluing with your set of forceps, and put a dab of glue either on the bottom of the figure or on the base where you plan to set the figure. I like to glue the base because then you avoid dripping the glue where you don't want it. You don't need to squeeze the glue gun trigger very hard at all. You only want a drop. Practice on your newspaper to get a feel for it."

She moved to the supply of glue guns. "I've got one for each table. Here, let me get situated with the extension cords. They should all reach just fine, but be careful if you stand up not to trip on one." Mark left his viewing stool to help her, but an incoming phone call interrupted him. He pulled his cell phone out of its holder and stepped outside to take the call.

I went with May's suggestion, doing a practice squeeze, then I held each of my figures, one at a time, over the spot I wanted to place it, applied a dab of glue there, and set it in place. Some people struggled a little; others were quicker draws with their glue guns. Erin and Pinky were both more adept than I was. Erin did crafts with her class, and Pinky was a bit of an artist with her baking.

"So we'll see how the snow is coming along." May looked at the clear glass pan, and we all followed suit. It seemed the snow making was a success. "When you are ready, the next steps work together. You'll put a thin line of glue around the outside edge of the base, then we'll add the snow-filled water to your globes and attach the base to the bottom of the globe. And I have more supplies if any of you want to make two. You can just reimburse me the extra amount."

Mark returned after his phone call, and when he noticed that Archie was doing his best to help some of the women, he joined in. I was too involved in my own project to pay much attention to how the others were doing, so I thought it was nice the men were lending a hand.

May moved from one student to the next, using a small measuring cup to dip the snowy solution from the pan to pour into our globes. Each person held a globe in one hand and its base in the other. Then after May filled her globe, she put the base in place. When they were all filled and attached, May instructed us to do a final sealing bead of glue where the base met the globe.

Not only had we all survived the class without incident, but we'd produced some wonderful products. I admired what the other crafters had come up with. The teenage girl had assembled a miniature train of three cars on tracks chugging past a group of trees as a gift for her brother. One church lady had placed a single silver, leafless tree with its branches reaching heavenward on her base. It was stunning in its beautiful simplicity. I could have happily put any number of them up for sale on the shop's display shelves. The class had gone along without a hitch, despite my concerns. But had I known what was about to happen, I would have tried to stop it before it started.

2

Most of the attendees had left by nine o'clock, and the rest of us were swallowing the last of our treats and putting away the supplies. Pam and Lauren thanked us then headed to the door. May called out to their backs, "You're welcome, ladies. You know, Pam, you seem like a nice person. Don't let Jerrell ruin the rest of your life, as he's sure to do if you stay with him."

Pam and Lauren both turned on a dime. Everyone's eyebrows shot up, including mine.

Erin's face paled. "Jerrell? As in Jerrell Powers? That Jerrell?"

Lauren reached over and laid her hand on her sister's arm. "That's why I'm really in Brooks Landing. To get my sister away from him," she blurted out.

"What's your connection to Jerrell?" Pam asked.

"He's my ex-husband."

Archie mumbled first to himself, then out loud, "Lordy, Lordy."

"Did you come to Brooks Landing to teach the class, or was it so you could check up on Jerrell?" Pam asked.

May's head went back like she was avoiding a punch and her face drew taut. "I didn't know where he was, and haven't seen him in forever—except today, that is—and I was more than shocked. I wasn't going to let him wreck this class. I had a say in that much at least. Not like when I couldn't control what he did. He ruined my daughter's life." She paused for a breath. "And mine."

Erin turned to Pam. "How about you? You and your sister sat with me at the same table and didn't say anything. You know who I am, don't you?"

Pam shrugged. "I thought it was you then knew for sure when you introduced yourself."

Erin pointed her finger at Pam. "For Pete's sake. And worse yet, you're in cahoots with Jerrell Powers. You're harboring a fugitive."

Pam's lips trembled and tears welled in her eyes, but didn't spill out.

Mark gave his hand a slight wave. "Technically, he's not a fugitive."

"Okay, a criminal, then. And a creepy one besides. If he comes near me or my things—"

"Then I'll handle him, Erin," Mark said, lowering his voice.

Pinky stepped in beside Mark. "Me, too. I'll protect you."

I rolled my eyes before I could stop myself.

"If we kick him out of Pam's house, he'll have to leave town and you won't have to worry about him," Lauren said.

"Lordy, Lordy," Archie said again.

Being caught up in dramatic scenes had followed me from Washington, D.C., to my hometown of Brooks Landing. At least no one was pointing fingers at me this time. I raised my hands for everyone's attention. "I think the best thing to do is put a little time and space between all that's gone down here. I don't think we're going to resolve this tonight, so we should all go home and try to get a good night's sleep. And remember what a nice class we had. We all have wonderful snow globes to prove it." My words sounded fake and shallow even to me.

"Sleep? Seriously, Cami?" Erin asked.

"A glass of wine might help, Erin. Do you want a ride home?" Pinky said.

Erin lifted her eyebrows. "No." She rolled her shoulders backward in a half circle. "But thanks." She looked at each of us in turn. She nodded then left. Mark followed her out the door.

May turned to Pam. "I'm sorry, I shouldn't have said anything. I wasn't going to, but it came out anyway. And Jerrell is a—"

"No-goodnik," Archie finished for her then slipped out himself.

Lauren pulled on Pam's arm. "Time to go." Pam nodded, and they left without another word.

Pinky brushed a crumb off a table. "Let me help you carry your things to your car, May."

"You know what? I have everything packed in my

suitcase on wheels, and I'm parked right outside. But thanks. It was a good class. I wish now that I had just left it at that."

"Yes, it was a good class," I agreed and zipped my mouth shut before I told her it was probably the last time she ever taught a class at our shop. Pinky held the door for May, who rolled her supplies out behind her.

"Well, that went well. Not," I said and sank onto a stool at the counter.

"Holy moly, Cami, our hopes of holding classes here may have died on the vine."

"Yeah, well, after some time passes, maybe we'll get our enthusiasm back."

"That's optimistic." Pinky adjusted her neck scarf. "Well, it's an early day tomorrow, getting up to bake my delicacies, so I'd better head on home."

I stood up and gave Pinky a light hug. "Rest well, friend."

"You, too."

Alone in the shop, I walked around to settle my nerves. The last thing I had wanted that evening was a conflict. And a fairly significant one at that. I checked to see that every electrical appliance was off, then shut off the lights in the coffee shop and headed into my more familiar territory on the curio side. I picked up a recently acquired snow globe on a shelf near the counter and gave it a shake. It snowed on the man and woman who were dressed in Victorian clothing, snuggled together on a rocking horse. Their expressions of both joy and contentment had been captured and preserved for at least a century, according to the best information we had from one of our dealers in Germany.

I carefully replaced the globe then sat down in front of the computer on the checkout counter. I read through and responded to some e-mails and read the featured news head-lines of the day. I was surprised when the clock on city hall chimed ten times. My hour online had seemed like half that amount of time.

"You need to head home yourself," I said out loud and shut down the computer. I went to the back of the store and used the bathroom then grabbed my jacket and backpack from the back room and slipped them on. When I returned to the retail area, I walked toward the front window to turn the security light on, but a snow globe sitting on a nearby shelf stopped me in my tracks. It was "snowing." I blinked, knowing I was imagining things, and watched until the last of the flakes had settled on the ground. I had never seen that particular globe before and wondered where it had come from. It was made of similar, or the same type of, materials we had used in our class. How odd. A chill ran up my spine as I reached for the front door to be sure it was locked. It was. I was relieved because I honestly could not remember locking it, no matter how hard I thought about it.

I picked up the foreign snow globe and studied the scene. Inside, there was a man sitting on a park bench with his head resting almost on his chest. He appeared to be sleeping. There was a streetlamp, several leafless trees, and a moon behind them. The scene looked familiar, like it could be in one of our town parks. I set the snow globe back on the shelf and let myself out. I locked the door behind me and double-checked it to be certain it was secured.

I went to the back lot, where I usually parked, and had a moment of panic when my Subaru wasn't there. "No. Of all the days not to drive," I chided myself. My house was less than a mile away, and I often walked or biked to work. It had been a gorgeous October morning, and it was an even lovelier evening, with a full moon overhead. And, as Archie had pointed out earlier, unseasonably warm.

Even though I generally felt safe walking after dark, I removed the small canister of Mace from my backpack and slipped it in the front pocket of my khaki slacks. It had been a long day on my feet, but I hadn't thought of bringing a change of shoes with me, so my walking sandals would have to do. I headed south on Central Avenue, glancing up at the top half of the old county courthouse building that sat on the rise of a hill, a block west of the buildings on the opposite side of Central. A bank building dating back to 1890 that currently housed an antique business was directly across the street. It still held the original internal vault, a feature that added to the building's charm.

The streets were mostly deserted at that hour, even though it was Friday night, and I wished there was more traffic. Why was I on edge? I crossed the street and walked on the sidewalk that ran alongside Green Lake. Not a soul was fishing from the public dock. During the summer months, it wasn't unusual to see fishers there late at night. But once school started in September, people were rarely there after dark, and the dock would be rolled in soon, before the winter snow fell and the lake froze over.

Where the sidewalk divided—one path ran alongside the highway, and the other turned and led into the park—I veered to the right and took the park pathway, a shortcut that saved me a fair distance. There were streetlamps every fifty feet or so, but because I felt more unsettled than usual, I wished there was one every twenty. I patted the cell phone in my left pocket and the Mace in my right pocket. I'd gotten in the habit of carrying a canister during my years in Washington, D.C.

As children, my friends and I had spent hours playing games in the park, sometimes after sunset, before we were beckoned home. Our favorite nighttime game was a version of tag called Starlight, Moonlight. *Starlight, moonlight, I hope to see a ghost tonight.* I thought about the words and raised my eyes skyward. *Just kidding.*

Something shiny on the concrete path caught my eyes. A penny. I had a thing for picking up pennies. I remembered my mother—my birth mother—telling me, "Find a penny, pick it up, all the day you'll have good luck." As a teenager, I had started to believe it was my mother who dropped the pennies from heaven just for me. I bent over quickly, snatched up the coin, and dropped it in the pocket with my Mace. The two items made a soft clicking sound as I picked up my pace.

At the bottom of the hill, before the ground rose again, I noticed a man sitting on the bench. I considered what I should do: sneak by him quietly or make enough noise so I didn't startle him when I walked behind his back. I pulled the Mace from my pocket and cupped it in my hand. "Hi, there! Beautiful evening, isn't it?"

No response. As I got closer, I saw his head was bent over, like he was reading a book. But it was too dark where he sat for that. I decided I had better cross in front of him so I could keep an eye on his movements, and be sure he didn't have any kind of weapon in his hand or stuck in the pockets of the windbreaker jacket he was wearing. I put my finger on the trigger of the Mace container, just in case. When I was about six feet away, little nerve prickles touched the back of my neck. I sidestepped toward the lake, not only to put more distance between him and me, but also so I could get a better view of him.

He appeared to be sleeping, with his head bent over and his hands resting palms up on his thighs. His ball cap hid his face. A cloud moved across the moon, and since the streetlamp was behind him, I couldn't see well at all. "Hello? Are you all right? Just to let you know, you can't sleep in the park. The cops in this town are pretty strict about that."

Still no response. The cloud moved and the moon's light came through the trees, shining down on us. "Oh, my God," I whispered. It was the scene from the new psycho snow globe in my shop. I pinched myself to be sure I was really awake and not in the middle of a nightmare. I squeezed enough to make it hurt. Ouch.

I was afraid the man might be drunk and vulnerable to . . . whatever. I braved a step closer and then another. My pounding heart threatened to break through my chest. "Sir." I didn't want to touch him, so I picked up a stick lying by my foot and gently touched his shoulder with it. Instead of lifting his head, he fell forward and toppled onto the ground, landing facedown. I jumped back and then screamed.

The handle of a knife was sticking out of his back. His jacket was a dark color, maybe blue. It was too dark to see much more, but I detected a wet, earthy scent that I guessed was blood. "Oh, my God!" I yelled. "Help." Was there anyone around to hear me? He must be dead, but I wasn't sure. Maybe the knife was in just a little ways, stuck to a rib. Instinctively, without thinking, I reached down and checked. It felt like it was very deeply and tightly stuck in place.

Oh, Lord, I'd never been alone with a dead body before. Somehow my reasoning kicked back in and I dialed 911.

Thankfully it went through to the emergency operator. I didn't know if the county had that capability with cell phone calls or not.

"Buffalo County, nine-one-one. Is this an emergency?" a woman asked.

"Yes, it is. I'm with a man who I'm pretty sure is dead. Someone stabbed him. Send the police to Lakeside Park right away. We're maybe two hundred feet in from the Central Avenue side. Hurry!"

"Ma'am, my partner is dispatching an ambulance and a Brooks Landing officer. Do you know the victim?"

"No. I mean, not that I know of. I can't really see his face."

"Are you in danger yourself?"

Dear God, was I? I looked around and listened for sounds, but the only thing I heard was a fish jump in the lake behind me. "I don't think so."

"And what is your name?"

"Camryn Brooks."

"Ms. Brooks, please spell your first name." I did. "And your middle name?"

"Jo. J-o." Why did they need that?

"Your date of birth?"

"A man might be dead here. He's not moving at all, and there's that knife sticking out of his back."

"Okay, well, yes, but you need to stay calm. The officer and ambulance will be there in minutes. I need your date of birth and address to start the report."

It was faster to tell her than to argue, and giving her the information helped distract me from the awful scene in front of me for ten or fifteen seconds.

"I'll stay on the line with you until the officer arrives. My name is Betty. Stay with me, okay?" Her tone was sympathetic and she sounded like my mother. I felt my knees start to buckle under me. "Okay." My own voice was weak and shaky. I heard sirens getting closer and turned to see emergency vehicles come around the lake from the north. There were three of them. I stole a quick glance at the body on the ground. Still facedown. He had to be dead, but my brain had trouble processing the whole thing.

"An off-duty officer is responding also. And I can hear the sirens over your phone so they must be close," Betty said.

"They're turning into the park."

"Oh, good. I'll leave you in their capable hands, then."

"Okay, 'bye." I hit the end button on my phone as the first police car pulled to a stop on the walking/bike path ten or so feet past me. Officer Mark Weston, wearing street clothes, jumped out and jogged toward me. An ambulance stopped behind him, and the second Brooks Landing police car parked behind it. Four people descended on the scene in seconds: Mark, a male EMT, a female EMT, and Clinton Lonsbury, another Brooks Landing High School alumnus. He was a year ahead of us, and Mark had told me he served as the assistant chief of police with the department.

"Cami, what in the heck?" Mark was first to reach the body. He knelt down and checked for a pulse on the man's neck as the EMTs looked on. He shook his head and looked up at them. "Nothing you guys can do for him. He's gone."

The EMTs nodded, but didn't make any attempt to leave. One did his own quick check of the body, probably a required procedure. They were the medical experts, after all.

Assistant Chief Lonsbury shined a bright flashlight around the ground and on the bench behind it. When he looked at me, his face was partially shadowed and far more handsome than I'd remembered. His large brown eyes studied me. "Mark said you were back in town." He cleared his throat. "Can you tell us what happened, Cami? When you called it in, you said you didn't know the victim's identity."

"It's Camryn now," I corrected him. I'd had my name legally changed to a more professional-sounding one when I lived in Washington. Only my family and oldest friends knew me as Cami. "No, I didn't get a good look—or any kind of look—at his face. His cap covered it almost completely. Then when he landed, his cap sort of moved, but as you can see, his face is in the grass and shadowed," I said.

"Go on."

"I was walking home—"

"Through the park, at this time of night?" Mark interrupted.

Clint shot him a look that said, *Be quiet.*

"I didn't mean to leave the shop so late, and wouldn't have if I hadn't forgotten I had walked to work—"

"Any one of us would have given you a ride home," Mark said.

"Officer Weston, quit interrupting."

"Sorry, sir." Sir. Was that how I should be addressing Clinton Lonsbury now?

"Go on."

I told them every detail of walking through the park and finding the body. I decided to leave out the part about seeing the same scene in the strange snow globe until later. "And I did something I knew right away that I shouldn't have."

"What was that?" Clint asked in an official tone.

"I touched the handle of the knife."

Clint looked from me to Mark then back to me. He let go of a grunting sound and must have counted to twenty before he spoke. "Why in the hell—"

"I panicked. I thought maybe if it was in just a little ways, I could pull it out. I know it was stupid."

He left that opening alone. "Have you ever been finger-printed?"

"Yes, for my last employment position."

Clint nodded, and to his credit did not yell or swear at me. He turned his attention to Mark. "We'll need the Buffalo County Major Crimes Team to help process the scene." Clint phoned Dispatch to get the crime team started. He flashed his light on the victim's jeans. "Doesn't look like he has a wallet in his back pocket. Mark, get pictures; then we'll move the body, see if we can make an ID. And we'll need to tape off a perimeter before anyone else shows up."

"Yeah, I'm surprised a Buffalo County deputy hasn't gotten here yet to check things out. Must all be out of the area on their own department calls." Mark grabbed the camera from his car and snapped photos from every angle.

"Okay, let's roll him on his side," Clint instructed.

Mark set his camera down, and the EMTs assisted him with the roll on the count of three. Clint kept his magnum steadied on the body.

"Jerrell Powers, in the flesh. Or in the spirit, as it were."

Jerrell Powers. I'd seen the newspaper clipping with pictures of him after his crime against Erin two years before, but this would be my first, last, and only encounter with him in person. Or spirit, as Clint had said.

"He was the topic of many conversations today," I said.

"Any of them positive ones?" Clint asked.

"Um, no."

Mark agreed with me by shaking his head.

"Any suspects, Mark?" Clint asked.

"A lot of 'em, I guess. Potential suspects. Real suspects with real motives? Not sure about that."

"Well, the supervisor at the halfway house phoned before Powers was released to tell us his enemy number one at the house had been released a week ago. He'd be a good one to track down and question. And we'll gather the evidence and interview everyone who knew him."

"That's right. I kinda forgot about that call from the halfway house. What's that guy's name again?" Mark asked.

Clint stuck his flashlight in his armpit and pulled a memo pad from his breast pocket. He flipped through the first few pages then stopped. He turned it toward the moon so he could read it. I was struck for the second time since he'd arrived how Clint had miraculously matured into an actual hunk. Maybe it was the uniform. "Benjamin Arnold, age forty-two."

"Not Benedict?" I asked. My nerves had brought out the smart aleck in me.

Clint lifted his eyebrows in place of an answer, and Mark said, "Very funny, Cami." I didn't remind my longtime friend about my name change.

The Buffalo County Major Crimes van pulled into the park about ten minutes later. I didn't know either deputy who got out of the vehicle. They were both males; one was around thirty-five, the other, late twenties. At age thirty-six, I was starting to think of anyone younger than thirty as a kid. The deputies asked me some questions and then told me I was free to leave. At that moment, I felt like I had nowhere to go. The EMTs got into their rig and drove off. As the city officers and county deputies went about their business—looking for evidence along the pathway, taping off the perimeter, looking at the body—I walked over to a bench ten or twelve feet away and sat down while I tried to comprehend the unbelievable situation I had gotten caught up in.

The air had cooled and I zipped up my hooded jacket to seal in the warmth around my middle then checked the time on my phone: 10:44. Too late to call Erin or Pinky, even though I knew both would be upset with me for not phoning, no matter what the hour. I mentally went through the day's events, from when we first heard of Jerrell Powers's release to that minute in the park. I thought of at least four people who would be glad Jerrell Powers was gone. But dead? Gone and dead were two completely different things.

A white unmarked van pulled in and parked behind the line of vehicles. A woman of perhaps forty, looking sleepy and tousled, got out. I often wondered what people on call in various professions might be in the middle of doing when they got called in. She'd apparently been in bed.

The group addressed her as Doctor, and I realized she was the county coroner. She did a brief exam and asked a number of questions. Then the crime lab guys got a gurney from her van, and in minutes Jerrell Powers was strapped on, on his side, and loaded into the vehicle. I heard the doctor say she would transport him to the Buffalo County Medical Examiner's Office for an autopsy. Before she left, she joined me at the bench I was sitting on.

The doctor's kind demeanor was evident when she reached over and put her hand on my shoulder for a moment.

"The officers said you were the one who found the victim, and that you didn't know him. Is that correct?"

"Correct. I only knew of him."

"It's quite a shock, I know." She moved her hand from my shoulder to her pocket, pulled out a card, and gave it to me. "Go home, drink some warm milk, or a hot brandy toddy with some honey, if you have any. Just one, mind you. And don't hesitate to give our office a call if you need to talk to someone about this. We have a number of good referrals."

Oh. She thought I might need psychological help to deal with what happened. And maybe I would. "Okay, thanks."

After Powers's body was taken away, the crime lab deputies resumed their work. One of them pointed at me. "Someone should give her a ride home."

Mark and Clint both looked at me like they'd forgotten I was there. Clint came over. "Let's get you home," he said.

I'd had a lot of time to think while I waited. "There's something I should tell you first."

"Like what?" His internal antennae seemed to sprout from the top of his head.

I told him about the class we'd had at the shop earlier and shared some of the details of the showdown over Jerrell Powers and how I'd stayed to relax before heading for home. "Then, right before I left, I saw a new snow globe on a shelf by the front door. It was snowing."

He cleared his throat. "Snowing as if someone had given it a shake?"

"Yes."

"Who else was in the store with you?"

"Just me."

"And Casper the Friendly Ghost?"

I shrugged.

His eyebrows came together. "It's an interesting story, I'll give you that. And there has to be a logical explanation. My question is, why are you telling me about it now?"

"Because it was the same scene I found here at the park. A man was sleeping on a bench with trees and a streetlamp"— I pointed to each—"there, there, and there. There was even a moon at the top of one of the trees." I pointed again. "But now the moon has moved to over there." I pointed for the last time.

"Let's see if I've got this straight. You're alone in your store and a snow globe that matches this scene, one you've never seen before, suddenly appears on your shelf and it is snowing—"

"It was made of the same materials we used in our class tonight, or at least something very like them. I know it sounds crazy—"

"And the doors were locked?"

"Actually, I didn't know if I'd locked the front door or not, but it was locked when I checked it. Before I left the store."

He crossed his arms on his chest. "When you're alone in your store late like that you should always—"

"I know, I know."

"I don't remember you being much of a risk taker back in high school, Cami."

"Camryn. That's my name now."

"So you fancied up your name in the big city, our nation's capital, and you got hooked on risky behavior at the same time."

"I did no such thing." My face reddened and I was glad

for the partial cloak of night but wished that bright moon wasn't ready to betray me. My mind traveled back to that awful time. . . . The senator's office had tried to keep the scandal quiet, but there were leaks. Plenty of them. Everyone with access to the Internet could have read the false version of the story that I had tried to seduce a married man, and my boss's husband, no less. What Clint classified as risky behavior, I guess I would, too.

He turned toward the concrete path. "We'll swing by your store first. You won't be able to sleep tonight anyway."

Good thing he hadn't gone into medicine; he'd get a zero in bedside manner. "That's reassuring."

Clint pointed to his police car. I stood and realized I was still wearing the backpack. I had forgotten all about it. "Anything dangerous in there?" he asked, nodding at my pack.

"Ah, no. You're welcome to look, though."

"Nah. Just don't try anything funny."

I didn't know whether to laugh or act contrite. "Yes, sir," was my middle-of-the-road answer.

I had never been in a police car before and had no idea there were so many buttons and blinking lights. How did officers keep them all straight and manage to drive at high speeds besides? Clint typed a message on the laptop computer mounted on his dashboard: *Clear the scene for now. En route with one to 18 Central Avenue on follow-up.*

I wondered why he'd sent a written message instead of giving the information on the radio, but there must be a reason. I knew a lot of people had police scanners they often tuned into, and it was fine with me that they didn't know the assistant chief of police was on his way to Curio Finds.

We were at the shop in less than two minutes, and I was

overcome by a reluctance to go in search of the evil snow globe. "Something wrong?" Clint asked when he opened his car door and I didn't move.

"Do you have to ask?" I didn't want him to know I was afraid. Afraid of too many things to name at that moment. Especially since a mysterious snow globe was at the top of the current list. Something that would not begin to frighten a police officer. I grabbed the door handle, used my waning energy to open it, and stepped onto the sidewalk. I slid my backpack off. "My keys are in here."

He patted his gun and nodded solemnly. Was he actually planning to shoot me if I accidentally pulled something else out instead? Could he really be this much of a jerk all the time, or was he making the extra effort for my benefit?

I fumbled through the inside pocket where I always put the keys. Not there. I searched the other pocket. Not there, either. "I don't need this right now," I muttered under my breath.

Clint whipped out his flashlight and turned it on. "Let me put a little light on the subject for you." One more minute with the man would be a minute too long. "Here." We both bent over at the same time and ended up cheek to cheek with our eyes peering into the pack. His face was smooth and warm, and if he'd been anyone but Clinton Lonsbury, I would have been tempted to ask for a comforting hug. I felt his jaw move slightly.

My face twitched in return. "Uh, you hold the light and I'll look."

"Good idea." He straightened up immediately.

"Thank you! They were mixed up with some junk on the bottom."

"Backpack: the new purse."

I turned the lock on the front door, pushed it open, reached for the panel on the immediate right, and flipped on the light. I blinked against the assault to my eyes. The shop had a surreal feel at that time of night. I walked over to the shelf where I'd seen the snow globe, but it wasn't there.

"That's odd. It's gone."

"The snow globe with the death scene?" Clint stood close beside me.

"Yes. It was right here." I touched the empty space.

Clint rested his hand on his gun. "Let me do a walk-through."

Aside from the main space, which was filled with shelves holding an assortment of items for sale, there was a bathroom, a small storage area, and a smaller office space in the back of the store. The coffee shop sat on the south side of the shared brick wall. It, too, had a bathroom, but only one storage area, which had once been a kitchen.

It took mere minutes for Clint to search the two shops. "Clear. The back room windows are secure. No sign of a break-in, Cami."

"Camryn. Well, someone was here after I left."

"You're sure the door was locked?"

"Positive."

"And you're sure no one was in the store before you left? They could have been hiding in one of the back rooms."

Eewy eew. "Um, I'd say no, but I guess I can't swear to it. I know no one was in my bathroom or storeroom because I'd been in both of them right before I discovered the snow globe in the first place. But the other rooms? I mean, I'm pretty sure everyone from the class left, and why would they hide here anyway? Plus, you need a key to lock and unlock my shop door from either the inside or the outside. So even if someone was in the store, they'd need to have a key to lock it after they left."

Clint pulled the memo pad and pen from his pocket. "And who all has keys?"

"My parents. Pinky—I mean Alice—Nelson. Me. Erin Vickerman. I think my parents gave one to Mark Weston a few years ago. Every once in a while they'd forget to lock up and he'd discover it on one of his evening checks. It was easier to just give him a key so they didn't have to get out of bed to come down here." My parents. What were they going to think of all this?

"Makes sense. Anyone else? Past employees?"

I shrugged. "Have to ask my folks."

"May want to change your locks, just in case."

Just in case. Didn't he believe me about the snow globe? Granted, if I were him, I'd have trouble believing it myself. But that raised a very important question. Which one of the trusted key holders had made a snow globe that depicted a murder scene before the murder had even occurred?

3

The long, emotion-filled day, a downright unbelievable night, and wondering if one of my friends had actually killed a man caught up with me. It seemed like a robe of weariness had dropped on my shoulders, and I leaned against the shop's front counter for support.

My exhaustion was obvious because Clint said, "Maybe you better sit down while I finish up. Unless you want me to run you home first."

I straightened my spine a bit. "How much more is there to do?"

"I'm going to check the shelf where you saw the now-missing snow globe and look for fingerprints."

"Oh. Well, I'm fine, really." I could pretend a while longer. "I can run a pot of coffee, if you'd like."

"None for me. You go ahead."

None for me, either, or I'd be awake the rest of the night for sure. In case the trauma of the evening alone didn't do it.

I sat down on the swivel stool behind the counter, where I had a decent view of most of the shop and a great view of the Brooks Landing assistant chief of police at work. He was busy with his flashlight looking at shelves from various angles. My parents had a mirror mounted high on the wall in a nook that was partly hidden from view. I studied that for a time. If anyone had been in the shop earlier when I was working on the computer, it would have been impossible for them to hide. In the public shopping area anyway.

Who had left the snow globe on the shelf for me to see before I left for the evening, but had come back to retrieve it before anyone else saw it when the store opened in the morning? What if I had taken it, knowing it didn't belong there? Had that same person known I'd be walking home that night? And did he or she know me so well that they knew I'd cut through the park and find the body? Or was it all one weird coincidence?

Maybe the person had left the globe accidentally and didn't expect or want me to see it at all. Maybe that person was watching from somewhere, and when I went to the bathroom, seized the opportunity to try to grab it. But I wasn't gone as long as they'd hoped, and they'd had to hide beneath one of the shelving units instead. But they could have grabbed the snow globe on the way to their hiding spot. Maybe they had tried and, because they were nervous, couldn't grip it, and bumped it instead. That's why it was snowing.

Nothing made sense. What kind of a person would make a snow globe of a murder scene? And the more I thought about it, the snow globe must have been made before the murder. I was alone in the shop after the class, and no one else had come in. I went into the back for only a minute or two before I left for the night, but the front door was locked anyway. And not long after that I discovered Powers's body. Could it have been a completely wild happenstance? One of the snow globe class members had designed a scene that turned out to be true?

I watched Clint work for a few more minutes. He looked like he knew what he was doing, and I was moderately impressed. When I asked if I could do anything to help him, he shot me a look that clearly said, *Stay as far away from me and my police work as possible.* What he said out loud was, "No, but thanks." Jiminy Cricket.

Clint tapped his flashlight against his cheek. "Martha Stewart work here, or what?"

"What do you mean?"

"Mr. Clean, maybe?"

"Oh, well, I did wipe off all the glass shelves earlier today." I glanced up at the clock on the wall to verify it was still the same day. Not yet midnight. The morning was long ago and far away in my memory.

"Are you for hire?" I think he meant it as a compliment, but I felt a little insulted.

"No."

Clint jutted out his chin. "If there was someone who placed, then later removed, a snow globe from your shelf, they did not leave any fingerprint evidence to prove it."

If? I would admit to a moment of forgetfulness here or there, but I have never had a hallucination in my life. The "visits" from my parents, mostly my mother, didn't count.

And it wasn't like I actually saw them; it was more like I knew they were there.

Well, if Assistant Chief Lonsbury did not believe me, he could conduct his own official investigation and I would conduct my own less-official investigation. He had a primary suspect. I'd figure out my own list. May the best man or woman win.

Why drag out this misery any longer? "So, if you're all done here, then I'm ready to go home."

He slipped his flashlight into its holder on his duty belt. "Yes. Long day, I'm sure. You have a shrink here in town?"

I sat on my hand to stop myself from throwing a stapler at him.

"No. Why do you ask?" I controlled my voice, which was difficult.

"Seems like maybe you've been under a lot of stress, what with what happened in D.C., and then tonight. . . . I just thought some counseling might be a good idea."

When the coroner had suggested it earlier, I'd thought of it as something to consider. When Clint said essentially the same thing, I wanted to run for the hills. "Okay."

"Okay?"

*"Okay."*

The ride home was even tenser than the ride to the shop. The front bucket seats in the police car were not far enough apart for my personal comfort. Clint drove with his left hand and rested his long, muscular right arm on the middle console between our seats. I scrunched my body as close to the passenger door as possible, but it made little difference. He could have easily touched me by simply waving his fingers to the right. Fortunately, he didn't.

After I'd given him my home address, neither of us spoke until he pulled up in front of my modest 1960s brick Tudor-style home. The motion detection lights on either side of the front door flicked on and lit up the front seat of the car. Both Clint and I flinched at its brightness.

"You bought the McClarity place, huh?" He shifted into park.

"Ah, no. I'm not sure how long I'll be staying here in Brooks Landing, so I'm renting for now."

Clint moved his jaw forward slightly. "Well, it'll at least have to be until our department gets through the murder investigation. You weren't thinking of leaving anytime real soon, were you?"

I reached for the door handle and pulled. "No. No immediate flight plans."

"Is your house locked?"

He would have to ask me that. "No, but—"

"We've had one murder in this town already today—"

"I have friends here, unlike Jerrell Powers, who seemed to have made enemies for himself wherever he went." I got out of the car.

"Like you?"

"Good night." I remembered my manners. "Oh, and thanks for the ride." I shut the door.

Clint jumped out from his side. "I'll go in with you, check things out."

"Why?"

"It'll make me feel better."

This day would never end. Clint followed me to the front door then put his arm in front of me so he could lead the way. He was a man on a mission and it was simply easier to let him do what he felt compelled to do. He turned the knob and pushed open the door. As he stepped inside, he drew his gun. It occurred to me he had been itching to do that since he'd first arrived on the murder scene. Police training, I supposed.

"Wait here," he whispered over his shoulder. As much as I wanted to follow him, I rested my back against the rough brick exterior wall by the door and waited. It seemed an eternity passed before Clint returned. His gun was back in its holster.

"Come on in, it's clear." *Gee, thanks for inviting me into my own home, Officer.* "You keep your house pretty much spotless, too."

"Cleaning is like therapy for me." I'd had no intention of giving him one iota of personal information about myself. Exhaustion must have lowered my defenses.

"Hmm. Looks like you're in therapy a lot."

"If there's nothing else . . ."

Finally he took the hint and walked to the door. "Lock up behind me."

"Yes, sir." I did as he'd instructed, then I dropped my backpack on a chair and plopped onto the couch. I turned to lean my back on the armrest and stretched out my legs. The house was still furnished with most of the owner's furniture. Sandra McClarity had died about two months before my return to Brooks Landing.

She had been one of my favorite people because my birth mother, Berta, had loved her so much. Berta and Sandra McClarity had been best friends from kindergarten until Berta's death over thirty years before. Sandra had been like an aunt to me while I was growing up, and she'd been privy to secrets I couldn't tell my real aunt.

The McClarity home had always had a warm, friendly atmosphere. I figured the reason was Sandra McClarity herself, but even after her death, the house smelled and felt almost the same. The family had removed the prized heirlooms, which included some of the antique furniture. I imagined as the rest of Sandra's possessions were moved out, it would gradually lose the built-in warmth.

"Well, this has been a day to make the whole D.C. scandal seem not so bad. Falsely accused is decidedly better than getting killed," I said out loud. I had lived alone so long, if I didn't talk to myself, I probably wouldn't exercise my voice box enough. I patted the can of Mace still in my pocket—I hadn't remembered that potential weapon when Clint had interrogated me. When I pulled it out, the penny I'd found on the pathway in the park came with it and dropped onto my lap. I picked it up, noticed the date on it, and smiled. It was my biological mother's birth year. "Thanks, Mama, for doing your best to stay close all these years. If you were trying to warn me to turn around because you knew Jerrell Powers's dead body was just a little ways down the path, then thank you. I'll try to pay closer attention next time."

I put the penny back in my pocket and pulled the warm fleece blanket that was draped on the back of the couch over me. I tucked a corner of it under my back and grasped part of the top in my folded hands on my chest. I didn't have the energy to get paper and pen, so I made a mental note of everyone I knew who did not like Jerrell Powers. Erin Vickerman was first on the list. Or maybe it should be May Gregors, followed by Pamela's sister, Lauren.

Then there was Pamela herself. She couldn't be ruled out yet, despite her apparent love for Powers. Not to mention Mark

Weston, who had been protective of Erin since high school. If he'd thought Powers posed a danger to her, what would he do? Of course, Pinky and I would do whatever we could to help defend Erin, if it came to that. Even Archie Newberry was there for all three of us. Actually, in a town like Brooks Landing, the list of others like Newberry who would show their support was probably a mile or two long.

Sandra McClarity's cuckoo clock startled me when the little bird popped out and crowed, followed by eleven more noisy appearances. Midnight. Yesterday was officially over and today had begun. I closed my eyes, convinced I wouldn't be able to turn off my brain long enough to sleep.

The ringing telephone awakened me Saturday morning. I sat up and glanced at the clock, amazed I had slept soundly for eight hours. I snatched my cell phone off the coffee table and braced myself when I read the display. I pushed the talk button and was greeted by a very upset Pinky on the other end. "Mark just left my shop and you are in the deepest doo-doo ever. I can't believe you didn't call me last night."

"I didn't call because you had an early day, and you needed your rest."

"Who died and made you my mother?"

"Pinky—" I kicked off the blanket.

"Sorry, that was mean. I shouldn't have yelled, but you were involved in a murder. Jerrell Powers's murder, to be specific. Oh, my God!"

"Not in the actual murder—"

"I didn't mean it like that. You have to tell me every single detail."

My phone beeped, alerting me I had another call coming in. I glanced at the caller ID. "Pinky, it's Erin calling, so I better take it. I'll be down at the shop by nine and we'll talk then."

"Okay," was her reluctant reply.

I hit the talk button. "Hey, Erin."

"Don't you dare try to act like nothing happened." Her voice rose and I had to move the phone away from my ear.

"You've obviously heard."

"Mark just called. It's actually on the metro news stations, but they didn't name the person who found the body. I couldn't believe it when Mark said it was you."

The media must have picked up the murder information from the Buffalo County Sheriff's Office. There had been no reporters on the scene the previous night. And thankfully none of them had called me. Erin sucked in a loud breath, then continued, "You didn't think that one of the first things you should do was to call your best friends? Especially since one of them was the victim's victim?" Victim's victim. That was a good way to put it, I thought.

"Erin. What would you have done about it anyway? And you know very well you got a better night's sleep by not getting a call like that at midnight."

"Well—"

"Why don't you meet Pinky and me at our shops about nine? I will disclose every single solitary sordid detail." Since it was Saturday, Erin had the day off from school.

"I'll be there."

We said our good-byes and hung up. I stood, folded the blanket, and smoothed it over the back of the couch. After a long, hot shower, I dried myself with a towel, then wrapped it around my body and made my way to the bedroom closet. Because of my previous career position, I had a wardrobe filled with suits, with both skirts and pants, and dresses with jackets that turned them into business attire; plus I had more casual, longer skirts and jeans. I no longer battled with my weight and I had finally accepted the fact that I had a curvy shape. My mother called it "an hourglass figure, like Marilyn Monroe's."

That had inspired me to dress up as the famous, although haunted, actress for a few costume parties over the years. When I styled my strawberry blond hair like Monroe's, covered the sprinkling of freckles across my nose and cheeks with makeup, darkened my eyebrows, and wore red lipstick, I passed. As long as you didn't look closely at my more generous mouth or my smaller ears with attached earlobes. And I'd gotten a pair of colored contacts to make my green eyes blue. Decked out as Marilyn from head to toe, I looked quite authentic, and almost fooled myself.


B oth Pinky and Erin were walking around in the coffee shop like chickens with their heads cut off when I got there at ten minutes before nine. Actually, in the bird world, Pinky was more like a swan, with her long, skinny legs and elongated neck, and Erin was more like a baby chick: small and compact. Pinky wore black leggings with a pink-and-purple-striped top that hung to her knees. Erin was in her usual outside-of-work outfit of jeans and a sweater.

Pinky opened her shop at eight o'clock for her clients, but I rarely had a customer before ten, so that was when the curio side opened. An occasional coffee shop customer would wander in and look around, but we were lucky if Pinky sold an item for us once a month.

As soon as she spotted me, Pinky grabbed my shoulders and steered me to a table. "You sit right down here. I'll get your coffee and scone."

Erin sat down opposite me. "You'll have to talk between bites."

Pinky plunked food and drink on the table, then slid onto the chair between Erin and me. "Shoot."

I gave each detail I remembered, starting with looking at my e-mails, using the bathroom, finding the snowing snow globe . . .

"Wait a minute. Say that again," Pinky said and reached over to check the temperature on my forehead. "You're not spiking a fever."

"One of your old snow globes just started snowing?" Erin asked in an "I want to believe you but can't" voice. Her frowning expression backed up her tone.

"Not one of the old ones It was one I'd never seen before. . . ." I filled them in on the scene, and how it looked like a snow globe made of the same materials we'd used in May's class. They glanced at each other in a way that made me curious if they knew more than they were admitting to.

"Did you see the globe?" Both Pinky and Erin shook their heads, but neither answered. I continued my story. When I got to the part of touching the body with a stick, and having it topple to the ground, they grabbed my hands— Pinky my left and Erin my right—and squeezed. "Ouchy, you're cutting off my circulation." They eased their grips a tad.

"Cami, you were alone with Jerrell Powers's dead body in the park at night and you lived to tell about it. I'd have died of fright," Pinky said. Her hazel eyes were as round as the moon had been the night before.

Erin slowly shook her head back and forth. "That is the creepiest thing I've ever heard in my entire life."

When I relayed that Clint and I had discovered the snow globe was missing from the shelf, they both squeezed my hands again. Pinky spoke. "And you're sure you weren't having some sort of premonition? Like when your mom comes—"

"I'm sure. More than sure. Positively sure." I hadn't used that expression since we were teenagers and I was trying to convince the others I was right. "And my mother's visits are not premonitions or hallucinations. And they are not even real visits . . . oh, never mind. After I'd watched the last of the snow settle, I picked up the globe and studied it. I know what I saw."

"Yes, but if you were having a premonition, you would see the scene. I mean, what if it was really one of your other globes, but the scene changed to show you what had happened, or was about to happen?" Pinky said.

I felt my eyes squint slightly. "Uh, no. I will say it one more time. I don't have premonitions."

"Then how do you explain it?" Erin asked.

"I have a theory."

"And that is?" Pinky said.

"Someone planned the murder, captured the scene in the snow globe, and realized they'd accidentally left the globe.

They saw me in here at the computer, waited until I went to use the bathroom, slipped in, and was about to grab it, but I came back faster than they expected, so they hid instead. Then, after I left, they took it and fled."

Erin shrugged one shoulder. "That sort of makes sense."

"And if that's what happened, I'm glad you didn't get bopped on the head. Or worse," Pinky added.

We all knew what worse meant. "There is one major flaw in that explanation to consider," I said.

Erin was the first to take a sip of coffee. "What's that?"

"My shop door only locks with a key from the outside."

"That's true with your door, but you can lock my shop door from the inside, then pull it shut from the outside. They could have gone out that way," Pinky said.

That widened the pool of suspects substantially.

4

A group of people came in for coffee, which put an end to our discussion. Erin left to run errands and I went into my shop to get ready for the day's business. I unlocked the shop door at one minute to ten and my mother called me at one minute after ten. They'd heard about my walk through the park from Mark, who had stopped by their house. "Thank God you weren't killed last night. Why didn't you call us?" Mom's voice was shaky.

Although I had planned to call my parents before they heard the news from anyone else, I was trying to think of a good way to do that without overly upsetting them. Plus, I needed to process major events for a while before I was able to talk to my parents about them. My dad had calmed down a lot over the years, but his Italian temper still rose quickly from time to time. I felt the need to phrase disturbing news in the most diplomatic way possible so neither one of them freaked out.

"Sorry, Mom, I meant to, but it's been a little hectic. Kind of a late night. And I really wasn't in any kind of personal danger." Not that I could tell.

"Your brothers and sisters, not to mention your nieces and nephews, are all buzzing like bees. Like half the people in Brooks Landing seem to be."

When I had gone to live with the Vanellis at age five, they had four children of their own. It was a busy, noisy household and a bit of a culture shock for me; I had been an only child in a quiet home.

"I'll talk to everyone in the next day or so," I promised.

"Yes, that's one of the reasons I called. Susan wants to have the whole family over to her house tonight for a potluck." Mom started coughing.

"Maybe that's not such a good idea, especially for you, Mom. You should concentrate on healing." Her coughing sound muffled, as though she had covered the receiver or moved away from the phone.

"Cami, it's Dad." He took over the conversation. "Your mom'll be fine. She caught a little cold with her immune system being down the way it is. But don't you worry, I'll keep a close watch on her. Come to Susan and Mick's place when you close up the shop. We'll see you a little after six, then."

That settled that. "Okay, Dad. I'll bring some muffins." We said our good-byes, and I moped about the whole thing for a minute. I dearly loved my family, but when I'd lived out of state I had more control over my personal life. With the exception of that one major incident, of course, but that was different. Another life-changing experience, but different. Maybe someday my parents would realize their baby was all grown up with a mind of her own.

After we'd hung up, I checked the phone messages. There was one from May Gregors, left at 11:57 the night before. "Hi, Camryn and Pinky, I must have left a bag of supplies in your coffee shop, maybe on one of the chairs. I am missing some figurines and snow globes. I know you're not still at the store this late, but please call me when you get this message."

Oh, my, Jerrell Powers's ex-wife. I wondered if she had heard the news that morning. Or had she already known about it last night because she was directly involved in the crime? She was definitely on my list of potential suspects. It seemed a little strange she had phoned late at night to ask a mundane question when she knew we wouldn't be there. Or was it a well-planned attempt to shift unwanted attention away from her?

I went into the coffee shop in search of May's missing supplies. Pinky glanced at me then back at the customer she was handing a bag of goodies to. I looked around for May's things, including under the tables and chairs.

"What are you doing?" Pinky asked when she was free.

"May is missing some snow globe–making supplies and thought she might have left a bag behind."

"That's strange. I didn't find any extras here, last night or this morning."

"Maybe they fell behind something, like these bags of coffee beans." She had large burlap sacks against the side wall.

Pinky lifted an arm and waved. "Have at it, sweets. I sure didn't see anything when I did my morning grinding earlier, but then again, I wasn't looking for them."

We searched for a couple of minutes, but turned up nothing that didn't belong to Pinky. There were not many potential hiding places in that area, and to our knowledge, no one had gone in her storage room. "I'm always relieved when we move things and don't uncover a mouse nest," she said.

"Pinky, ew. What would make you think of such a thing?"

"Out in the country, living next to a field, mice would crawl in sometimes in the fall to find a warm spot to have their babies. I remember my mother moved the couch one time to clean and there was a nest underneath. I can still hear her screaming." She shook her head and smiled at the thought.

I gave her a single pat on the back. "Okay, this is an old building, like, ninety years old, but I have never seen any sign of a mouse."

"Good point. And I don't see any sign of May's supplies, either."

"I'll let her know we looked. Hopefully she misplaced them when she packed up last night and has found them by now."

A pale Lauren Engle and a paler Pamela Hemley appeared from seemingly nowhere. I hadn't heard the customer alert bell on the door ding and, judging from her look of surprise, Pinky hadn't, either. Pam put her hand on a table for support and collapsed onto a chair. Lauren hovered protectively near her.

"Jerrell didn't come home last night and I thought it was because he was afraid of . . . I mean, that he was worried about what Lauren would say," Pam said in little more than a whisper.

Lauren rested a hand on her sister's shoulder, then looked at me. "The assistant police chief paid us a visit very early this morning. He told us about, um, your, um, discovery in the park last night."

"Jerrell's dead and they questioned *us*," Pam said.

"God rest his sorry soul." Lauren mouthed the words so no one would hear, but I read her lips. She caught me staring and lowered her eyes to look at Pam.

"I can't believe he's really gone." Pam grabbed a napkin off the table and buried her face in it. She sobbed and Lauren patted her back. When Pam lifted her head and found my eyes with her own red, puffy ones, she sucked in a big gulp of air. "Tell us how he was."

I searched for a word other than "dead." But that was the one that was most accurate and summed it up the best: dead. That was how he was. "Well, when I saw . . . Jerrell, he was sitting on a park bench. And I honestly thought he was sleeping. But then he fell off, and didn't move at all, and that's when I realized he had . . . passed on."

"They wouldn't even say how he died. Just that it was being investigated as a homicide," Pam said and more tears rolled down her face and dropped on her chest.

The police hadn't told me to keep how he'd died a secret from anyone. I had no idea why they couldn't give the poor ladies the basic facts. I'd heard somewhere, maybe from a movie, that there were sometimes key pieces of evidence that only the killer would know about. Maybe that was the case.

And it was something for me to consider in the investigation I was secretly conducting. Maybe the police didn't want Pamela and Lauren to know because the two of them were on their radar after all. They were surely on mine. "I'm sure the police will reveal whatever details they can when they can. But of course I can't speak for them," I said.

Lauren gave Pam's shoulder a squeeze. "We should get you home, and let these ladies get back to work."

"Home." Pam said the word then wailed, "It'll never be the same, knowing Jerrell will never be there again."

Lauren rolled her eyes. "Come on, Pam."

I raised my hand. "Oh, if you have another minute—this isn't a very good time to ask you this, but did you happen to accidentally pick up a bag of May's snow globe–making supplies? She's missing some things."

Lauren shrugged. "I don't know how we could have, but things got a little confused before we left. We'll check our bags when we get back to Pam's and let you know if we did."

"Thanks. She said it's some figurines and globes."

Lauren nodded then helped Pam get to her feet and guided her out the door.

"They are quite the pair of opposites," Pinky said.

"They really are. And Lauren acts more like her mother than her sister."

"Let's face it. If you had a sister who took to the likes of Jerrell Powers, you'd be doing your darnedest to get her away from him."

"I guess I would. But to what lengths?"

"What are you getting at?" Pinky bent over slightly and leaned her face closer to mine. "You think Lauren had something to do with Jerrell Powers's murder?"

I shrugged. "I missed that part—you know, the actual committing of the crime."

Pinky folded her hands. "And thank the good Lord you did."

Yes, indeed. It was bad enough coming on the scene after the fact. "Well, I'll go call May to tell her we didn't find her supplies."

May's voice was shaky when she answered. "The police just left. I can't believe Jerrell is actually dead. I mean, not that I'm really that sorry he's gone for good, but . . ." I gave her a minute to finish, but she had quit talking. She must have figured she had said enough.

"It's a pretty big shock, I'm sure. I didn't even know him, and I'm bowled over," I said.

"Now I won't have to make excuses to our daughter about why her father never comes to see her, or never makes any kind of contact with her."

My own father had always been there for his children. "That must have been tough for you all those years."

It sounded like May sniffled. "It's all behind us now. It would have been easier if he had moved to the North Pole, or some other remote place that was hard to get to or from, but that was not to be."

The way she talked about her ex-husband's shortcomings, I half expected her to confess that she had been the perpetrator of the crime. After all, she had a stack of reasons, happened to be in Brooks Landing, and had even seen Jerrell Powers. She could have arranged an opportunity to meet him and then killed him. I wished I had been a fly on the wall when the police had talked to her. If she had told them the things she'd told me, maybe they would have arrested her. I moved her up to the top spot on my list of suspects.

I thought I'd play an angle. "Well, as difficult as it was to see him yesterday, at least you did get to see him one last time before he died."

"What do you mean?" Her voice was hesitant.

"In the post office, before you came to the coffee shop."

"Ah . . . yes, that's right."

"Or maybe you saw him after that. After the class?"

"After the class?" she repeated. "Uh, no. No, I didn't."

We were both quiet a while. "Before I forget, I wanted to tell you I got your message about the missing supplies. Pinky and I searched around and didn't find them." Should I tell her about the two sisters stopping by? Why not? "Oh, and I happened to see Pamela Hemley and Lauren Engle this morning and asked if your things had accidentally gotten mixed in with theirs. They didn't think so, but they're checking."

"Hmm. Well, if they find them, ask them to bring them to your store and I'll stop by the next time I'm in town. I do not care to have another run in with either one of them, which I'm sure you can appreciate."

"Yes, I can. Okay. We'll check with the others who were at the class last night and hopefully we'll be able to locate your things."

"I'd appreciate that." She paused then said, "The police told me that it was a woman who found Jerrell last night. Can you imagine a woman walking through the park all alone in the dark, at that time of night?"

I was more embarrassed every time that question was

posed. Mark had told Lauren and Pamela it was me, but the officer who'd talked to May had just said it was a woman.

"Actually, I can. I have the bad luck of being that woman."

"No. *You?* Are you serious?"

"Unfortunately, I am very serious."

"So you know what happened? The police wouldn't give any details."

"I don't exactly know what happened, but I was the one who found him. I guess if the police are keeping certain things about it quiet, I'd better not say any more, for now."

"All right, then, I won't try to pump you for information. I wouldn't want you to get into trouble."

Too late. I was up to my neck in trouble. Starting from the minute I'd spotted Jerrell Powers sitting on the bench. "Thanks." A customer came in the front door. "I need to hang up and get to work."

"I'll let you go. And thanks for calling me back. I don't think I'll be able to get much of anything done myself today. This whole thing is kind of starting to hit me, I think."

"I'm sure it is. Take care, May. 'Bye."

"Bye-bye."


Pinky ran to the bank shortly before noon, and I had the shops to myself for a few minutes. There were no customers so I went to the back office and found an empty spiral notebook and pen. I carried them to my front counter, where I could watch for any shoppers, and slid the stool over in front of a clear writing surface and sat down. I opened to the first page and wrote, *Who killed Jerrell Powers?* That was blunt, and maybe too specific of a question. I tore out the page and put it through the shredder located on the floor behind me.

I wrote a new heading on the new page. *Who wanted Jerrell Powers out of the picture?* I had to consider that the person or persons who had killed him may have set out only to convince him to leave town, but the encounter became violent. Not necessarily premeditated. On the other hand, it could have been planned years before. From what I had learned in the past twenty-four hours, Powers was not the kind of guy you'd want on your team. He'd be the last pick, or asked to leave the lineup altogether.

I debated about whose name to write down first. I settled on Clint's choice of Powers's halfway house roommate. He had an easy-to-remember name, Benjamin, not Benedict, Arnold. That was how I remembered his name and that was what I wrote down. For all I knew there could be more than one halfway house resident who had it in for Jerrell Powers. It was just that Benjamin, not Benedict, happened to spout off about it.

There was still the mystery of the snow globe appearing then disappearing in my shop. If a stranger to the town was the guilty one, he'd likely need a local accomplice. Hmm.

Suspect number two: May Gregors. She'd said Jerrell had ruined their daughter's life and hers at the same time. May had also told us she didn't know Jerrell was in Brooks Landing. Maybe that was true. Maybe not. And to my way of thinking, it was a little suspicious that she just happened to schedule a class in the same town Jerrell had been living in, and committed a crime in, and still had a girlfriend in. More than a little suspicious. And she had certainly not been saddened to learn he'd been killed. Quite the opposite.

I put Lauren Engle down as suspect number three. She was obviously upset with her sister's choice of Jerrell Powers as a boyfriend. With good reason, it seemed to me and everyone else. I would have felt the same way if one of my sisters had fallen for a loser. But was she against it enough to actually kill the man? With her size and muscle strength, Lauren would have no trouble handling just about any man. And she was roughly the same height as Powers.

And really, Pamela was not completely off the list, either. She was under pressure to give Powers the shove. Maybe she tried, but Powers wouldn't budge, so she gave him the ax. Or the knife, as it were. It was possible she and her sister had worked together to commit the dastardly deed. Pam could have lured Powers to the park, where Lauren planted the knife. That would make it premeditated. Lauren did say she was in Brooks Landing to do her best to convince her sister to get rid of Powers. Maybe she had done just that, in the literal sense.

Who else needed consideration? I hated for even a moment to ponder that either Pinky or Erin was involved, but there was that remote possibility. If they were connected to the crime in any way, I had to believe Powers had not been killed on purpose. It would have to have been a meeting that went downhill fast, past the point of no return. I thought better of writing their names down in case they happened upon my notebook, which I vowed to keep as securely hidden as possible.

And the last two people I thought of were also unlikely suspects: Officer Mark Weston and Archie Newberry. Both were obviously protective of Erin. And of Pinky and me, to a lesser extent. Mark held a long-burning torch for Erin. He had the training to take down suspects, but would Mark risk jeopardizing the career he dearly loved to get rid of Powers?

Archie had no children of his own and spent a fair amount of time at the coffee shop, especially when Erin was there. He seemed to genuinely enjoy and appreciate our company. He even called us his "almost family friends." But could Archie hurt a fly, much less a man?

I knew the police were hot on tracking Benjamin Arnold down, so I'd steer clear of that avenue. I was curious about other possible halfway house suspects, but thought I'd better stick closer to home first before broadening my horizons. I had a healthy list of people to investigate.

The little "ding" of a bell alerted me the coffee shop door had opened. It also reminded me that if anyone had come or gone through that door while I was in the store the previous night, I would have heard them. Unless I was in the bathroom with the door closed. Which I was for a brief minute. So that basically confirmed the person either had a key or was hiding in the store waiting for me to leave.

"It's me!" Pinky called out as I was getting up. I shoved the notebook under the counter on the shelf.

"Okay," I called back.

She came through the archway. "You cannot believe how everyone in town is talking. I mean, when is the last time anyone was murdered around here?"

"Um, never?"

"No, not true. We had one umpteen years ago. Remember old widow Calder? Poor thing. That was never solved."

"Yeah, I'd forgotten about that."

"People are talking about locking their doors and getting watchdogs and everything."

Drastic times called for drastic measures. "Pinky, who do you think did it?"

She scrunched up her face. "That's a funny question to ask me."

"If you had to guess."

"Cami, I don't want to guess."

The coffee shop door opened and the two new customers saved her from having to answer.

Erin phoned in midafternoon to see if I wanted to go out for a bite to eat after work. "I wish I could, but I've been summoned to a family dinner. You're welcome to come. You can make sure I live through the interrogation of the masses."

"Gee whiz, tempting, but no, thanks. You can stop over after your dinner instead." She gave a single chuckle. "If you live through the interrogation, that is."

"You have no idea. Okay, I will make every attempt to break away from Susan's before nine o'clock and will see you then."

"Sounds good. I'll be waiting in my quiet house."

We hung up and I puzzled over why Erin was so keen on getting together that night. Usually when I had other plans, she left it at that. Unless she really needed to talk to me, which must be the case.

Pinky came into Curio Finds and plopped down in one of the chairs we kept off to the side, mostly for the men who tagged along with their shopping wives. She stuck her feet straight out and stretched her arms above her head. "I am beat and we've got a couple more hours yet."

"If you're tired, go on home. You'll be back here early tomorrow, and I'm sure I can handle things. There's not all that much going on."

"I suppose. I just feel like I should keep you close. Keep an eye on you."

"What for?"

"I don't know. Maybe to keep you safe."

"Pinky, that is sweet, but totally unnecessary. I promise I will not be taking any late-night treks alone. Unless it is on a main road."

"That's not good enough."

"Okay. I will not go out walking alone at night until Jerrell Powers's killer is found."

She reached up and adjusted her pink headband. "And what if that doesn't happen? What if they are never found?"

*They?* Did she think there was more than one person involved, or was she doing what most of us did, saying "they" instead of "him" or "her"? I shrugged. "Chances are they will find the killer, and if they don't, we take it from there." I thought of something else. "Oh, I meant to ask you this morning. Do you have the list of people who were at the class last night?"

Pinky's eyebrows drew together. "Was it really only last night?"

"I know, it seems like last week. Anyway, I thought we'd better call everyone to see if they got the extra supplies May is missing by mistake."

"I don't think that's necessary. If someone has them, they'll return them."

"Not everyone would do that. Okay, maybe the ones who were here last night would. But if her stuff got mixed in with their stuff, they might not notice for a while."

"I say let it go. We don't want anyone to think we're accusing them of anything, or they'd never come to another one of our classes again."

"Golly, Pinky. You are really thinking of having another class in this same century after all that happened last night?"

"We'll talk about it when we can all think a little better. They say time heals all wounds. We'll see. And maybe we won't do snow globes next time. I thought learning how to make them was kind of fun, and not as hard as I figured it'd be. Mine looks really cute on my dresser at home. The other members in the class seemed to enjoy themselves, too."

"I was distracted knowing who was who, waiting for the proverbial shoe to drop. But if it wasn't for all that, I'd have to say the class itself was fun."

Pinky pushed herself out of the chair. "All right, then, I'll head on home. I hear my oven calling out to me."

"You are a dedicated baking machine."

Pinky smiled. "That's me, for sure." Her smile faded. "On second thought, maybe you'd rather I hang around so you don't have to be alone. I bet you're still in shock about last night."

"To tell you the truth, the whole thing seems more like a dream than reality. I feel okay, but I'll let you know if, or when, I don't."

Pinky came over and gave me a hug. "Good. Hang in there, Cami."

Pinky was barely gone before Mark Weston stopped by. He was out of uniform, dressed casually in jeans and a hooded sweatshirt, more like the Mark I remembered. I sometimes wondered why he and Erin had never married. He'd be a great catch by most people's standards. Above average height—five foot ten, lean and muscular, attractive features, especially his sky blue eyes.

He glanced around the shops. "You're here alone? Where's Pinky?"

"I sent her home. Not much going on this afternoon."

He sat down on the chair Pinky had vacated. "Clint was smart not to release your name to the media, and there haven't been any big leaks yet so it keeps the gawkers at bay. But when word gets out, people will be flocking in here big-time."

"Really? Like, they want to see what a person looks like after they've had a traumatic night in the park, or what?"

"Guess so." Mark crossed his arms on his chest. "I sure didn't think you'd be at work today, not after everything that happened."

I sat down on the stool behind the counter. "I was just telling Pinky that last night seems like a dream—actually, a nightmare. I wouldn't have wanted to hang around the house by myself all day, thinking about it."

"I can see your point. I wouldn't, either."

"So were you and Clint busy talking to Jerrell Powers's friends and family members this morning?"

Mark's eyebrows rose. "Me? Nah, that was just Clint. He was up at the crack of dawn, determined to crack the case. I had my regular shift."

"But you did tell my parents, and Erin, and Pinky."

Mark raised his right hand. "Guilty as charged."

"Pamela Hemley and her sister stopped by all upset and said the assistant police chief had questioned them. Then I returned a call to May Gregors, who was not quite as upset and said the police had talked to her. I didn't ask which officer. She wasn't exactly sad Jerrell was dead."

"Is that right?"

"That's what she said. So what are your thoughts on the whole deal?"

"I'm deferring this one to Clint. He's mostly looking for that Benjamin Arnold. And we haven't gotten the official autopsy report. That'll be a day or two yet, or so I'm told. I know they performed it this morning and have some initial findings, but I'm not authorized to say anything."

"That's understandable. And I personally don't care if I ever hear those details."

"No need for you to."

He was right. I'd had a close-up view of the victim and saw what had likely caused his death. "Mark, this isn't exactly police business, but May is missing some of her snow globe–making supplies."

"Is that right? She had a lot of stuff. How could she even know her exact inventory?"

"I have no idea. Just telling you what she told me. Pinky and I looked, but we didn't find anything in her shop. I told Pam and Lauren about the missing items, and wanted to call the others who were here, but Pinky didn't think that was a good idea."

He frowned. "Why's that?"

"She didn't want them to think we were accusing them."

"Yeah, it might seem like that, and the stuff may turn up after all. No one in the group struck me as a thief, but that doesn't mean one of them wasn't. Pinky's probably right about dropping the issue."

"Yeah, I'll think about it some more." I got up and pointed

to the decanter on Pinky's counter. "Go ahead and help yourself to a cup of coffee or something."

He shook his head. "Nah, I've got some things to take care of. Hey, do you want to do something later on, so you don't have to be alone?"

All my friends were thoughtful. "Thanks, but I'm having dinner with the whole family."

"Your *whole* family? You better bring your earplugs." Mark gave his forehead a bop with the heel of his hand.

I reached over and gave his forehead a mild bop of my own. "It's not that bad."

"That's because you're used to it, but don't say I didn't warn you. I'm gonna run, so I'll catch up with you later, Cami." He got up and headed for the door.

I smiled and waved. He gave a nod on the way out.

It was not two minutes later that Archie walked into Pinky's shop. I had to wonder if all my friends had decided someone should keep me company today. Like the old telephone game; as each one left he or she called the next one, and so on. I went into Brew Ha-Ha to wait on him.

"I heard you found that no-goodnik in my park last night." Archie talked about all the city parks like they were his personal property. "Sorry you had to go through somethin' like that. I know with all I saw when I was in the war, those kinds of things are hard to forget. You put 'em out of your mind and they pop back in."

I walked over and rested my hand on his shoulder blade. "Thanks, Archie. I'll be just fine with all the support from my family, and friends like you."

The expression on his wrinkled face was earnest when he turned it toward mine. "You know you're almost like a daughter to me."

"I know that, and thank you." I gave his shoulder a squeeze then went behind the counter. "So, how about we have a cup of something and sit and talk for a while?" I glanced up at the Betty Boop clock and saw it was thirty minutes until closing. "What can I get you?"

He looked at the menu of beverages posted on the wall above the serving counter. "You know one of them fancy chai teas would hit the spot on a cool fall day."

"Mmm, that does sound good. You should work here, Archie. You've sold me on one, too."

I mixed up the concoctions and set one frothy drink on the serving counter in front of Archie and kept the other for myself. "So, Archie, what'd you think of the class last night?"

"Accordin' to my way of thinkin', it never hurts to learn a new skill. And I thought it was kind of interestin' the way that teacher made that snow. It did seem like magic." Archie pronounced the word "interesting" as "inneresting."

"We had kind of a big surprise after the class, huh?"

"It was a durn big shock is what it was."

"No, not what happened with Jerrell Powers. I meant the whole thing with May Gregors and Erin and Pamela Hemley and her sister."

His lips pushed out and formed an O. "That whole fiasco was quite the deal, at that. Those women involved with the likes of that no-goodnik. If a guy had to die, out of all the guys I know, I guess he'd be the best pick."

Archie had a simple, sometimes even simplistic, way of looking at things.

"When you put it that way, I can't argue with you. But I would have voted for running him out of town instead."

"He'da probably only come back anyway."

# 5

Mark was right: if wearing a pair of earplugs wouldn't have been obvious and rude, they might have prevented my eardrums from pounding at the family gathering. All the immediate Vanelli family members were loud and expressive. Except for Mom and me, that is. We both clung to our more quiet Scandinavian—Norwegian and Swedish— roots. On top of that, my biological father was of English descent. Consequently, loud and expressive was not in my gene pool, or part of my experience in the first five years of my upbringing.

When I first moved in with my new family at the young age of five, I was on sensory overload. It seemed like everyone talked at once, and I couldn't figure out how anyone heard what even one other person was saying. Eventually I sorted it out and came to love the way my father and siblings were so passionate about things. And Mom's low-key demeanor kept it all from getting too crazy.

I opened the door of my sister's large, two-story house undetected and stood in the entryway, taking a second to inhale the combined smells of garlic, tomatoes, olive oil, and herbs. When I walked into the living room, Susan was the first one to grab on to me. She took the bag of muffins out of my hand and gave it to one of her daughters. Then she hugged me so tightly I could barely breathe.

"Okay, okay," my other sister, Debby, said, "my turn."

I was passed down the line until everyone—my brothers, brothers-in-law, sisters-in-law, nieces, and nephews—all had physical proof I was all right. Mom was sitting on the couch, and Dad practically carried me over to her.

"Cami, you sit down here so I can hold you a minute," Mom said. When she put her thin arms around me, it was like I was that scared and lonely little girl again. Tears filled my eyes, surprising me. Besides being worried about Mom's health, the emotions connected to all I'd experienced the previous day caught up with me. Dad sat down on my other side and laid his large, muscled arm across me then rested his warm hand on Mom's. In minutes, I felt calmer.

"We are so grateful you weren't harmed," Mom said, her blue eyes bright with unshed tears. Her head was wrapped in a stylish multicolored scarf I'd given her from my seldom-worn collection.

"But we're mighty troubled to think we have a killer who lives among us in our community," Dad said.

"They don't know if the killer lives here or not. The

police think it might have been someone from outside of Brooks Landing. They're looking for a man Jerrell Powers knew from the halfway house they were both in."

"Let's hope that's the case," Dad said.

I had an inkling that wasn't the case, but there was no need to mention that.

"Soup's on," Susan called above the rising volume of twenty or so voices talking at various decibel levels. We gathered in the country-style kitchen for our mealtime prayer, then Susan guided me to be the first in line for the buffet assortment of hot dishes, salads, and breads. I dished up portions of Susan's always-in-demand lasagna; Debby's romaine and provolone salad drizzled with an herbed dressing; ricotta and fruit salad; manicotti with mozzarella cheese oozing out the sides of the pasta; and a piece of crusty bread. A culinary heaven for Italian food lovers like me.

"You go sit next to Mom at the table tonight," Susan instructed. Her extra-large dining table held sixteen people comfortably, so there was room for all the siblings and their spouses, plus a few nieces and nephews. The others sat at card tables in the living room.

Eventually everyone got through the line, and Dad filled a plate of food for Mom, which she picked at and pushed around more than she ate. I wondered if it was good for her to be surrounded by all the potential germs in the room, but she wouldn't have it any other way.

Dad sat at the opposite end of the table from Mom. He clapped his hands together three times, which was the signal we all recognized as *Attention, please.*

"Children, Cami has the floor and will tell us of her unfortunate experience last night. And we will listen without interruption so she can get through her whole story before the cows come home." My dad had never owned cows, but it was an expression he preferred over "it gets too late."

I walked the family through the entire "Friday from hell," beginning with Pinky's news that Jerrell Powers was once again wandering the streets of Brooks Landing. But for a very limited time, as it turned out. There were loud gasps when I told them the class instructor was Powers's ex-wife, and about the confrontation at the end of the class. But the snowing snow globe got the biggest response, until I filled in the details of finding Powers's body in the park, that is. My family members were shifting, visually itching to ask questions along the way, but Dad's command kept them in check. When I finished by telling them that when Clint took me back to the store, the snow globe had disappeared, the normal unchecked family gusto returned.

And it seemed I answered questions, and repeated key parts of my story, until the cows did come home. "Okay, everyone, enough! We can all see we are wearing Cami out," Dad said.

I smiled a thank-you at Dad then gave him and Mom a kiss and a hug.

Mom's eyes misted. "Besides being my daughter, you're the only living connection I have to Berta. I need you to stay safe, my dear."

"I will, Mom." And for the second time that night tears welled in my eyes.

Instead of the usual thirty-minute Minnesota good-bye, I slipped away quietly into the night. The cool evening air was refreshing after the warmth of the house. I threw my head back to look at the moon and the stars and sucked in a big breath of air. On my way to the car, my phone beeped, alerting me I had a message. It was Erin wondering how much longer I'd be. Instead of texting a reply, I phoned her, said, "Five minutes," then hung up.

Erin handed me a bottle of my favorite brand of beer while I was still in the entry, after I'd slipped off my jacket. "Thanks, I think this will really hit the spot tonight."

"I got nervous waiting for you so I already had one," Erin said as I followed her to her den. We sat in her comfortable overstuffed wing chairs and plopped our feet on the matching ottomans. She pulled at her straight black hair, gathered in a ponytail at the nape of her neck. "I didn't exactly want him dead, you know. I actually feel bad about it."

*Didn't exactly want him dead?* "I think I know what you mean. There have been people in my life I hope I never see again, but that doesn't mean I want them to die." I took a sip of my drink. "So who do you think did it?"

Erin's dark eyebrows shot up. "For Pete's sake, Cami, what a question! I think we should leave that up to the police to figure out."

Her reaction was so similar to Pinky's, it stopped me in my tracks. It wasn't like either of them not to answer a direct question, especially from me or someone else who was close to them. Erin and Pinky had returned to Brooks Landing after their years away at college, and they'd continued spending time together all the years I'd been gone. They were still the best friends I had in the world, but the two of them had more history, more memories, probably more secrets, that I hadn't been a part of.

I wanted to get to the bottom of what had really happened to Jerrell Powers. I needed to know the truth, even if it meant my friends were involved. The fact that both Erin and Pinky were reluctant to offer their opinions of what they thought may have happened was just plain odd. Everyone seemed to have a theory, or at least a guess, when a major crime went down. Maybe they'd be willing to talk about it in a few days.

There was no need for me to keep pressing her. "Erin, you didn't happen to find extra snow globe–making supplies with your things last night, did you?"

"Extra supplies?"

"May is missing some from her stash."

"Hmm. It's funny she'd even notice with all the stuff she brought." She shifted then studied my face and changed the subject herself. "How are you doing, really? And tell me the honest truth, Cami."

"I'll be okay in time. The whole thing does not seem like it really happened. At all. But I've told the story so many times already, it's bound to sink into my thick little brain eventually."

She smiled and shook her head at my last comment. "You mean your thick *big* brain. I don't think that the whole thing is real to any of the rest of us, either."

"And how about you? I mean, first off, you heard Jerrell Powers was back in town. And then the whole ordeal of finding out who was who before and after our class. May, Pamela, Lauren. You had a few shocks of your own, huh?"

Erin looked down at her dainty hands then nodded. "That's for darn sure. Nothing that compares with yours, but it was one thing after the other once we heard the last person in the world I ever wanted to see again was back roaming our streets." She reached over to the end table that stood between us, picked up the snow globe she'd made, gave it a shake, and set it back down. We watched the snowflakes settle over her scene of kids sledding down a hill

"I'm glad I was in the dark about who May was when I signed up for the class because I really liked learning how to make these. And my students will get a kick out of making something this special. They'll be cool gifts for their parents."

"No pun intended?"

"What? Ahhh, cool. No, no pun intended. And Pam and her sister being there added another strange aspect, but neither one will have to worry about Jerrell Powers anymore."

"That's one way to put it, I guess."

Erin gave the snow globe another shake. "Who's manning the shops tomorrow?"

"Pinky."

"Good. You need a day of R and R. I was planning to meet one of my friends from school to do some hiking, but I can cancel and spend the time with you instead. Or do you want to come along? Physical activity is a great stress reliever."

"No. You go have fun. I have a date with a dirty house."

"Whose?"

"Mine."

"Cami, you never let your house get dirty and you know it."


Sunday morning, just before ten o'clock, I was scrubbing away in the kitchen, pondering who may have been involved in the murder, and otherwise minding my own business, when I heard a car pull up and park on the street in front of my house. I looked out the window and was not at all pleased to see it was Assistant Chief Clinton Lonsbury's police car. He got out of it and shut his door. I threw the rags and cleaning bucket under the sink, and pushed the vacuum into a nearby closet a second before the front doorbell rang.

I took my time walking to the door, as much to slow my breathing as to make Clint wait an extra minute. He rang the bell again. I steeled myself and opened the door. "Good morning," I said, with not a trace of a smile on my face.

Clint raised an eyebrow. "Am I interrupting your cleaning therapy session?"

"What?"

He pointed at my jeans. "You have a rag stuck in each of your front pockets."

"Oh." I patted the telltale evidence.

"And the smell of citrus fruit is the second dead giveaway."

"Do you feel safe coming into my lemony clean house?"

"If you feel safe against any invisible germs that might be clinging to my body."

I stepped aside and bit my tongue to hold in a rude remark while he braved a step inside.

Clint pulled his memo pad from his front pocket, flipped to a page, and glanced at his notes. "I wanted to give you an informal update on the case."

"Informal?" I waved my hand toward the kitchen, and then I led the way there.

"Rather than asking you to come to the PD."

I pulled a solid wood chair back from the small table for

him. "I see. Here you go, have a seat. How about a cup of coffee? I have the beans from Pinky's special supply."

Clint's nostrils flared slightly and he blinked. As I waited for his answer the thought crossed my mind that he might be wondering if I was thinking of poisoning him. It made me smile. He smiled back. "Something funny you'd like to tell me about?"

"No, it wasn't all that funny. Coffee, no coffee?"

"Coffee. Thanks." Clint settled onto the chair and crossed his arms on his chest. I felt his eyes boring into me as I turned my back, pulled a mug out of the cupboard, and filled it with a Guatemalan-blend medium-dark roast from Pinky's last delivery.

"Do you take cream or sugar?"

"I drink it black."

I set the mug on the table and sat down across from him. "Take a sip and if it's too strong and you need to add milk or cream, I have both."

Clint noisily slurped a bit of the hot brew and frowned slightly. "It's good. I don't usually go for the fancy stuff, but . . ." He took another loud sip.

"Do you always do that?"

"What?"

"Slurp. That loud sound when you suck in your coffee."

"Never thought about it, but yeah, I guess I do. To cool the hot coffee before it hits my mouth."

"And that works?"

"It does. Why, does it bug you?"

I considered denying that it did, but "yes," came out instead.

Clint shrugged and slurped some more. "I thought I'd let you know Benjamin Arnold has slipped off the radar."

"What do you mean?"

"We haven't been able to locate him yet. Not since Powers's murder anyway."

"Really? How do you go about looking for him, anyway? Aren't they required to give a forwarding address when they're released from the halfway house?"

"Not to the halfway house, but to his probation officer, yes. Arnold will be on probation for a while. The address he provided is his parents' home in Atwood. Seems he was there for one night then didn't go back. He's allegedly been gone over a week."

"So you talked to his parents?" I took a sip of coffee.

"Not yet. I called his hometown police department yesterday and talked to the police chief down there. I wanted to get a hold of his probation officer but since it was Saturday, the courthouse was closed. I will drive down to Atwood and have a chat with the parents myself. So I can get a feel for what they're like, get their take on their son and where he might have gone. It's about two hours south of here." He took a larger slurpy sip.

I moved my elbow to the table and rested one ear against my hand, partially blocking my hearing. "Can I get you some crunchy carrot sticks, maybe some peanuts or almonds to go with your coffee?"

One eyebrow shot up when he realized what I was hinting at. "No."

"When are you going to Atwood?"

"Right after I leave here. Based on my experience and professional opinion, the fact that our prime suspect is missing increases the chance that he is up to something. It sure doesn't put him in a good light."

He had a point. But I kept going back to the now-missing snowing death scene snow globe. It didn't mean Benjamin Arnold wasn't involved. But if he was, there had to have been someone in town he was working with. And who might that be? Even though I was not a police officer, it seemed to me that first checking then eliminating the people who were closest to Jerrell, or were affected by his crimes, made the most sense. At least we knew how to find them, for the most part.

Clint cleared his throat and put the memo pad back in his pocket. "So you about finished up with your therapy session?"

"Uh . . ." What was he getting at?

"If you are, I thought maybe you'd like to get out of town for a few hours. I know you've been spending a lot of your time at Curio Finds since you've been back."

*How would he know that?*

"According to Mark Weston, anyway. He says you're always there. In fact, that's where I thought I'd find you today. But when I stopped by, Pinky said to check here."

"Pinky and I trade off on Sundays, and sometimes a day off during the week, so we don't both have to work all seven days."

"Sounds like you have a worse schedule than I do. Ever thought of hiring someone to cover some of those hours?"

"We've thought of it, yes. But that involves a whole other level of issues, like workers' comp insurance and finding someone we can completely trust. We'll see. What did you mean about getting out of town for a few hours?"

"I thought you might want to ride along with me to Atwood when I check in with the Arnolds."

That was unexpected. Did he feel sorry for me, being stuck at Curio Finds month after month with little time off, or was he planning to pump me for information, convinced that I was somehow involved in the murder of Jerrell Powers? I figured that was probably it. But that didn't stop me from saying yes. After all, it would be a nice break from Brooks Landing.

Even if it was with the irritating, but nevertheless handsome, assistant chief of police. Maybe I could pump him for a little information in return. And I had gotten in a calming cleaning session. Which would be helpful before my hours-long journey with Clint, especially if he drank a hot beverage on the way.

I left Clint to finish his coffee and slipped into the bedroom to get ready. I changed quickly out of my jeans into gray slacks, a black sweater, and black boots. Not too casual, not too dressy. I brushed my teeth and hair, put on a little makeup, and was set to go in no time. Clint looked from me to his watch when I returned, gave a short nod and a small smile of approval, then stood.

"You might want to grab a jacket. It's about sixty degrees."

I knew what the temperature was, but decided at that moment I would have to pick my battles with Clinton Lonsbury, or we would be bickering over every little thing, instead of every other thing. On the way out, I pulled a gray, thigh-length rain-or-shine coat from the entry closet and threw it over my arm.

As I settled in the front seat of a police car for the second time in my life, I felt much more relaxed than the first time. When Clint turned the ignition, a voice crackled and made me jump. A Buffalo County dispatcher was sending a deputy to check on an open door at a business in a nearby town. Clint pulled the radio mouthpiece from its holder on the dashboard. "Brooks Landing PD Three-one-two to Buffalo County Dispatch."

"Go ahead, Three-one-two," a deep male voice answered.

"I'm ten-eight with a rider, en route to Atwood, Minnesota. Starting mileage: five-eight-six-two-two."

"Copy, at ten twenty-three."

Clint retrieved a logbook from the inside pocket of his door and jotted the date and mileage on the top sheet. "We're off," he said as he fastened his seat belt then put the car in drive and pulled onto the road in a seemingly simultaneous motion.

He glanced my way when he pressed down on the accelerator. "Have you recovered from your major shock the other night?"

I shrugged. "I don't know if it will ever seem real."

"It's the kind of thing *real* therapy might help with."

*Pick your battles.* "Have you ever had therapy to help you deal with things you've been through as a police officer?" My words came out with sugar coating around them.

It took Clint a minute to answer. "Well, um, no."

*Aha.*

The time and miles passed with not much dialogue between us, outside of observations about the small towns and countryside along the way. As I stole the occasional peek at

Clint, it struck me that he was even more attractive when he was in the role of a strong, silent type. I was relieved when we finally reached our destination at the Arnold home in Atwood, so I could quit fighting the urge to look at the guy.

The house was an average-looking middle-class rambler most likely built in the 1960s. It had a large picture window framed with black shutters that looked nice against the gray siding. We got out of the police car and followed the sidewalk to the front steps. I stayed back a ways to give Clint room when he rang the doorbell.

Mrs. Arnold opened the front door and stared at Clint's uniform for a second then gave me a quick once-over. Without a smile or a greeting, she let us into the house and led the way to the kitchen, where Mr. Arnold was reading the newspaper at the table. He stood and shook Clint's hand and nodded at me. I nodded back and we all settled on chairs around the table.

Morton and Penny Arnold were a couple that seemed ill matched, at least appearance-wise. He was well over six feet tall with a barrel chest and long stray gray hairs that poked out from his nose, ears, eyebrows, and throat area. She was thin and over a foot shorter than her husband. All her visible hairs were on her head and neatly combed into a severe bun. I challenged myself to spot a single errant strand, but there was not one to be found.

If Assistant Chief Clint Lonsbury were part of an interrogation team, he'd surely be the one who would take the "bad cop" role. I doubted he had a charming, schmoozing bone in his professional body. I folded my hands and kept them on my lap so I wouldn't bump elbows with either Mrs. Arnold or Clint. Both of them were serious—"stern" would be more a more accurate word—during the interview. I was the innocent observer who'd gotten out of Brooks Landing for a little break but was wishing I was back there. Or anywhere else. Morton moved his eyes from his wife to Clint and back again, as each one spoke. He appeared as uncomfortable as I was.

Clint squeezed his eyebrows together and leaned closer to Mrs. Arnold. ". . . So you have had no communication whatsoever with Benjamin in over a week?"

"Officer Lonsbury, that is what I have told you two times already: when you phoned, and not one minute ago when you asked again. I see no reason to repeat myself a third time."

"How about his friends? If you give me their names, I'll follow up with them."

Mrs. Arnold shook her head and shrugged. "We learned the hard way that birds of a feather do flock together. Our son fell in with some hooligans in high school, and he's been skirting the law ever since. He made one bad choice after the next. We tried to do right by the boy, but he turned his back on all of it. We told him he always had a place here if he was willing to toe the line, but we've had to accept that might never happen." Her face softened a tad.

Clint turned his focus on Mr. Arnold. "And the names of Benjamin's friends, if you would?"

Mr. Arnold lifted weary eyes and met Clint's. "We don't know of any. Ma's right. Benjamin burned about every bridge he crossed since high school. As far as his friends, we sure don't know any by name."

Clint squeezed his lips together then relaxed them. "Do you have photos of Benjamin we can have a look at?"

Mrs. Arnold squinted her eyes together as if she were in pain. "You're a policeman. You must have seen those pictures they take. What they call mug shots."

"I have seen Benjamin's photo, but appearances can change. Back when those were taken, two or three years ago, he was sporting a reddish auburn beard and had longer bleached blond hair. His face looked like it was sunburned and had an angry expression on it."

*Not unlike the current one on Mrs. Arnold's face,* I thought.

Mrs. Arnold raised her eyebrows. "Well. I guess Father and I have not seen him with that look before." She left the room and returned with a small photo album a minute later. She set it gently on the table and opened to the last page. It was a professional high school picture, the kind that went in a yearbook.

"This was taken his junior year. He didn't want to get one taken his senior year. He dropped out as soon as he turned eighteen at the end of September. Once he became an adult, there was not much more we could seem to do with him. He moved out, and you know the rest of the story," Mrs. Arnold said.

I knew very little of his story, but it was not my place to ask questions. I looked at Benjamin's photo. He could have been nice looking if he'd smiled, or at least hadn't tried so hard to look like a thug. He had large, close-set brown eyes and an intense stare. Without the beard, I noticed his chin was small and would have given his face a weak appearance if it weren't for his strong, cold eyes. His hair was a reddish auburn, and his skin was fairly light, and apparently prone to burning instead of tanning.

"He was always a handful," Mr. Arnold added.

Clint reached over and turned back a few pages and glanced at the photos. There weren't many, and none of Benjamin in groups, like at a birthday party or a ball game. Was that because of the type of kid he was or because his parents limited his activities?

"Your son must've been kind of a loner," Clint said.

Mrs. Arnold seemed taken aback. "Well, there weren't many playmates in the neighborhood." She left it at that.

Clint nodded. "You have my number so be sure to call if Benjamin shows up or if you hear from him. As I told you over the phone, I need to talk to him before I can clear him of any involvement in Jerrell Powers's death."

The way Mr. and Mrs. Powers each barely nodded, I wasn't sure if they would contact Clint or not.

We stopped by the Atwood police station before we left town. It was housed in an old building that likely dated back to pioneer days. An older gent sat behind a desk the size of a judge's bench. His few remaining hairs were snow-white and it was entirely possible he was eighty years old. I'd never seen a more ancient man in uniform, but he was as distinguished looking as could be.

"What can I do for you folks?" His voice was clear, and so were his royal blue eyes.

Clint hesitated a minute before he stepped up to the desk. "I'm Assistant Chief Clinton Lonsbury, Brooks Landing PD, and this is Cami Brooks."

"Camryn," I said.

"Oh, yes, Assistant Chief Lonsbury and . . . Camryn. I'm Bill. I'm retired from the force, but I couldn't let it go completely. So I help out here and there at the office." He shifted his full attention to Clint. "I understand you're on the lookout for one of our former, more infamous citizens. Benjamin Arnold."

"Correct. He seems to have gone missing."

"That's what I heard. Have you talked to his probation officer?"

"Not yet."

"Well, I know that she's looking for him, too."

Clint nodded. "You got her name and phone number handy?"

"Sure." He tapped his left temple. "Right in here. Want me to write it down?"

Clint pulled out a memo pad and pen from his pocket. "I got it. Go ahead."

Bill recited the information and Clint wrote it down. "Appreciate your help, Bill."

"That Arnold boy has been in trouble since he was a young'un in high school. A real shame for his parents and the whole community. And for him, too, of course. That goes without saying. Now to think he might be mixed up in a murder, that just takes the cake."

"I can't say he's my prime suspect at this point. But he is my prime person of interest. Some evidence at the scene was compromised. . . ." My mind drifted to the moment I had grabbed the knife and I knew that was the evidence Clint was talking about. I broke out in a full-body flush, drawing first Bill's, then Clint's attention. Clint studied me for a second before he went on, "He's at the top of the list of people I still need to talk to."

Bill nodded slowly and surely. "Understood, and I'll pass it on to our chief that you stopped by. And on a Sunday, too. I like a dedicated officer."

Clint lifted a shoulder in a half shrug. "It's part of the job." He left Bill with a reminder to call if Benjamin Arnold showed up. Especially if he was spotted at his parents' house. They had agreed to call the Brooks Landing police in the unlikely event that they heard from their son, but Clint was not convinced they would do that. Neither was I.

When we were back in Clint's police car, he started the engine then jotted something on a logbook that lay on his center console. I looked out of the corner of my eye and saw he was recording the times of when we were at the Arnolds' house and the Atwood police station.

"The halfway house where Jerrell Powers and Benjamin Arnold spent quality time together is in Hassock, about a twenty-minute detour on the way back to Brooks Landing. I wasn't planning to stop there today, but it might not hurt. Unless you need to get back home at a specific time for something, that is."

There *was* the cleaning, but on second thought . . . "No, I'm good." I'd never been to a halfway house before, and I was curious what it was like. Clint threw me a questioning look, so I added, "No pressing plans for the rest of the day."

He nodded and focused on the road ahead. "So how did you end up in our nation's capital?"

That came out of left field. "Um, well, it sort of evolved. After my high school graduation, I moved to Chicago and attended the University of Illinois. I liked the art and the culture there, so I stayed. It was far enough away so it gave me a little break from frequent visits from family members."

Clint threw me a sideways look. "That's a problem for you?"

"Not anymore. Back then, with my brothers and sisters being so much older than me, it was like having six parents who were always giving me advice about nearly everything. What car to buy, what career to go into, what schools were good, what schools were bad, what kind of people to avoid, and so on. It was wearing on me. Putting a little distance between us was a little lonely, but freeing at the same time."

"So you were in Chicago . . ."

"Yes. I majored in public affairs and did an internship for Ramona Zimmer, who was a state senator at that time."

"In Minnesota or Illinois?"

"Illinois. Her husband had a job transfer to Minnesota toward the end of her second term. She stayed behind to finish her term when he moved, then joined him. Two years later she had made enough connections to run for the senate seat and won. It was a highly contested race and lots of money flowed to both her campaign and her opponent's."

"I remember that."

"After she'd won the election, she contacted me. She'd liked my work ethic and offered me the position of legislative director."

"As the top dog, huh?"

"No. That'd be the chief of staff."

Clint nodded. "Shows you what I don't know much about. What does the legislative director do?"

"You have to keep abreast of the issues, monitor the

legislative schedule, make sure the assistants are doing their homework."

"Sounds boring."

"I liked it, and I didn't have time to be bored."

He grunted and pointed at a road sign. "Hassock. The name kind of makes me want to put my feet up."

"It is Sunday. The day people are supposed to rest."

"I guess." He turned, headed down a long driveway, and parked in front of a brick building.

"It looks like an old schoolhouse," I said.

"That was its original purpose, back when it was built. It was also a brothel at one time, but the pious folks around here got it shut down. Then the state bought it and turned it into a semisecure facility."

"Which means?"

"The inmates are not locked down, like in other correctional facilities. But if they break one of the major rules, like not being in their bunks by eight o'clock at night, their probation is revoked and they go to jail."

"Without passing go?"

Clint sort of smiled. We got out of his car and walked up to the steel entrance door. There was an intercom with a camera lens mounted on the frame next to it. Clint pushed the button.

"Can I help you?" The voice sounded like it belonged to a younger man.

"I'm Clinton Lonsbury, assistant chief of the Brooks Landing PD. And this is my partner for the day, Cami Brooks."

"Camryn Brooks," I corrected, as if anybody cared.

"I'm investigating a homicide and would like to talk to the person in charge, if he or she is available."

"Will you hold up your ID in front of the camera, Assistant Chief Lonsbury?"

Clint pulled out his wallet and opened it, revealing his official police identification. Then he held it up for the person monitoring the security system.

"Okay, I'll buzz you in."

The door made a clicking sound and Clint pulled it open. He motioned for me to go first, and we stepped into a large area that held a number of seating possibilities. There were tables with chairs, couches, and stuffed chairs with varying amounts of cushioning. Two men sat at a table playing checkers, but the place was otherwise deserted. They both looked at me like I was the best thing they'd seen in a long time and I repressed the urge to hide behind Clint so they'd stop gawking.

"Greetings. I'm Officer Davis," a voice called from an open window of a booth-size room to the left of where the men were sitting. I hadn't noticed it until he'd spoken.

Clint headed over and I followed. A man in his late twenties stood up from his swivel chair. When we got to the booth I noticed a control panel with buttons and a number of security camera monitors he had been watching.

Clint rested his elbow in the ledge of the opening. "Good afternoon. As I mentioned, I'd like a few words with the person in charge about a couple of your former residents here."

"Jerrell Powers and Benjamin Arnold," Davis said.

"Correct." News got around fast in the crime-fighting world.

"I should be able to help you with any questions."

"Good. They were both here together during what time frame?"

Davis sat down and typed on his computer keyboard. He had an answer a moment later. "From February to October of this year. Arnold was released a week before Powers, on October fourth. Powers was released October eleventh." The same day he wound up in Brooks Landing.

Clint pulled his memo pad from his breast pocket and wrote down the information. "I understand Arnold threatened Powers."

"It was an ongoing thing between the two of them. They started out in the same dormitory, but we had to separate them pretty soon after."

"They could have been twins," one of the eavesdropping men at the table called out.

Davis shrugged a little and lifted his hand toward the man, indicating to Clint that the halfway house resident might be a better resource for information than he was.

Clint nodded and turned toward the men. "You don't say. And why is that?"

The man, with a prickly-looking short gray beard, pushed out his lips. "They had the same sort of rascally disposition. Not mean, but on the ornery side. And they took things from each other. You might expect that with the bunch of lawbreakers we got in here. But most of us try to follow some code of leaving other folks' things alone."

The other man, who was clean shaven and neat in appearance, added, "Mac's right. They could have been cut from the same cloth. They were born just one day apart. Even looked alike. Different coloring, though. Arnold was a lot heavier, but had trouble with the food here. Didn't like it. So he lost weight, and the more he lost, the more he looked like Powers."

The other man jumped in. "Yeah, that was a strange thing to see. Lord above, those two fought like teenage brothers, instead of the forty-year-olds they were. And made each other mad as hell about the dumbest things."

"Like what?" Clint asked.

"One of the first days they were in the same dorm together, Arnold got sick—some kind of stomach bug. He accused Powers of swishing his toothbrush in the toilet. The way I figured it is Arnold would've had to have done that to someone himself to come up with a crazy idea like that."

Yes, who would think of such a yucky thing?

The clean-shaven man went on, "They mostly kept their fights pretty quiet so they didn't lose privileges, but once in a while one or the other would flare up. The kicker was when Powers went into Arnold's dorm when he wasn't there and snooped through his things. The control officer saw him on the camera and Powers ended up losing a week of good time. But that wasn't enough for Arnold. One of the guys overheard him say, just before he was released, that he would hunt Powers down when he got out and take care of things once and for all."

Clint nodded. "That sounds like a terroristic threat to me. But he wasn't arrested?"

"No, the guy who overheard him didn't say anything to the officers for a couple of days. By then, Arnold was released and word had it that he'd disappeared."

"For now, maybe. We'll find him."

The bearded man raised his hand. "Can you send him somewhere else besides here?"

"I have a pretty strong indication the judge will do just that."

We were back on the road a short time later. Clint looked at his watch. "It's getting late and we haven't had lunch. Want to stop?"

The toothbrush story had quelled my appetite. "I'm really not hungry, but go ahead if you are."

"I got a bag of trail mix in the glove box, if you'd get it out. I'll share."

I opened the box, pulled out the bag, opened it, and handed it over.

"Thanks." Clint set it on the center console and reached in for a handful. "Help yourself."

I took some, mostly to be polite. The salty nuts and sweet chocolate chips tasted surprisingly good after I'd pushed the toothbrush incident to the back of my mind.

"I can't call this a wasted trip, but I'd hoped to shake loose some more useful information from the parents," Clint said between bites.

"The guys at the halfway house seemed helpful."

"They were. Arnold's definitely our prime suspect. This disappearing act he's pulled makes him look all the more guilty. Unfortunately, your fingerprints were the only readable ones on the knife they pulled out of Jerrell Powers's back."

I reddened. "I admitted that was a dumb thing to do."

"The question is, when you reached for it, did you put your hand on top, or under the knife?"

Where was he going with this? "I have to think." I closed

my eyes to go back to that careless moment. "I guess my fingers were underneath, and my thumb was on top. Why?"

"That's the way the medical examiner said it went in. An underhanded thrust, not an overhanded one."

The knife was still in the victim's back when the coroner had arrived on the scene, so there was no argument there. The way Clint described it made me realize he still considered me a potential suspect despite the fact that I had no motive whatsoever. And I had just admitted grabbing the knife in the same way the killer had pushed it into Jerrell Powers's back. Lord help me, if the man had a charming bone in his body I'd like to know where it was.

"Oh," was the only word I could force out of my mouth. I contemplated whether it was feasible to hope that I would never have to set eyes on Clinton Lonsbury again after today.

6

Pinky was on a tear when I got to the shop Monday morning. "Cami, a hundred people have been in looking for you already today. And I'd swear to that on just about whatever you'd want me to."

"Really, Pinky, one hundred people were here to see me? Before ten o'clock on a Monday morning? And they weren't searching for unique snow globes, I have a feeling."

She waved her hand at me. "It was a hundred, more or less. Okay, I won't swear to it. First it was all the early birds who stop by before work. Then there was a whole bunch of other people who I don't remember ever seeing in here before. And they all asked for you specifically. They wanted to hear the story firsthand of what it was like finding Jerrell Powers's body late at night in Lakeside Park."

The scene that I continued trying to put out of my mind

popped back in full living moonlit color. "Jeepers creepers. I guess the word must have really spread like wildfire yesterday. I had to quit answering my phone last night, except when it was someone in my family. Even the local reporter, Sandy Gibbons, wants to interview me. She left two messages, which I need to return as soon as I can make myself do so."

"Maybe you should have one of those press conferences—you know, where you talk to everyone at once, and then you can be done with it."

"Pinky, I just want all this hoopla to die a natural death and be laid to rest."

"The trouble is, you came upon a murder victim and most people seem to have a morbid curiosity, which actually kind of surprises me. I mean, even my minister's wife was here asking questions. They want to hear all the scary details."

The bell on the door dinged and three women dressed in workout clothes came in, chattering a mile a minute. One singled me out. "Ooh, you're Camryn Brooks. We read the article in the Minneapolis paper yesterday about how you were the one who came upon that criminal's body in Lakeside Park."

I looked at Pinky and she shrugged. Apparently she hadn't seen the newspaper, either. Someone had obviously released my name to them.

The woman went on, "And it was on the ten o'clock news last night."

Pinky and I exchanged another look of ignorance.

"Not to mention that everyone was talking about it at the health club this morning," the second woman said.

"A lot of us had gone to our cabins for the weekend, so

we had no clue what had happened in our sleepy little town until we got back last night," the third one added.

"We came in for our lattes and here we get the bonus of talking to you besides," interrogator number two gushed.

Number one moved close to me. "Especially since the paper said you couldn't be reached for comment. . . ."

Like the last time I was caught up in a major news story. I guess having a quiet life was too much to hope for, even in sleepy Brooks Landing, Minnesota. Being reached for comment was, in my opinion, highly overrated. When something big happened, I'd found out the hard way that people jumped to their own conclusions. And the truth of the matter was that those conclusions often had little to do with the real facts. As much as I disliked discussing my dreaded discovery, at least I could give this small group of women a true account.

There was no reason to fill them in on the drama of what went on before and after the snow globe–making class between the teacher, students, and observers. Nor did I need to go over the whole burglary ordeal my dear friend had suffered at the hands of the murder victim some time before. Instead, I simply shared the fact that we'd hosted the class after work and I'd stayed later than usual. And when I remembered I'd walked instead of driven my car to work, I hiked through the park to save some time.

When I got to the part about Jerrell Powers falling forward off the bench, they all gasped and one of them, a red-haired woman wearing a black headband, jumped up and down a few times, flapping her hands in the process. I thought she might actually lift off. "Oh, my gosh! You *have* to come to our Halloween party. We'll turn the lights down low and you can tell your story. Everyone will absolutely flip. It'll be the best party we've ever had for sure."

Her two cohorts both leaned closer and gave their two cents' worth of agreement. I figured we were all about the same age, but I felt ten or twenty years older as they gently pleaded with me. Like kids begging their parents for something.

It was probably the most unusual request I'd ever gotten. "I'll have to think about that one."

"Of course you do. We kind of sprang the whole thing on you. How about I check back with you on Thursday? The party is on the twenty fifth, the Friday before Halloween, starting at seven. Ooh, I am so excited." Red jumped up and down a few more times. "I'm Tara, by the way. And this is Emily; and Heather." The others smiled and nodded when she said their names.

Pinky stood behind the counter watching the whole exchange with her mouth open.

I nodded and tried to smile in an attempt to look less dumbfounded. "Okay."

The three women chattered about the party possibilities for a minute, thanking me a dozen times, then turned their attention to Pinky and gave her their drink orders. I slipped away to my half of the building and the relative safety of shelves full of snow globes and other finds that I could hide behind in a pinch.

When they'd left with their beverages, Pinky found me behind my shop counter and dug her hands into her hips. "I suppose you're going to need a booking agent."

It took me a second to figure out what she meant. "For the scary party circuit, you mean? 'Come and hear Camryn

Brooks relate the sordid details of her late-night discovery. You'll never walk alone through Lakeside Park at night again.'"

I expected Pinky to laugh, but she grew more serious instead. "Cami, I still can't believe you walked through that dark park alone in the first place. What on earth got into you to do such a thing?"

I shrugged. "It was a shortcut. Brooks Landing feels safe to me, especially compared to Washington, D.C."

"Well, duh. That's not any kind of a comparison, and you know it."

"It is to me. We grew up here. How many times were we in that park after dark when we were kids and teens?"

Pinky flapped the dish towel she was holding. "There were at least two of us together when we were there late. And the curfew whistle blew at nine o'clock back then, so we had to get off the streets before that."

I chuckled. "You're right. I'd forgotten all about the nine o'clock whistle. We were back in our own yards by the time it blew, and we didn't even question the curfew, or what would happen to us if we didn't follow it."

She partially smiled at the memory, then her serious expression was back. "Cami, back to that party invitation: you're not really thinking of going there, are you?"

"I'm not sure. I'll have to ponder it some more. Weigh the pros and cons."

Pinky narrowed her eyes at me, but her door's bell dinged so she left to take care of her customers. Monday was not normally a big business day for Curio Finds, which I had counted on, except a steady stream of customers changed that. It felt more like a Saturday. Most people who came in said they were just looking around. But it wasn't the merchandise they were interested in. It was me. And I felt almost as uncomfortable with the attention as when I'd been accused of being involved with Peter Zimmer.

Back then it was mostly the people in high places who gave me accusatory looks and spoke in low voices to others. Now it was the folks around Brooks Landing who studied me like I was a science fair project. Both experiences reiterated for me that I was more of a behind-the-scenes, low-profile kind of person. I remembered reading that the majority of people were more afraid of public speaking than of dying. That'd be me. If it came right down to it, I'd choose giving a speech to a large group of people over death, but my knees would be knocking, my hands would be shaking, and my face would be twitching. Being raised in the Vanelli household had helped me overcome some of my innate shyness, but not all of it.

A little after noon, I headed to Pinky's side to get a muffin and coffee and saw Mark Weston standing close to her. They both wore a serious expression and were talking about something seemingly important. Pinky saw me first and nudged Mark, who almost knocked Pinky's head with his own when he turned to face me.

"What's going on?" I asked.

"Nothing," Mark said. Clearly there was *something*.

"What do you mean?" Pinky's shoulders lifted a little.

"You two look like you're plotting something. Not that it's any of my business if you're having a private conversation."

"No." Pinky used the cloth she was holding to wipe the counter.

"Private? Is that what it looked like?" Mark's laugh sounded forced and fake.

Pinky looked up. "We were just talking about all the extra customers today. And hoped you were holding up okay."

"That's right," Mark agreed.

I knew they were not telling me everything, but I was not going to keep coaxing them. "Well, thanks. It has been trying having half the people in town walk through. But I'm looking at the upside of it. If a bunch of them happened to notice any of the neat things we have for sale—in between staring at me, that is—maybe they'll be back to actually shop sometime."

"You're absolutely right. You need a cup of coffee?"

"I do. And a muffin; maybe blueberry today."

"I hear you took a trip with our assistant chief of police yesterday," Mark said.

Pinky raised her eyebrows. "You didn't tell me about that."

"I was going to, but we haven't had any real time yet to talk today." I turned back to Mark. "Clint's your boss, so I'm not going to say anything against him. But I think I'm still on his suspect list."

Mark shook his head. "Cami, we all know you couldn't have done it."

Pinky nodded. "We know that for a fact."

"Well, I did have the opportunity, it seems."

"Never mind about that. Tell us about your day with the luscious, eligible Clinton Lonsbury." Pinky nearly drooled.

"You can't be serious. Do you have a crush on him?" I said.

"I don't really, but he is one of my favorite pieces of eye candy." She stretched her long neck to the side.

I put my hands over my ears. "I did not hear that."

"Me, either," Mark said and made a face. " 'Eye candy'?"

I changed the subject by filling them in on the previous day's adventures: first the visit with the Arnolds, then the stop at the Atwood police station and the ancient officer we talked to. I ended my recitation with the halfway house experience.

"Wow, you had quite the day, Cami. I'm feeling a little jealous. How did Clint happen to take you along in the first place?" Pinky asked.

"I think it was to pump me for information. You know, see if I'd spill any beans on the long ride there and back again."

"Nooo." Pinky drew out the denying word.

But Mark's silence backed up my theory.

I shrugged. "No matter. It was good getting out of Brooks Landing for the day, and I got to see another small-town police station and a halfway house. I don't care what our assistant chief thinks of me."

Erin stopped in after she had finished at school for the day. "Cami, I'm glad to see you made it through the rest of the weekend in one piece."

"I only had to endure Clinton Lonsbury for about six hours yesterday. But other than that, I ignored all unknown phone calls so the evening was fairly peaceful."

Erin grabbed her ponytail and pulled it in front of her

shoulder. "You said you'd be cleaning all day. Instead you spent six hours with Clint? Do tell."

I summed up the day for my friend, then a few more customers strolled into my shop and Erin left to talk to Pinky. Erin was still there at quitting time, a half hour later. When I walked into Brew Ha-Ha, I heard Pinky utter two words that made me tune in—"Jerrell Powers." She and Erin stopped talking and looked at me.

"I am developing a strange complex."

Pinky frowned slightly. "Over what?"

"It seems like every time I enter a room, strangers and friends alike stop talking and stare at me."

"That'll pass when the whole matter of you-know-what dies down. People will forget about it and life will go on. At least that's what I'm counting on happening," Erin said.

"Maybe for people I don't know. But what about you guys?"

"What about us?" Erin said.

"You're keeping something from me."

Pinky looked down and Erin picked up her mug before she answered. "If you must know, Pinky was just telling me about those ladies who want you to be the entertainment at their Halloween party. And we were saying we didn't think that would be a good idea."

Pinky agreed with a nod.

For some reason—maybe it was their overprotectiveness; maybe it was their interference—my dander went up and I decided to make them think I was planning to go to the party, even if I wasn't. "It might be fun."

"You really think so?" Pinky said.

"Cami, it's a *social* event with people you don't even know," Erin added.

"I attended more social events during my years in Washington than I will ever remember." I threw up my hands. "Hey, it's not so bad. There is always someone at any given gathering who's interesting to talk to."

They both shook their heads.

Sandy Gibbons blew into the coffee shop like a whirlwind, reminding me I had not gotten around to calling her. "I'm sorry, Cami, but my editor is going crazy. I left a bunch of messages on your home phone, then one of my friends just told me you were at work. I usually try not to bug people when they're working, but it's almost six and you're about to close up shop for the night anyway, right?" She spit out her whole monologue in about three seconds.

Sandy had been reporting for the *Brooks Landing Weekly News* since I was a young girl. She was a short, pudgy ball of energy in her early sixties. I smiled at the enthusiastic, expectant expression on her face. She was flushed and her eyes were open as wide as could be.

Pinky and Erin moved in closer to me as if they felt they needed to, in case Sandy attacked or tried to kidnap me or whatever else they thought she might do.

I lifted my hands. "Sandy, I honestly meant to call you—"

"She honestly did and told me so this morning." Pinky defended me unnecessarily.

Sandy flapped her hands then lowered the briefcase she had strapped over her shoulder onto a counter stool. It swiveled a bit so she steadied it as she reached in and pulled out a notebook. It had a pen clipped to the front of it, ready for action. "You'll give me the story, won't you? If I get my article in by ten o'clock tonight, it'll be in the paper tomorrow."

I was momentarily torn. Clinton Lonsbury hadn't told me to keep my account under wraps, even from the media. Having the story in the local newspaper might somehow prompt the person who had committed the crime to slip up and say something incriminating. I'd heard those stories a number of times over the years. It had to do with bragging rights, which I didn't understand, but then again I did my best to live inside the law, not outside of it. "Let's have a seat and I'll tell you what happened."

We went to the same table Pinky, Erin, and I had sat at two days before when I'd relayed Friday night's events out loud for the first time. It seemed like a week or two ago. Pinky and Erin sat down with us, not considering whether they were invited or not.

Sandy plopped down like she was carrying an extra one hundred pounds then blew out a loud breath of air that lifted the first few pages of her open notebook. "I can't believe the biggest story to break in our town in a long time, and where was I? At my annual quilters' retreat up north, where I had no cell phone reception. And neither my husband nor my editor thought to call the resort."

The newspaper came out weekly, not daily, so even if news was breaking, it would not be reported in print until Tuesday afternoon. Why wreck a high-strung woman's chance to relax by telling her news that would surely have her scrambling to get back home for every juicy detail?

"Okay, Cami, take me through that fateful night and then I'll ask you any questions I still have."

I told her as much as I could, leaving out details like

finding the penny on the pathway and picking it up; grasping the knife in that unthinking moment; the snowing globe in my shop; and my fact-gathering trip to southern Minnesota with the infuriating Clinton Lonsbury.

When Sandy finished jotting notes of what I'd said, she looked up and shook her head. "Who are the police investigating?"

"You know I couldn't answer that, even if I knew."

"Off the record?"

"Sandy, it would be pretty obvious who you got the information from, and I am trying to avoid any further trouble with the Brooks Landing Police Department."

"You said 'further trouble.' You don't mean they think you had anything to do with Jerrell Powers's murder, do you?"

"I didn't say that—"

"Oh, my goodness, Cami!"

"That reminds me, I'm Camryn now. Just for the record."

I lay in bed that night pondering what was really going on with my friends. I'd shredded the pages of the notebook where I had started listing possible suspects—in case it fell into the wrong hands. Without a doubt, Mark, Pinky, and Erin had some kind of secret information they were not telling me about. If they thought they were shielding me from something, they had another think coming. Unless they were somehow involved in Jerrell Powers's death after all. I hadn't wanted to consider such a thing the night it happened, and I didn't want to now. And the possibility that all three of them had played any kind of part, no matter how small, was especially troubling.

Clinton Lonsbury's prime suspect was Benjamin Arnold, which was understandable from a police perspective. It was easier for me to see where he was coming from, particularly after what we'd learned on our visit to Atwood and Hassock. Arnold had threatened Powers and that was witnessed by several semireliable sources. From what little I knew about Powers, he had likely pushed Arnold to the limits. Maybe what Arnold and Powers didn't like about each other was that they had nearly identical personalities. At least according to one of the halfway house residents who'd spent time with both of them.

My mind drifted to Pamela Hemley. She was an enigma. Why was she so taken with Jerrell Powers anyway? I knew that bad boys were magnets for some women and maybe that was the case. Her sister had, in no uncertain terms, made it clear she had not wanted Pam to continue seeing Powers. And I had to agree with her. She had legitimate reasons. From all I'd heard, he was definitely a bad boy.

I heard a crashing sound outside my window and jumped out of bed. It was most likely a cat who was in pursuit of a mouse or other small creature and had knocked something over. But what? The backyard border was an alley that separated my house from the backyard of my neighbor's. A detached single-car garage, accessed from the alley, was where I usually parked my car. I opened the bedroom blinds enough to sneak a peek. I didn't see a cat, but I did see a man running away from my house, down the alley.

Goose bumps popped up all over my body. It was highly unlikely the guy was out for a jog at eleven p.m. on a chilly night. And it was a little early for trick or treat. I wondered if there was a peeping Tom lurking in the neighborhood. As much as I did not want to call the police, it was my civic duty to report unusual and suspicious activities, especially when they were happening right outside my house.

I picked up the phone from my bedside stand and punched in the critical three numbers.

"Buffalo County, nine-one-one. Is this an emergency?" As luck would have it, it was the same dispatcher who had answered my call a few short days before when it was a real and critical emergency.

"Um, no. But I just saw a man running from my backyard and I thought you should know in case he's up to something."

"Yes. Your name, ma'am?"

I gave her all the key information, including my address, so she wouldn't have to ask me for it.

"Okay, I will send an officer over."

"I don't think that's necessary. If you could just have him drive around the area, maybe."

"It's standard procedure, Miss Brooks. It shouldn't be more than a few minutes."

"All right, thank you." I hung up wishing my friend Mark worked the night shift. He and Clint were the only two officers in town I really knew. It was a small department and Mark had made mention of the other five members who worked there, but I had never met any of them, officially or otherwise. I'd known Chief Hermann from when I was a teenager and he was a Brooks Landing police officer in a much smaller department.

I got out of bed, grabbed the blue flannel robe I had lying on top of the covers, pulled it around me, and cinched the sash around my waist. Then I stepped into the pink furry slippers Pinky had given me the previous Christmas. They were more her color and style than mine, but they were warm and she was my friend.

A police car pulled up to the curb and parked in front of my house right after I'd turned on the lamp in the living room. I glanced out the window and who got out but Clinton Lonsbury. I had almost made it one whole day without seeing him or hearing from him. Drat, drat, double drat. I immediately felt underdressed and wished I'd put on some clothes.

I opened the door to save him from knocking. "Good evening, Assistant Chief Lonsbury. You're working late again."

Clint's eyes roved from my head to my toes in a split second. "One of the officers called in sick and there was no one else to cover. Rather than making one of the others work a double, I thought I'd be a nice guy for the second time in less than a week, and work the first half. Then Mark's starting four hours earlier to cover the second half of the shift."

I came close to liking Clint when he said that. I hadn't thought about why he'd been on duty late the night Jerrell Powers had died.

He waved his hand at my robe. "You were getting ready for bed and you saw someone in your backyard?" His eyebrows came together and the tone of his voice sounded like he didn't quite believe my report to the dispatcher.

He made it easy to go from almost liking him back to not wanting anything to do with him. "No, I was in bed when I heard a crashing sound out back by my garage. I thought it was a critter and got up to check. That's when I saw a man running away."

"Can you give me a description of him?"

"Not a good one. He had on dark pants and a dark jacket and a dark stocking cap. Maybe they were black, but he could have had on jeans. It happened so fast, he was gone before I knew it."

The inside corners of Clint's eyebrows touched. "You're saying he ran fast?"

"Pretty fast, I guess."

"Approximate height, weight?"

Oh, boy. "Well, he didn't seem really tall—like, I doubt if he was much over six feet—but he wasn't short, either."

Clint cleared his throat. "How about his build? Can you give me an estimate of his weight?"

"I'd say average. So if he was six feet tall, he'd maybe weigh around one-seventy, one-eighty. But with a jacket on it was hard to tell because that adds bulk."

"Did you happen to notice if he was carrying anything?"

"Like what?"

"Anything. I don't want to put ideas in your head, but something that could be used as a burglary tool, maybe."

"Oh." I closed my eyes, hoping to squeeze whatever I could from a scene that had lasted just a few seconds. "He may have had a backpack, but I can't swear to it."

"Or to any of the rest of it, either, it sounds like."

"I can swear that there was a person who I'm pretty sure was a man that took off and ran down the alley."

"I drove around the area and didn't see anyone on foot, but he could be a neighbor who is back at home by now."

"Could be." But the man in the alley had acted more like someone who was running away from something.

Clint pulled a magnum flashlight from his duty belt. "I'll

go take a look around out back, see if he left any evidence behind." He started for the front door.

"Why don't you go out the back door in the kitchen?" I headed in there and turned on the light. When I turned to see if Clint was following me we almost collided. "Sorry."

He shook his head to brush it off. "I'll come back in before I leave to tell you if I find anything."

"I'll grab a coat and go out with you."

"You should stay inside."

"I need to know if he broke into my garage. There was that crash." I ran to the front closet and found a long wool coat. I put it on over my robe, but didn't take the time to find a pair of shoes. Clint had already gone outside and I didn't want to miss anything.

The air was nippy on the bare skin of my lower legs, hands, and face. Clint was flashing his light on the ground by the garage. The moon was behind some low-hanging clouds, but there was a streetlight about halfway down the block, so it wasn't completely dark. I tagged along at a safe distance behind him as Clint followed the length of the garage to the alley where the garage's overhead door was located. He directed the flashlight's beam to a bicycle that was lying on the ground in front of it. "That your bike?"

I'd never seen it before. "No. And I know it wasn't there when I got home from work because I drove my car into the garage."

Clint shined his light on a plastic bag that was slung to hang from the handlebars. Then he turned around and studied the area to the north. "I think I know what caused the crash. He was riding and hit that wet clay, skidded, and wiped out."

"Why didn't he just get back on the bike again, instead of running away?"

Clint reached into a pocket and pulled out a pair of latex gloves. He put them on before he slid the bag off the bike's handlebars. He looked inside. "Aha. The bike crash might have stopped him before he committed a crime after all. He's got a flashlight, bolt cutter, box cutter, picks. A nice assortment of tools for breaking into buildings, cars, storage units."

"Have there been burglaries in town?" I hadn't heard of any.

"Not a rash of them. But we get reports of one every so often."

"I guess people should lock their doors at night."

Clint shined his light on the garage. "I don't see any damage to your garage. I'll check out the rest of the houses around here and then get this stuff loaded up. Losing his tools will hopefully curtail that guy's criminal activities for the night."

"Besides crashing and losing his bike."

"That, too. After I finish up here and get back on patrol, I'll be on the lookout for a man on foot, dressed in dark clothes."

"Thanks."

I started to turn to go back to the house when Clint said, "You get those from Pinky?"

"Get what?"

"Those fuzzy things on your feet. They're not quite your style, somehow."

"I like pink bunnies, too." There was no way I was going to tell Clint he was right. I liked the slippers just fine as long as I didn't look at them. "Good night."

"Lock your doors."

I didn't want to be caught gawking out the windows while Clint went about his police business, but watching him work was somewhat interesting. I went into the bathroom, left the lights off, and pulled the shade back a little—enough to see the beam of his flashlight moving around the alley. When he walked by the side of my house to cut through to the front where his car was parked, I let go of the blind and stepped back.

A minute later I heard his car idling in the alley and resumed my spying position. He loaded the bag of tools and bicycle into the trunk of his car. Then he climbed behind the wheel and sat there for what seemed like ten minutes but was probably closer to five. I figured he was writing notes on the incident, what I'd seen, and what we'd found. About the time I decided the action was over, he shifted into drive and rolled on down the alley and out of sight.

After all the late-night activity and being outside in the cold air, I was too keyed up to go back to bed. I went into the kitchen, made a cup of cocoa, carried it to the living room, and curled up on the couch. The eyes of my bunny slippers looked up at me, so I pulled the blanket over them.

As I sipped my cocoa I realized how wrong I'd been when I'd thought living in Brooks Landing after my years in big cities would be boring. Of course, the scary things that had happened the past few days were not the kind of excitement I welcomed in any way, shape, or form.

A wave of emotion rolled over me from out of the blue and I started shaking. Then tears spilled from my eyes and ran down my cheeks. It may have been another reaction to finding Jerrell Powers's body, triggered by seeing a man running behind my house and learning he was a potential burglar that had crashed his bike by my garage.

Once the tears started, I had trouble making them stop. *Okay, deep breath, you need to focus on positive things instead of negative ones,* I told myself. I started with my family and thought of how much I loved them. Next, I admitted I actually enjoyed working at Curio Finds. It may not have been my career of choice, but it was where I was supposed to be for now.

And it was good to be back with old friends again. Little had I known, a year ago, I would have an adjoining shop with one of them. None of us had planned to be small business owners when we were growing up. I uncovered my feet, took off one of my bunny slippers, and laid it on my chest. I put my arm around the little pink guy, tucked the blanket around my body, and fell asleep.

7

The *Brooks Landing Weekly News* was on the stands and in the stores by three p.m. Tuesday. I had taken a break from work and went to spend a few minutes with my parents. I was on my way back from the visit at 3:20 when Pinky called my cell phone. "Clint Lonsbury was here looking for you and he did not look happy. Not even a little bit. He said you are to call him the second you get back to the shop."

"Did he say what it was about? Like, have they found the burglar from last night?"

"Nope, not a word. I even asked him a few different ways, but he would not tell me."

"Okay, well, I'll be there in about two minutes."

I was on Fourth Street, a block from Central Avenue, when I noticed flashing lights in my rearview mirror. I pulled over and stopped, wondering what driving offense I had possibly committed. I was going under the speed limit and hadn't rolled through the stop sign. When I saw Clint get out of his police car and walk toward mine, I didn't know whether to feel mystified or miffed.

I remembered my brother-in-law telling all of us at a family gathering that if we ever got stopped by a police officer to be sure to stay in the car and let the officer come to you. He'd learned the hard way what happened because he'd gotten out of his car and had a pair of handcuffs slapped on him before he'd a chance to take a breath, much less say, "Good evening, Officer." Police officers had strict rules about traffic stops.

I rolled down my window and the smell of burning leaves drifted into my car. It was the time of year when people raked the fallen leaves and either bagged them or burned them in their fire pits.

Clint opened my door. "I need to talk to you. Get out, and we'll go sit in my car."

When I saw the sober look on his face, I was not about to argue. I turned off the engine and slipped out of my car. I glanced around, hoping no one was watching the action and might start a rumor that I had gotten arrested. At least I hoped it would be a rumor. With the way Clint was hovering over me, maybe that was exactly what was about to happen. "After you," he said in a quiet, deep voice.

I walked as fast as I could without running and climbed in the passenger seat of his car. The faster we got it over with, the better. Whatever "it" was. When Clint sat down in the driver's seat, the entire car was filled with his presence. He picked up a copy of our local newspaper from the center console and held it up so I could see the article Sandy Gibbons had written of my account. "If you would, please explain why in tarnation you'd tell the town gossip that you are considered a suspect in Jerrell Powers's murder."

"What?" I was flabbergasted and grabbed the paper out of his hands to read it for myself. I couldn't believe Sandy would write such a thing after I'd asked her not to. I scanned through the article, using my finger to help keep my place. Clint's close proximity made it difficult to concentrate. The last paragraph contained the lines that had Clint all fired up. I read it out loud. "'An unnamed source revealed that the police consider Camryn Brooks a possible suspect in the case.'" I looked at Clint and tried to appear as imposing as he did. "You think *I'm* the unnamed source?"

"Aren't you?"

"When I gave Sandy the story, I did not tell her anything like that. Maybe one of your officers did."

"No, they know better than to give statements to the press without approval from the chief. What exactly did you say?"

"I can't remember exactly, but if she got that"—I stuck my finger in the paper—"from anything I said, then . . . then . . ."

"Then what?"

"She was using artistic license, narrative license, or whatever it's called." I took a final look at the paper, folded it, and laid it down. Then my cell phone rang. I picked it up to shut it off and saw the incoming call was from Pinky. Something may have happened at one of our shops. "I should take this, if it's okay to answer. It's Pinky."

Clint nodded.

I pushed the talk button. "Hello."

"Holy moly, Cami, are you all right?"

"Pretty much."

"You don't sound all right. Did you have an accident? It takes, like, three minutes to drive from your parents' house and it's been fifteen. I'm dying to find out what Clint had his drawers tied up in a knot over. Where are you anyway?"

"In Clint's police car."

"She's safe, Pinky," Clint added. He'd obviously heard the entire conversation. Cell phones were not very private.

"Ahhhh, okay, I'll let you go, 'bye." Pinky's words were rapid-fire and she'd hung up before I even had time to process them.

"Maybe Pinky is Sandy's source," Clint said.

"I don't think so. She may get caught up in gossip from time to time, but she is very loyal to her friends. And protective."

Clint nodded. "It sounds like you'd better get back to work. And try to stay out of trouble."

I wanted to ask if he'd found out anything about the would-be burglar, but his words irritated me out of his car instead.

I parked in back of the shop and when I walked around to the front, who had pulled up to the curb and was getting out of his police car? None other than the man I was annoyed with himself. I tried to ignore Clint, but he followed me into Curio Finds.

"I'm back," I called to Pinky through the archway. She popped her head in, but when she saw Clint behind me, she backed away without saying a word.

Clint stopped and struck a pose that made him look like he was at some official event: he stood with his legs a few feet apart and clasped his hands behind his back. "I meant to tell you about the owner of the bicycle we found by your garage, but the article in the paper distracted me."

"Oh, who was it?"

"The bike belongs to a ten-year-old boy. His mother called to report it was stolen last night. She correctly described it, and the two of them picked it up from the station a while ago. The little guy, Jacob, was pretty happy to get it back."

"The would-be burglar stole a little boy's bike? That almost seems worse than breaking into someone's garage. Why would he do that?"

"If I had to guess, I'd say it boils down to perceived need and opportunity." Clint sounded like a college professor.

"Which means?"

"He's equipped with burglary tools and has no wheels to drive around searching out a good place to break into. He spots a bike sitting in a yard and grabs it. It speeds up his mobility—until he crashes it. He's worried the noise alerted the neighbors so he takes off while the getting is good."

"Any ideas yet who 'he' is?"

"No, he was clever enough to wipe the bike clean. We only found one partial fingerprint that was too big to be the boy's. I lifted it, but it's not enough to positively identify anyone, unless you knew who the person was and could compare one partial print to another.

"He must have been planning to dump the bike when he was done with it or he wouldn't have wiped it. I'll even give him the benefit of the doubt and say he might have wanted to return it to the kid's house. Who knows? In any case, he must have been wearing gloves."

I envisioned the running man and would agree that was possible. "I can't say for sure, one way or the other."

"Most likely. I think gloves are included in a burglar's toolbox."

I thought Clint was being facetious, but I didn't dare smile in case he was serious.

"The good news is that there were not any reported break-ins last night or so far today. He might have been passing through town and is hopefully long gone by now."

"That'd be a good thing to hope for," I said.

"I'll leave you to get back to your business." He gave me a single nod then yelled, "Good-bye, Pinky."

She stuck her head around the corner, which proved she had been listening in. "'Bye, Clint."

When Clint was safely back in his police car and out of earshot, Pinky jogged over to me with the ends of her head scarf flying around her. "What in the world did he talk to you about in his police car? If you can tell me, that is."

"It was the last line in the newspaper article our dear friend Sandy Gibbons wrote."

"Which was . . . ?"

"That an unnamed source revealed that the police consider me a possible suspect in Jerrell Powers's murder."

"*No.*"

"Yes, and Clint figured it was me."

"The only thing you did when Sandy asked you that question was change the subject."

"I know."

"Well, I'm glad the little boy got his bike back and no one else had a break-in." She smiled when she realized she was confessing that she'd overheard what Clint had said.

"Me, too."

"Hey, maybe we should catch a bite to eat somewhere

tonight. We could both do with a little relaxation. And Erin might want to join us."

"It's a school night."

"I know for a fact she eats dinner whether it's a school night or not."

I laughed. "Yeah, I guess we don't have to get wild and stay out late."

Pinky shook her head and lifted her eyebrows. "I have not stayed out much past midnight in probably ten years."


Pinky, Erin, and I met at Sherman's Bar and Grill at 6:30. The building, which had been a department store when we were kids, had been converted to look like a ski chalet with interior walls of old, dark wood and decorations that celebrated Minnesota winter sports like antique sleds, ice skates, toboggans, snowshoes, skis, and hockey pucks. I'd been told they changed the decorations for the summer months. Crowds of people were milling at the bar, talking and laughing. It was busier than we'd figured it would be on a weeknight.

The hostess greeted us with a smile. "If you'd like to wait at the bar, it shouldn't be more than five or ten minutes before we have a table ready for you."

Pinky led the way and found two remaining seats in the horseshoe arrangement. "You two sit down; I'd rather hover," she said.

"With your height, it's easier to scout around for men if you're standing, you mean," Erin teased as she climbed onto a bar stool.

"That's true, but then what if I find one?"

"When Mr. Right comes along, you'll know what to do," I said, speaking from years of observing the relationships my parents and other committed couples shared; not from personal experience.

Pinky sighed. "I thought Kirk was Mr. Right all through high school and our first six months of marriage."

"We all thought he was a nice guy. He had everybody fooled," Erin said.

Pinky flicked her hand as if shooing an insect away. "Water over the dam."

The bartender, a young woman, laid napkins on the bar in front of Erin and me, and one in between us for Pinky. "What can I get you ladies?"

"Orange juice for me," Erin said.

"I'll have a glass of whatever beer is on tap," I said. I'd grown up in an Italian household where wine was the alcoholic beverage of choice, but I preferred beer.

Pinky laid her hand on my shoulder. "And I'll have what she's having."

"Coming right up."

Pinky bent her head down between us. "Don't look now, but Eye Candy Clint is over there, having dinner with Mark."

Erin turned her head toward Pinky. "*Eye Candy* Clint?"

"Don't ask," I said.

"You don't mean . . . our assistant chief of police?" Erin said.

"One and the same, because he is," Pinky said and gave us each a pat on the back.

"As long as you don't call him that to his face," I said.

Pinky laughed. "I may be dumb, but I'm not stupid."

"He is your basic hunk," Erin said.

I groaned. "Not you, too."

"Just making an observation. And no, he's not my type."

*I don't think he's anybody's type. Unless you're attracted to eye candy police officer hunks.*

"Mark just spotted me and waved. Now Clint is looking this way," Pinky said out of the side of her mouth.

Erin and I both swiveled in our seats. "That man is everywhere," I said then turned back when the bartender said, "Here you go," and set our drinks down.

Erin paid for our drinks before Pinky or I had the chance. "It'll be my turn next time," Pinky said as she leaned in and picked up her glass.

"Fancy meeting you girls here," Mark said behind us.

Erin turned around, and I braved a look myself. Yup, Clint was with him.

"Busy place for a Tuesday," Pinky said.

"Sherman's is always busy," Mark said.

A middle-aged woman squeezed in between Clint and Mark. "Excuse me." She looked directly at me. "Would you autograph this for me? Right at the end of the article." She handed me a newspaper and pen.

The request caught me off guard, to say the least. The look on Clint's face told me he was a little surprised himself. And so were my friends. I had a split second to determine what to do, and I decided granting her wish was not that big of a deal after all. I penned my barely legible signature and handed it back to her. She smiled broadly. "Thank you so much!"

"Okay, that was strange," Pinky said after she'd left.

"For Pete's sake, Cami. I mean really," Erin said.

Clint scowled at me. "You could have refused."

"And disappoint my fans?" I knew that would irritate him, and from the look he gave me, I'd say it did.

The hostess picked that convenient moment to pop her head around Mark. "Okay, ladies, your table is ready."

Erin and I picked up our drinks and slid off our stools. A man near the back wall caught my eye. He appeared to be watching us then turned and headed out the door. "Do any of you know who that was?" I pointed to the door. They all turned around to see who I was referring to.

"You mean that woman, your new groupie?" Pinky said.

"No, the man who just left. He looked familiar, but I can't seem to place him."

"Sorry, I didn't see him," Erin said and the others shook their heads and said they hadn't, either.

"He acted like maybe he knew us, but took off as soon as I looked at him."

"What did he look like?" Clint asked.

"I'd say he was around forty years old, maybe six feet, short dark beard, Buddy Holly–type glasses."

"I can't think of anyone I know who fits that description," Mark said.

None of the rest of them could, either. "Well, maybe he just looked like Buddy Holly with a beard, then," I said.

"Could be," Clint said.

The hostess was patiently waiting by the table she was holding for us, and our group moved over to her. Pinky and Erin sat down. As I moved to the other side of the table, Clint pulled a chair out for me then pushed it in when I sat down. I couldn't remember the last time a man had done that for me. "Thanks."

"So what do you guys recommend?" Pinky asked the men.

"It's hard to beat a burger and a beer," Clint said.

"Burgers are their specialty; they use Black Angus beef. With about any topping you can think of. My favorite is the one with Swiss cheese, fried onions, and sautéed mushrooms," Mark said.

"Ooh, that sounds nummy," Pinky said.

"I'd recommend the provolone cheese, tomato, cucumber, and avocado myself," Clint said.

That sounded good to me.

Clint gave Mark a light slap on the back. "We should shove off so these ladies can get to their dinner."

Mark gave Pinky and Erin each a little nod. "Catch you all later." Then he and Clint made their way around the tables to the door.

"Do you two have plans with Mark to do something later tonight?" I asked.

Pinky raised her eyebrows. "Huh?"

"Why do you ask?" Erin said.

"He gave each of you a little look."

"Cami, I think you've been letting your imagination run wild lately." Pinky picked up her glass and took a sip of brew.

I looked at Erin then Pinky. "Are you saying Mark didn't do that?"

"He was saying good-bye and I didn't notice anything special about it," Erin said as she reached for the menu.

Either my friends were keeping something from me or I had developed an increased sensitivity to every nuance of their interactions when they were together. Maybe I was just overreacting because I'd been on sensory and emotional overload the past few days.

I brushed aside my doubts for the moment and picked up a menu. "So, what are you girls going to have?"

By the time the server came by for our order, we'd made our choices. Pinky went with Mark's suggestion, I went with Clint's, and Erin picked a burger topped with a marinara sauce and mozzarella cheese. We decided to split a large order of French fries.

"Can I get you another round of drinks?" our server, Donna, asked as she jotted our food choices on her pad.

We all said we were fine with what we had. Donna gathered up the menus and moved to the next table.

"I was kind of surprised to see Mark here with Clint," I said.

"They aren't exactly close, but they do stuff together once in a while," Pinky said.

"Like my colleagues at school. One of them will ask me to go to a concert or craft show here or there, but it's not a regular thing," Erin said.

I shrugged. "I guess that makes sense, grabbing a bite to eat together after work."

Erin held her hand over her mouth. "Speaking of my colleagues, here comes one of them now."

The words "perky blonde" popped into my brain as a woman in her midtwenties stepped up behind the vacant chair at our table and smiled. "Hi, Erin. Hope I'm not interrupting, but I spotted you and wanted to say hi."

"Hi, Paige, I'm glad you did." Erin looked from Pinky to me. "Paige is new to our school district this year. She teaches kindergarten." Where her obvious energy and enthusiasm would be a necessary attribute.

Pinky and I smiled and welcomed her. Erin lifted her hand to Pinky. "This is Alice Nelson, otherwise known as Pinky. She owns Brew Ha-Ha downtown."

"Oh, sure, I thought you looked familiar. Your cherry vanilla chip scones are the best I've ever tasted."

"Thank you." Pinky beamed from the compliment.

"And Cami—Camryn—Brooks, who—"

"Really?" Paige pulled out the chair she was leaning against and slid onto it. "Really?" she repeated and stared at me like she didn't dare let me out of her sight. "You finding that man in the park is all the teachers have been talking about during lunch the past two days."

I took a quick look at Erin, but she had her eyes fixed on Paige.

"I mean, everyone tells me this is a safe community, but it's pretty scary when something like that happens right after I move here. And right in the park, too, where kids go to play every day. That's all I could think of when I heard. I'm sure glad a little one didn't find him. Can you just imagine?"

No, I couldn't, and I shook my head. Our server, Donna, appeared with a tray of food propped on her shoulder. She lowered it to her forearm then set the plates down in front of Pinky, Erin, and I. She glanced at Paige. "Something for you?"

Paige seemed flustered. "No, thanks, I ate."

"You got ketchup, mustard. Anything else I can get you right now?"

"We should be fine," Pinky said for all of us, and the server left with a smile.

Paige stood up. "I'm so sorry I butted in like that. Nice to meet you both. See you tomorrow, Erin." She rushed off to another part of the restaurant.

"I always feel pretty young until I meet someone who was probably born when I was graduating high school," Pinky said.

Erin smiled and nodded then reached over and patted my hand. "Cami, Paige is naturally enthusiastic and I know she'd feel bad she brought up the park incident if she knew how uncomfortable you are with all the attention you're getting."

*Park incident? That was a gentler way to phrase it, I guess.* "It's okay. Not a big deal."

Pinky took a handful of French fries from the generous plateful and passed the plate to Erin, who did the same, then handed it to me.

"I will be so happy when this whole thing is just a bad memory," I said.

"We all will," Erin said. She lifted her burger and took a bite. "Mmm."

We ate as much as we could and made an attempt to clean our plates, but it was impossible. "I am too stuffed to finish." Pinky pushed her plate back a few inches.

Erin stretched her body back against her chair and patted her stomach. "I'll take the leftovers for lunch tomorrow, minus the bun, which would be pretty soggy by then."

"Good idea," I said.

Pinky snuck a peek at her watch for about the fifth time since our food had arrived.

"Why do you keep looking at the time? Do you have a hot date, or what?" I asked.

"Cami, you would be one of the first to know if I had a hot date. No, just thinking about organizing my muffin and scone ingredients for the morning."

"You could make those in your sleep," I said.

"I do, every day. You think I'm awake when I bake?" she said and laughed.

Erin got a text alert and pulled her phone out of her jacket pocket and looked at the message. "It's from . . . ah, my mom." She bent her head over her phone and thumbed out a return message.

"Your mother texts you?"

"Um, sure."

"Since when?"

"I don't know, exactly."

Pinky waved her hand at our server. "Well, I say more power to her. More and more older people are texting, I've noticed."

Donna brought us doggie bags and our checks, and after we'd settled up we headed out to the parking lot. "Where'd you two park?" I asked.

"Over there, in the back row of the lot. I picked up Erin, since I practically had to go right by her place to get here," Pinky said.

"Well, I'm over here." I pointed to the right. "Thanks for introducing me to a new restaurant. It was really good."

"We should do this more often," Erin said.

I waved to my friends then found my car and unlocked the door. As I climbed in I felt the strangest compulsion to follow Pinky and Erin. They had both acted strangely at dinner, like they were up to something they couldn't tell me about. I started my engine, but sat there until I saw Pinky's car leave the lot and drive away. She headed west on Eighth Street. Twenty seconds later, I pulled out and followed them; they turned south on Central and west on Maple. When Pinky turned into Erin's driveway, I pulled over to the curb, two blocks away.

It wasn't ten seconds later that Mark drove in from the opposite direction and parked behind Pinky. The three of them got out of their cars and filed into Erin's house. I knew when Mark had said good-bye at the restaurant he had given Pinky and Erin a special look. And when I'd asked them about it, they had both denied it. Well, maybe not in so many words, but that was the way it had come across loud and clear.

Pinky had kept checking the time, and Erin had received a mysterious text from someone I knew was not her mother. I had known both of them since childhood and neither was a good liar. What in the world were they keeping from me? And it seemed that Mark was right in the thick of things with them. If I asked any of them point-blank if they'd had anything to do with Jerrell Powers's death, I was convinced I'd know by what they said, or how they said it, whether or not they were telling the truth. And how could I ever do that?

There I was, spying on my friends, who should have all been in their own houses by now, according to what they'd said. Instead they were all at Erin's, which was just plain strange. If Erin had said that Mark would be stopping over to help her get something out of the attic or whatever, I would have thought nothing of it. What were they up to, and why couldn't they tell me, their best friend? At least, I'd always thought I was; now I wasn't so sure. And who could I confide to about all of this?

My three closest friends, the ones who knew almost every

one of my deep, dark secrets, had met up at Erin's house without me. I took a deep breath through my nostrils and pondered my options. I didn't want to talk to my parents, with all they had going on with Mom's illness. My siblings were busy with their own families and lives. Assistant Chief Clinton Lonsbury? He'd probably laugh at me if I tattled on my friends to him, and then he'd ask me what I had to base my suspicions on. A secret nod? Or one giving another a ride home, and then the third happens to pull into her driveway a minute later? Pinky, Erin, and Mark were my friends, and if they were in some kind of trouble, I decided I'd better try to figure out what it was they were hiding before I confronted them with it.

8

As I got ready for work the next day I was still puzzling over Erin, Pinky, and Mark's secret meeting the night before. I wasn't hurt they hadn't included me. Exactly. Okay, if I was honest, I'd have to admit my feelings were a little hurt, and I chided myself for being immature. It wasn't like we were all still kids back in high school. And the bigger picture issue was I worried they were keeping something major under wraps. All three of them were well-known in the community and respected in their careers. I couldn't imagine any of them doing something that would throw that in jeopardy. At least not by choice.

Out of all of them, Erin had the biggest beef with Jerrell Powers. She had been one of the victims of his crimes. She lived fairly close to the park, about a half mile closer than I did, and not far from downtown. She may have walked to class on Friday night and then detoured through the park herself. Pinky lived another mile past me and would have had to drive by the park on her way home. It was possible Erin had walked to the shops and Pinky had given her a ride home. I remembered Pinky had offered, and Erin said no, but Pinky may have picked her up along the way.

In some ways Mark seemed the most suspicious of all. After my 911 call, he was the first to arrive on the scene, dressed in his street clothes and ready to go at the drop of a dime. It almost seemed like he had been waiting for the call. Was it because he was directly involved with what had happened to Powers, or was it because he had helped Erin and Pinky after the fact? Which of course made him an accessory.

I was officially driving myself crazy and figured the best way to prove they were innocent was to find out who was guilty. Aside from the few minutes when Pam and Lauren had stopped by Pinky's shop Saturday morning, I hadn't really talked to either one of them. I had no clue what Pam did for a living or if she would be home on a Wednesday morning.

After I'd finished dressing, I went into the spare bedroom, which also served as an office. I sat down at the small maple desk and fired up my laptop. When the search engine was ready, I typed in Pamela Hemley's name in hopes of locating her address. No problem. She lived in a newer neighborhood on the northeast side of town. I found a Post-it Note pad and pen in the top desk drawer and wrote down her address. Two other people were associated with her name. Given their surnames and ages, I presumed they were her children. Pamela was fifty-two, ten years older than Jerrell Powers.

Her supposed son and daughter were twenty-one and twenty-two. If they lived with her and were not pleased that Powers had returned, that could have thrown another monkey wrench in the works.

I had no clue about Pam's history with men, but the fact that she was involved, both before and after his incarceration, with a criminal who was ten years her junior made me wonder why. It didn't take a genius to know it wasn't for the financial support. Love really was blind for too many people. In Pam's case it seemed a lack of common sense went along with that. Even her sister had trouble convincing her that Powers was not good boyfriend material.

Lauren was the more likely suspect of the two. She'd said she lived in St. Cloud, a city about thirty-five miles away. I looked her up next. When I found her address, I jotted it down on the notepad under Pam's. If I decided to drive up to see her, I'd get the directions then.

Curio Finds didn't open for an hour and that gave me plenty of time to pay Pam a visit. Of all the people on my personal list of suspects, she seemed like the easiest nut to crack. I logged off the computer, grabbed my jacket and purse, and headed out the back door to the garage. I pulled the garage door opener out of my purse and pushed the button.

I'd found out from Sandra McClarity's daughter that Sandra had rarely parked in the garage, even though her car would have fit just fine. Janie didn't know why, but I figured it was because the old wooden overhead door was on the heavy side and must have been difficult for Sandra to manage. One of the first things I'd done when I moved into her house was to have an automatic opener installed. It made my coming and going much easier. And I felt better storing my car in the garage overnight, especially so after the bike thief had crashed there a couple of nights before. I kept going back to the question of why he was in our quiet little neighborhood at eleven o'clock at night riding someone else's bicycle without permission. I couldn't think of one good reason.

I always backed my car into the garage because I felt safer driving out rather than backing out blindly into the alley. Even with minimal traffic, I still worried about kids and dogs and others walking through. I climbed into my car and drove off to the northeast side of town for a surprise visit, where I got a surprise of my own.

When I was a block from Pam's house, I saw May Gregors on the front stoop. I stopped in the middle of the street then checked my rearview mirror to be sure no one was behind me. Fortunately, the coast was clear. I pulled over to the curb, trying to figure out what was going on. Pam's front door opened a few seconds later. I couldn't see who was inside, but May went in, so it was someone she knew. Most likely Pam.

May and Pam had acted like they'd never met before the snow globe–making class on Friday. Was that a ruse so the police wouldn't link the two of them together as partners in crime? And if you threw Lauren in the mix, oh, my. Another trio of potential suspects to consider. First it was my friends, and now it was this unlikely team.

I glanced at the clock on my dashboard: 9:10 a.m. There was a forty-minute window of time before I needed to be at work. I couldn't call Pinky to tell her I was running late because I was staking out Pamela Hemley's house. And that I just happened to see May Gregors go inside. And she hadn't forced her way in, either. Someone had opened the door for her.

It was a brisk morning, in the low forties, but I didn't want my car to idle for long. I turned off the engine and pulled my cell phone out of my purse to monitor the time. At 9:24, I rubbed my hands together to warm them. I was about to start the car and crank up the heat when May stepped out of the house and back onto the stoop. She waved to the person inside, then turned and headed down the walk at a medium pace toward her waiting car. She was carrying a brown paper grocery bag that she hadn't had going in. I tried to read the expression on her face, but it was blank. She wasn't smiling and she wasn't frowning. Whatever she was feeling, she didn't let it show. May's emotionless face struck me as odd, given the fact that she had just left the house of the woman her ex-husband had been involved with. The woman she'd advised to leave the relationship while the getting was good.

May drove away and I considered my options. On the one hand, I wanted to talk to Pam, especially now. On the other hand, would it seem like too much of a coincidence if I showed up two minutes after May had left? Even though it truly was a coincidence, pure and simple.

I started the car, drove the short distance, parked in May's vacated spot, and hurried to the door. As I reached for the doorbell, I heard voices inside. Who was in there with Pam? I pushed the button and the bell's chiming momentarily covered the sound of the voices. I waited for a minute, but no one came to the door. It was possible the voices were from a radio or television and Pam was in there alone. Or she didn't want to talk to anyone right then. May's visit could have easily upset her. It did me; and it made me wonder what in the world had brought her back to Brooks Landing.

Then it dawned on me—I bet Pam had found May's missing snow globe–making supplies and May had stopped by to retrieve them. Why it had taken fifteen minutes to do that was another question. I waited a minute, but if Pam wasn't going to answer the door there was no point standing there. I got back in my car and headed to work.

Pinky looked like she was upset with me when I walked through Brew Ha-Ha's shop door. I was thinking I was the one who should be upset with her after what had happened the night before.

"Cami, those women were in again looking for you."

"What women?" I slipped my coat off.

"The Halloween party planners."

Their request was the last thing I was worried about. "Oh. I thought they said they'd check back Thursday. It is Wednesday, right?"

"They stopped in for coffee and asked me if you'd made up your mind. I told them they'd have to ask you, of course, but I didn't think you wanted to attend their little soiree."

My friends were not only meeting behind my back, but had also started monitoring my social events. What was up with their weird behavior? Until I had more information, I was not about to make accusations that I hoped against hope were wrong. "Why would you tell them that, Pinky?"

"Well, everyone seems to think it's a bad idea." She half turned and filled a cup with coffee.

"Who's everyone?"

"Erin and Mark and me. Even Clint."

*Even Clint,* like he should have a say in whether I went to a Halloween party or not. Why was everyone making such a big deal about it anyway? "Pinky, can you give me a good reason why all of you are up in arms about this?"

She turned back to me, pursed her lips, and made a little "hmm" sound. "It just doesn't seem like a good idea." She handed me the coffee, maybe as a truce.

"Do you know something I don't?" The aroma tickled my nose.

"Well, no, and that's my point. I mean, what do we really know about those women anyhow?"

"How about I go check the police records and see what turns up?"

Pinky dug her hands into her hips. "Sometimes, Cami . . ."

Movement outside the shop's large front window caught my eye as a man walked by. "Do you know who that is?" I moved my head in the direction of the strolling stranger.

Pinky glanced at the window. "Who?"

"It was that same guy I've seen before, but can't place."

We walked over and looked out, but he was gone. "I didn't see him. What does he look like?" she said.

"Tall, broad shoulders with a thinnish build, like, narrow through the hips. Slightly hunched over. Long arms and legs. Somewhere in his late thirties, maybe early forties, I'd guess. Short, dark brown hair, close-cut beard. Glasses."

Pinky bobbed her head up and down. "Sounds like a few guys around town. Even Jerrell Powers. And we know it can't be him."

"Yes, we know that for a fact."

"So where have you seen him?" Pinky said.

"At the bar and grill last night—if it's the same guy. And . . . you're going to think I've got a big imagination, but from the side view, he reminds me of the would-be burglar from the other night. But I didn't get a good enough look at either one of them to swear they're the same guy."

"Cami, you do have a big imagination at times, and they are probably different people."

"I was trying to think if it was one of our classmates who looks a little older than we do."

Pinky raised her shoulder, leaned the side of her head on it, and winked. "Yes, not everyone our age is as youthful looking as we are."

I reached over and gave the other side of her head a light cuff. "Dream on, Alice Pinky Nelson."

"I will, Cami Jo Brooks. I mean Camryn." She went back behind the counter and started straightening cups. "You know what you should do? The next time you see that dude stop him and tell him he looks familiar."

"He'll think I'm trying to pick him up."

"That's not the worst thing in the world, is it? To repeat what my mother tells me about once a week: you aren't getting any younger."

"Gee, thanks, no one's reminded me of that for a month or so." I rolled my eyes.

"We both know that being single is way better than being married to someone like Kirk." Pinky's long-term sweetheart and short-term husband.

"That's for sure. So that's what we'll keep telling ourselves, and each other." I remembered I hadn't unlocked my shop door or turned the Closed sign to Open. "I better get to work."

"Nobody breaking down the door yet, at least."

"Not much going on this morning, huh?"

"It's been fairly quiet so far. The usual early rush, but not much after that. Except for your fan club, that is."

I smiled, turned, and set about opening my shop for business. My mind took a run-through of the past few days—the trip to Atwood with Clint, the bike thief in the alley and Clint responding to the call, Clint stopping me to ask about the newspaper article, dinner out at Sherman's, my friends' strange behavior. And then May paying a visit to the last person on earth I'd expect her to. I couldn't get that out of my mind, so I gave in to my urge to call Pam.

I'd kept the copy of the class list, which included all the attendees' phone numbers, and found it in the short stack of papers on the counter. I waited until Pinky was talking to some customers then carried my phone to the back of the store and dialed Pam's number. After five rings, it went to voicemail. Leave a message, or not? "Hi, Pamela, it's Camryn Brooks. I wanted to see how you're doing. Please give me a call at my shop anytime before six. Thanks."

After I'd hung up I thought about the fact that she hadn't answered her door, and thirty minutes later, she didn't answer her phone. It was entirely possible she was avoiding me. After all, I was the one who had made the awful discovery about her boyfriend, and she may not want to have anything further to do with me. I wandered back to my counter, sat down, and picked up the class list. Pinky had told me not to call any of them to ask about May's missing supplies. May was perfectly capable of handling that, plus she'd know the value of the items. I didn't feel compelled to hunt down her things, anyway.

I was more interested in finding out if one of the attendees had made a snow globe with a man sleeping on a park bench under a full moon. And if so, why would they leave it on a Curio Finds shelf, and how had they gotten it back later that night when the doors were locked? At least mine was. I hadn't personally checked Brew Ha-Ha's door, which happened to ding at that moment.

I poked my head into Pinky's space and saw she was alone. I needed her blessings on an idea that had popped into my head, a way to talk to the class members without raising any red flags. At least that was what I hoped. "Pinky, you mentioned hosting another class down the road, so I was thinking we should do a little phone survey of everyone from our last class."

"What kind of a survey?"

"You know, like they do at seminars. But there you have to fill out an evaluation form before you leave."

"Cami, I haven't taken a class since my brief stint in college umpteen years ago, and I don't have a clue about what to ask on a survey."

"Things like, was the space adequate? Did the instructor know her stuff? Would you attend another class if it was offered? What classes might you be interested in in the future?"

"Ooh." She tugged at the wide pink headband that kept her unruly hair away from her face. "Okay. If you write up the questions, I'm game."

"You know what? I'm having a slow day and I'm looking

for something to do. I'll take care of the calls and will tell you what everyone has to say."

"If you want to, sure. Why don't you see if they'd like to learn how to make perfect scones?"

I shook my head. "You don't want to take away from your own business."

"Oh, yeah, I guess that could. Well, then, maybe they'd want to find out more about coffee beans, how they're grown and selected—"

I interrupted her. "Maybe." I headed back to my own counter and the class list. I took out two legal pads and jotted down a few class-specific questions on one of them and left the other one blank for other information that might come out during the conversations.

I picked up the phone, hoping to catch someone at home on a weekday morning. The two older ladies from my church were the most likely to be available, but then again, I knew a lot of seniors were always on the go. I didn't suspect either woman of anything, but knew I'd have to call everyone on the list to be fair. People talked, and if the little old ladies realized they hadn't been asked to participate in the survey, they might feel left out. I dialed the first one's number.

"Good morning," Rena answered, and the smile on her face came through her voice.

"Good morning, it's Camryn Brooks."

"Oh, yes, Camryn. How wonderful of you to take the time to call, what with all you have going on in your life since the other night. Wasn't that a fright?"

"Yes, Rena, that's a good word. Things are settling down a little, so I wanted to call everyone who came to the snow globe–making class and ask how they liked it."

"Oh, my, it was such a treat to be there and learn all about making snow and putting the globes together. Edie and I were talking about it, and we're going to get together and make some more, one for each of our grandchildren." Edie was the other church lady.

"How fun. What scene did you do again?"

"I used an old white country church set with pine trees."

I remembered that one. "You didn't have time to make two?"

"No, no, I don't think anyone did. I know the teacher said she had extra supplies, but I didn't see anyone buying any." I hadn't, either, and that reminded me I should ask May that very question.

We chatted for a few more minutes, and Rena assured me the space was fine, the teacher was helpful and knew her stuff, and she'd love to take another class at our shops. If Rena had heard the gossip about how teacher May and student Pamela were connected, she did not let on.

I phoned Edie next and had a similar conversation with her. She and Rena were looking forward to making snow globes and taking whatever class we may offer next time around.

I spoke with the mother who had brought her crafty teenage daughter to the class. From what I learned, their family was fairly new in town, and the two of them had been looking for something fun to do while her husband and son were at a high school football game. She told me what scenes they had each chosen, and neither was a guy sleeping on a park bench.

The fourth call was to Kim, one of Pinky's regulars and someone I knew casually because she stopped in nearly every day for coffee and a muffin. She wasn't home, and I decided not to leave a message. It was better for me to try back later than to risk her returning my call when I was busy with customers.

The oldest of the class attendees was a frequent window shopper at Curio Finds. Emmy would come in and shake one or two or three globes and watch them snow over the various scenes. She was sweet and meek and told me she didn't have room for more things in her small house. I suspected the two real reasons were she had little means and browsing helped ease her loneliness. I was glad she had attended the class. We talked for a long time, which lightened my mood, and I think made her feel better, too. Emmy had made a wildlife scene with deer licking a salt block and kept it on the end table by her recliner chair. She had no plans to make more snow globes, but might come to another class to get out of the house.

The last attendee was a crafter who lived in the area and traveled all over to sell her goods at arts and crafts fairs. We talked for a minute, but she was busy packing up her wares for an event the next day and seemed distracted. I went quickly through the questions. She had enjoyed the class, but was in the middle of too many projects to think about making any more snow globes until probably next spring so she'd have a good supply for the following fall sales.

I finally reached Kim at about 5:40 in the afternoon, and she sang praises for the class, even though she had gotten the nitty-gritty from Pinky on what had happened with May and Pamela and Erin and Lauren. But that hadn't taken anything away from how much fun she'd had in the class or how much her daughter loved the Cinderella snow globe she'd made for her. She went on about Jerrell Powers until I had a beep telling me there was another call coming in.

"Kim, sorry, but there's a phone call I have to take."

"Okay, thanks, Camryn. Bye-bye for now."

I smiled when I saw who it was and pushed the talk button. "Curio Finds, Camryn speaking. How may I help you?"

"Hi, it's Pam Hemley. You called?" Her voice held little emotion, as though she were weary or depressed.

"Yes, thanks for calling me back. I wanted to see how you were doing."

"Not all that well, to be honest with you. I didn't know it would be this hard."

"You mean Jerrell's death?"

"Yes, I mean, he was gone for those couple of years and all. When he came home last Friday I didn't really know what to do. I wasn't expecting him for a few days yet. But he wanted to surprise me so that's why he didn't tell me his real release date."

"I imagine it was a big surprise."

"Yes, especially since Lauren was there. I still loved Jerrell and all, but Lauren had pretty much convinced me he wasn't good for me. His homecoming was not the way he hoped it would be, I know that much. He and Lauren argued. And then she brought up the class I was signed up for, and Jerrell said that was fine, I should go, he had things to take care of anyway."

"Did he say what kinds of things?"

"No, and when I asked him, he wouldn't tell me."

"Then what happened?"

"He left and we went to the class."

And we all knew how the night ended. "Thanks for

calling me back, Pam. I have to be honest and tell you I thought either you were avoiding me or you weren't up to opening your door this morning."

"Opening my door?" She sounded puzzled.

"Yes, I stopped by, and I thought you might be home, but no one came to the door."

"What time was that?"

"Around nine thirty."

"I was at work by eight. No one was home."

I wasn't sure what to say. "Oh. Well, I didn't know your schedule so I took a chance you'd be there."

"That was kind of you. I didn't feel like going in today, but Lauren said being busy is the best thing I can do right now."

Lauren. Her name kept coming up in the conversation. "Lauren isn't still staying with you?"

"No, but she checks in a few times a day and has been down a couple of evenings. She's got her own family to take care of, but with my kids away at college, she doesn't want me to be alone."

"Where do your kids go to school?"

"They're both at UND." University of North Dakota, almost three hundred miles northwest of Brooks Landing in Grand Forks. "And I didn't want them to take off school to be with me. They have midterms."

Lauren wasn't staying with Pam and her kids were over four hours away. So who had been at her house earlier? It was someone who knew May Gregors well enough to invite her in and spend fifteen or so minutes with her. And send along a brown shopping bag with her when she left. I was in a quandary over what to tell Pam, but she had the right to know what had happened at her own house that morning.

"Pam—"

She cut me off. "I've got to go; the police are here. Thanks again." She hung up before I could say "'bye."

I hung up myself. Maybe the police had gotten a tip from a neighbor about suspicious activities going on at Pamela's house, strangers coming and going when she was at work. Or they may have learned she was involved with Jerrell Powers's death after all and were there to arrest her, although that seemed unlikely.

Pinky had left about an hour before. She rarely had much business near suppertime, so it usually worked for me to be on my own for the last couple of hours. I glanced at the clock and smiled when I saw it was 5:55. I turned off the lights, flipped the Open sign, and checked to be sure the coffeemakers were shut down, then I locked the doors and was in my car by six o'clock on the dot. The sun was low in the sky on this cloudy evening. I felt fairly anonymous driving to Pam's neighborhood in the fading light.

A police car was parked on the street directly in front of her house. I drove on past, but her drapes were closed so I didn't see which officer, or officers, was inside with her. I went around the block then stopped at the stop sign on the cross street a half block from Pam's house. If someone came up behind me, I'd move forward. A few minutes later, Assistant Chief Clinton Lonsbury exited the front door. All alone, with no one in handcuffs. Pamela Hemley was not under arrest. Not yet anyway.

I didn't want Clint to see me, but I had no magic means to disappear into thin air. I had worn out my welcome at the stop sign and eased forward, hoping he wouldn't notice it was my car driving past his. No such luck. He turned on his flashing lights for a second. I pulled over to the curb before he made a bigger deal of getting my attention and alerted the entire neighborhood.

Clint walked up to my car door and tapped on the window. I rolled it down. "Miss Brooks, what are you doing on this side of town?"

"Just driving through."

"You're not following me, are you?"

"Following you? No." I needed to change the subject fast. "Assistant Chief Lonsbury, don't officers need a good reason to stop a person?"

"Yes, we do, and this wasn't a stop. I accidentally bumped the switch that activated my lights, and you'd pulled over by the time I'd flipped it back. I thought you must have wanted to talk to me about something."

"Oh, well, no. And not that it's any of my business, but isn't that Pamela Hemley's house?" I pointed my thumb back.

"It is. I gave Ms. Hemley the official death report on Powers and told her the medical examiner has released his body so she could go ahead and make the funeral arrangements."

"Is it secret, the medical examiner's report?"

"We're not withholding the cause of death. It was a stab wound to the heart." With the knife I'd tried to pull out.

I nodded. "Making any progress? Like, with finding Benjamin Arnold?"

"Not yet. But we're working on it, trying to dig up leads, so it's only a matter of time." Saying the word must have prompted him to look at his watch. "I need to push off. Drive safely."

Clint walked back to his car and I turned my head for a look at Pam's house. No one was looking out, thank heavens. I didn't want to have to come up with an explanation of what I was doing there talking to the assistant chief of police. Especially since she knew I'd been at her home that morning and she'd told me not thirty minutes before that the police were there. I'd have to get a lot better at spying on people.

I put on my turn signal and pulled away from the curb. Clint was still sitting in his car when I drove away. He'd given me the reason for his visit and it didn't include suspicious people in Pam's house. What was a good way to talk to her about that? I'd forgotten May Gregors's phone number at the store and swung back to get it.

As I pulled up to Curio Finds, I noticed a man on a bike on the other side of the street going the opposite direction. He was lanky and I was almost ready to bet it was the same guy who'd crashed in my alley. Then it dawned on me he might also be the same one I'd seen the other two times: at Sherman's and outside Pinky's coffee shop window. There were no cars coming from either direction. I did a quick U-turn to follow him, but he had disappeared. I took a gamble and turned right on Division Street, but there was no sign of him. I drove around the area for a while, but had no success finding him.

Who was that elusive guy? And what was it about him that drew my attention? He seemed to be everywhere and nowhere at the same time. He showed up places, but acted like he didn't want to be seen. It was entirely possible I was blowing the whole thing out of proportion. I went back to the store, found May's number, and headed home.

My house felt more lonely than normal as I wandered

from the living room to the kitchen. Maybe Sandra's spirit or essence, or whatever it was, was fading. I grabbed a glass of water and went back to the living room and plopped on the couch. I pulled the paper with May's number on it out of my pocket and programmed the number into my cell phone. For future reference. I dialed and waited.

"May Gregors and Distinctive Crafts." She'd added her business name to her greeting.

"Hi, May, it's Camryn Brooks."

"Oh, Camryn, your name didn't come up on the display."

"I'm on my cell phone. Anyway, I thought I'd check back with you to see if your missing supplies turned up."

"No, they haven't."

"I happened to see you in town today and thought maybe someone had found them and you were picking them up."

She was silent a minute. "Oh, well, yes, I was in Brooks Landing today to, um, take care of some business, but not about the supplies."

"To let you know, I surveyed everyone in the class about how they liked it, and if the space was okay, things like that. Everyone enjoyed it and you as the instructor."

"Well, thank you, I appreciate hearing that. The fun we had at the class paled with the confrontation after, and I apologize for that."

"No need to, really. Oh, and when I talked to the class members, I didn't come right out and ask them if they had somehow ended up with your missing supplies, but I didn't get the impression any of them did."

"I didn't mean to make such a big deal out of it. They probably amounted to around twenty, maybe twenty-five dollars' worth. If they turn up, great; if not, it's not going to make or break me."

"I'm just sorry it happened at our class."

"Not to worry, really. I was mostly puzzled about it."

"Did you have anyone who wanted to make a second snow globe on class night?"

"No, I didn't."

"Like I said before, when I saw you in town earlier today, I had hopes it was to pick up your lost supplies." There, I'd given her another chance to tell me the truth.

"I get to Brooks Landing every once in a while. You know, they sell my things at Crafts Landing."

Pinky hadn't told me that. "No, I didn't know. I'll have to check out that store."

"It's fun. Not as quaint as your shop, but fun."

"Are you doing okay, with your ex-husband's death and all?"

"My daughter is pretty broken up. Mostly for the relationship she *didn't* have with her father. But I would be lying if I said I was sorry he's gone." At least she was honest about that.

"I've taken enough of your time so I'll let you go. Take care, May, and have a good night."

"You, too."

I pushed the end button on my phone with more force than was necessary.

I was frustrated with May for not telling me the truth, and more frustrated with myself for not telling her what I'd observed. Pam had told me she wasn't home, so whoever May met with was still in question. She wouldn't reveal where she had been or why. Which meant she did not want me to know she'd been to Pam's house or she didn't want me to know who she'd met there. Or both. What was that tangled web saying?

I got up and went to the living room window to close the drapes. A penny lay on the floor on the carpet. I picked it up, fingered it a moment, then dropped it in my pocket. When I looked outside, I saw the same guy—and now I could swear it was him—ride by slowly on his bike on the other side of the street. He turned his head toward my house, but his face was in shadows. A chill streamed from my shoulders down my spine and raised goose bumps on my skin.

It was beginning to feel like the man was spying on me. If he was the same guy who'd given me a brief stare at Sherman's, and the same guy who had looked in Pinky's shop window, and the same guy I'd seen those few times riding by on his bike, then I'd gotten a fairly good look at him. It was possible he was one of our classmates, one who was scoping me out for one reason or another. Over the years a few of the boys from our school had contacted me and eventually asked me out on dates, which had taken me by surprise each time.

My school yearbooks were in a rubber storage tub in the spare bedroom closet. I went in there, closed the curtains to keep others from looking in, then flipped on the lights. Was I getting paranoid or what? I opened the closet door and surveyed the rubber storage tubs, trying to remember where the one I was looking for had ended up. I slid the tub closest to the door out and found the purple one marked *High School Mementos* on the floor behind it. It was easy to spot since purple was one of our class colors and I'd selected that bin color because of that.

I plopped down on the floor, stretched out my legs on

either side of the tub, and pulled it close to me. I flipped off the cover and studied the top layer. There were a number of certificates, awards, and club membership pins: choir, student council, debate club, drama club, junior class president. Activities my dad thought would help me overcome my shyness. And they did, to a great extent. The more time I spent in front of people, the easier it became.

I glanced at each item as I removed it until I got to the yearbooks on the bottom. There was one for all four years, freshman, sophomore, junior, and senior. The books had padded purple leather covers with silver lettering depicting the school and year in a variety of ways. I started with the most recent. It was a trip down memory lane paging through the book, reminding me of all the sporting events, band and choir concerts, school plays, teachers, classmates. Events and people I hadn't thought about for a long time. I looked at each face, studying more closely the faces of the boys I didn't know very well. I tried to imagine what some of them would look like eighteen years later and made a mental note to check on them to see what they were up to.

I looked through the pictures of the juniors, sophomores, and freshmen and got more confused than anything else. No one jumped out at me as a probable match to the mysterious bike rider. I closed that book and picked up the one from my junior year. I turned to the seniors' pictures and found Clinton Lonsbury looking at me with a half smile on his face. His family had moved to Brooks Landing when he was a sophomore or junior. I hadn't hung around with him much in high school, but enjoyed watching the basketball games, where he was a standout player. He had pumped up his muscles quite a bit since those gangly high school days.

After forty minutes perusing the yearbook photos, including the ones of various school events, I had a few leads to pursue, but none that seemed very promising. Maybe I would ask Mark to be on the lookout for a lanky man walking or riding his bike around town. But if the guy wasn't committing a crime, Mark would have no reason to stop and question him. And I had no real reason to suspect him of anything, either; it was more of a hunch. I reached in my pocket and touched the penny. *Is there something about that man I'm supposed to be paying attention to?*

9

My "fan club," as Pinky had called the trio, was waiting for me in Brew Ha-Ha when I arrived for work Thursday morning. They were dressed in their workout clothes. When the three women turned and rushed me, Pinky stared at me and snapped her dish towel.

"Camryn, we're here for your answer." Tara looked like she was going to start jumping again and I was tempted to tell her to save it for her aerobics class.

Instead, I said, "The party is on the twenty-fifth? What was the time again?"

"Seven o'clock. Does that mean you can make it?" Heather asked.

"Sure, why not. It'll be good to meet more people in town." And there was always the remote possibility a lanky guy would be there in a Buddy Holly costume. Ha.

Heather gave me a light hug. "I am sooo excited."

Emily moved in closer and put one arm on Heather's shoulder and one on mine. "It will be the best party ever. And if you'd like to come in costume, that'd be great. I think most everyone else is." Mmm. Buddy Holly, meet Marilyn Monroe. A kickback tribute to the fifties.

"But you're the guest of honor, so you wear whatever you like. We usually have one or two who opt out for one reason or another," Tara said.

They gathered together, ready to move on to the next adventure, then called out their thanks and good-byes and flitted out the door like little sparrows.

"Well, that was a treat. I can't believe you agreed to that whole fiasco they have planned." Pinky struck her favorite "I'm upset" pose—her head tipped to the side with her hands on her hips. "Do you have their phone numbers so you can cancel?"

We had never exchanged numbers, nor did I have the address of where the party was being held. Maybe I wouldn't be going after all. "I'm sure they'll be back with the details," I said.

"Hmm."

I left to open my shop for the day and was struck by an odd snow globe sitting on the shelf closest to the coffee shop. I picked it up and studied it. "Pinky, come here."

"What?"

I handed her the globe. "Any idea where this came from?"

"Why, no. It's your shop, after all."

"But it doesn't belong here; it wasn't here yesterday."

"How would you know that for sure with the hundreds you've got in there?"

"Because I dust the shelves and pick each one of them up."

*"Boring."*

I shrugged. "That's beside the point. Don't you think it looks like it could be one of the snow globes we made last week?"

Pinky looked more closely and gave it a shake. "It does, doesn't it? The snow could be the same stuff May whipped up."

"Another park scene, but it's daytime and there's a cop walking through in this one, and three kids playing," I said, more to myself than to Pinky.

Pinky handed the snow globe back to me and grabbed my arms. "Cami, by 'another park scene,' do you mean like the other one someone left on your shelf?"

I nodded. "When I locked up last night, I didn't notice it in here, but it's possible it was left on the shelf sometime yesterday. I'm positive it wasn't there yesterday morning, so it wouldn't have been left here Tuesday. Help me think of everyone who's been in here yesterday and today, so far."

*"Cami,"* was her one-word protest.

I put my hand on her back, steered her to a table in her shop, and pulled out a chair for her to sit on. "I know the ten o'clock coffee break rush is about to start, but let's take a minute to think about this. Pinky, you know most of the people who come in here—the regulars, at least. Who's been in here today?" I set the globe on the table and studied it while I waited for Pinky's answer.

She rattled off a dozen names of people I knew or had at least met, and a few I didn't recognize. "Then of course, Erin, Mark, and Archie all came in for their morning special. Oh, and Pamela Hemley stopped by on her way to work, which was kind of a surprise."

"Pamela? Really? What did she have to say?"

"Not much. There were three or four people in line, so I pretty much just took her order and said, 'Take care,' and that's about it."

Pinky's door's bell dinged and six local businessmen charged in, carrying on at least two, maybe three separate conversations. They ranged in age from forty to late sixties and were some of her faithful ten o'clock regulars. I left the snow globe where it sat on the table and joined Pinky behind her service counter to help dish up muffins and scones while she served each of them the coffee choice of the day: Jamaica Blue Mountain Blend, a medium-body, rich flavor that had a smooth chocolate finish. When I added a little cream, it was one of my favorites.

The men wanted a recap of my late-night discovery in Lakeside Park and asked if I had any updates on the investigation. Of course I wasn't about to reveal I was conducting an investigation of my own. "I know the police have a prime suspect, but the guy sort of fell off the face of the planet. They figure he'll surface one of these days."

"Yeah, I've seen his mug shot on the news and in the papers. Kind of a tough-looking character," one said.

"My friend in the PD, Jake, told me a lotta guys put on a mean face to change their appearance somewhat," another man said.

The most senior of the group nodded. "That's right. A guy walking around with an expression like that would have people running for cover. I'd be freaked out, and I'm almost too old for things to scare me."

The youngest in the group gave him a slap on the back. "Our fearless elder."

I looked up and saw a customer in my shop so I excused myself and went next door.

Business was fairly steady until midafternoon when the shop cleared of customers and I had time to think about May not disclosing her visit to Pam's house and about the new mysterious snow globe, which reminded me I'd left it on one of Pinky's tables. I slapped the counter when I realized we had messed up the evidence by touching it and leaving our fingerprints all over it. I'd know better next time even though I prayed there wouldn't *be* a next time. The first globe depicted a death scene; the second one signified— what? When I went into Pinky's shop to retrieve the mystery item, it wasn't there.

"Pinky, where'd you put that snow globe, the one we found this morning?"

She shrugged. "I didn't touch it. I noticed it wasn't on the table and thought you took it."

"Is someone trying to push me over the edge or what?"

"That'd be a short shove," she quipped and smiled.

"Very funny."

"Well . . ."

"You may be right, but that's why I need all the help and support I can get around here."

"At least this time I can testify that you did find a snow globe in your shop that wasn't part of your inventory, and then it disappeared from where it was sitting in my shop."

"How many customers have you had since ten?"

"Gosh, I don't know. Maybe thirty."

"Any of them a shady character who would steal a snow globe?"

"Holy moly, Cami. No one was wearing an 'I am a snow globe thief' T-shirt, if that's what you mean."

"Okay." I looked up at Betty Boop, and the hands on her clock said it was 3:40. "It's just about time for you to go, but do you mind if I take a little walk first? I'm going nuts over that snow globe, not to mention everything else."

Pinky put some cups into her sink. "Sure, that's fine. Take your time."

I grabbed my lightweight rain-or-shine jacket and took off like a bat out of hell. Nearly a week had passed and I felt compelled to return to the scene of the crime. I headed to Lakeside Park. When I reached the path that led into the park I felt a twinge that was hard to describe. A sense of fear mixed with curiosity and a little repulsion. I glanced down at the path every few steps, thinking there might be another penny from heaven. No penny. Instead there was a different kind of surprise altogether. A young and burly Brooks Landing police officer was walking toward me. That was peculiar. I had never seen an officer on foot patrolling the park before, unless there was a community event there. Normally, they'd pull their police cars in one of the two adjoining parking lots and scan the park from there.

I tried to appear as nonchalant as possible when we met, and intended to say hi and keep walking, but he stopped. "You're Camryn Brooks."

"I am. Officer . . . ?"

"Dooley. Jake. They say they always return to the scene of the crime."

How does one respond to that? "Um, I've heard that."

"At least that's what we're hoping for. That the killer won't be able to resist coming back at some point."

I'd thought he meant me.

"What brings you to the park today?"

"I often go this way."

"I see." Jake got a call on his police radio and I took the opportunity to smile and mouthed, "Keep up the good work," and walked away like I had someplace to go. Up ahead, there was a group of middle-school-age children running and goofing around. Another freaky snow globe scene that imitated real life: a police officer and children at play in the park. Who in the world was creating those scenes and leaving them for me to see? And in each case, the globes disappeared before I could turn them over to the authorities.

I picked up my pace and when I reached the end of the path, I turned around to go back to the shop. About five minutes later I went in my door and heard Pinky talking to someone as I headed to the back room to hang my coat. "I don't think Cami suspects a thing, but who knows for sure?"

I snuck up to the side of the archway and hung back to eavesdrop on her conversation.

"Cami's awfully smart, and intuitive to boot, so we just have to be careful not to say anything about it at all." It was Erin's voice.

"Mum's the word."

Pinky's door's bell dinged and they stopped talking. I went back to my own door and pretended like I had just gotten in. "I'm back, Pinky," I called out.

Erin appeared in the archway. "Hi, Cami. Pinky's with a customer."

"Hey. Done with school for the day?" I looked down and unzipped my jacket to compose myself. My friends were keeping something from me and I'd heard it with my own ears.

"Pinky was telling me you had another snow globe appearance and disappearance. Only this time, she saw it, too."

"I think I need a vacation. And maybe when I get back things will be normal again."

Erin frowned. "After what happened last week, it doesn't seem like things will ever be normal again." Her eyes focused on the door then she nodded and smiled. "Your mom and dad are here."

I turned, and was reminded in that second that no matter how confused things got, my parents were the safe harbor in my life. I couldn't begin to count the number of times I had sought refuge in them. Mom's illness had stopped me from burdening them with all the madness of the past week, but perhaps I shouldn't have let that stop me from seeking their advice. As soon as I sorted out a few things, we'd sit down for a heart-to-heart.

Dad was a big man, towering over Mom, but he seemed even more so since Mom had lost weight. She looked about half his size. And ten years older, with new wrinkles brought on by the weight loss. The doctors were confident she was on the road to recovery, and we all held on to that hope. Even with all they'd been going through, they still seemed younger than their early seventies.

Mom and Dad looked around and smiled broadly. "My, everything is sparkling," Mom said.

"Your daughter is the queen of clean, as you well know," Dad said.

"Yes, I do. A woman after my own heart."

I reached over and took her in my arms for a gentle squeeze then gave Dad the bear hug he liked.

"Good to see you, Erin. How is your mother doing?" Mom walked over to her.

"Well, I think. She's busy with her new life. Her husband likes to go, go, go. And they have a lot going on with his kids and grandkids."

Mom reached over and picked up Erin's hand. "It sounds like a big adjustment for you, dear."

Erin shrugged. "I have to admit it's been hard. Losing Dad was the worst thing I've ever gone through. And I know it was for Mom, too. But after three years of being alone, I can't blame her for wanting another chance at happiness. And they are making the most of their new lives together. Don't get me wrong, I'm very happy for her. But a little sad for me now that she's moved out of town and I don't see her as much as I'd like. Thank God for good friends like Cami."

I thought back to the story the Vickermans had told me over the years about Erin's arrival in the United States. Mrs. Vickerman had brought a small entourage to the Minneapolis–St. Paul airport to greet her husband and new daughter when they got off the plane. I'd loved seeing the pictures of the dark-eyed beauty, with black hair that stood straight up, and a look of sheer awe on her face.

Dad gave Erin a hug. "You stop over anytime you like.

It'll be like the old days when you kids were always playing and running around together."

"What are you two doing out and about?" I asked.

"I had my weekly checkup with the doctor, and we hadn't been by for a while so we thought we'd stop in and see if you needed anything," Mom said.

"Not a thing, except maybe some help ordering more snow globes."

Dad nodded. "That we can do. When your mother feels stronger, we'll be getting out to more auctions and estate sales. I've gone to a couple myself in the last few weeks and picked up some knickknacks; I got a mantel clock and an old covered crock that might have been a cookie jar. A few odds and ends. We'll get them cleaned up, figure out the right price, and bring them in."

"That'll be good."

Dad put his arm around Mom. "I guess everything is under control here, Beth. Why don't we grab a cup of coffee and one of those blueberry scones you love so much?"

Mom put her hand on his chest. "I'd love that, what a nice pick-me-up."

All four of us descended on Pinky, who was setting mugs of coffee in front of a pair of young women. She smiled at my parents. "Beth, Eddie, what a nice surprise. It's been a while. Holy moly, I miss seeing the two of you next door in your shop. Not to say that I don't enjoy Cami being there, of course. Find yourselves a seat at a table and Cami can take your order."

"Well, I need to run so I'll catch you all later," Erin said and held up her to-go cup as she headed out the door.

My parents and I waved our good-byes, then they sat at their favorite table in the middle of the shop. "Okay, Mom, you want chai tea with your scone?"

"Please."

"Dad?" He changed up his order from one time to the next. He had no "usual."

"I'll go with a cup of the daily special and a cherry vanilla chip scone."

"Coming right up." I fixed their order, made a chai tea for myself, then sat down with them. We chatted for a few minutes until Pinky joined us.

"You are really looking good, Beth." Pinky rested her hands on Mom's shoulders for a moment then sat down.

"Thanks. It's been a challenge, but I'm tolerating the chemo fairly well." She picked up her scone and took a bite. "Mmm, this is so good."

"Did Cami tell you about the new snow globe that appeared on her shelf this morning, and then disappeared?" Pinky said.

I wasn't ready to share the latest surprise with them, but my blabbermouth friend didn't know that. Mom and Dad looked at me for the story. After I'd given the details, Mom reached over and held my hand. "I don't like all the shenanigans that have been going on around here."

"That's a great word, 'shenanigans.' I like it," Pinky said.

"Mom, I'm not sure what they are, or what's really going on. Maybe someone is pulling pranks, but I have no clue why."

"It seems more like they're sending messages than pulling pranks, if you ask me. The first snow globe for sure. At least from the way Cami described the scene. It all fit, in a really scary way," Pinky said.

"And the second snow globe scene had to have been just a weird coincidence," I said.

"How is that?" Pinky said.

"When I took that break a little while ago, I walked down to Lakeside Park—"

"You went *where*?" Pinky's hands dropped on the table.

"Don't say it like that. You know very well I wasn't going to stay away from there forever. I've probably been there thousands of times in my life."

"I might stay away from there for good after everything that's happened." She crossed her arms on her chest.

"No, you won't. You love the summer concerts there."

"Oh, yeah."

My parents had shifted their eyes back and forth from Pinky to me during the conversation.

"Why did you go back there?" Dad asked.

"I felt I had to. Someone had left another park scene, and after what happened the last time . . . I just had to, that's all. And what I found out made me wonder if someone around here has ESP."

"Extrasensory perception?" Mom echoed.

"You mean someone besides you?" Pinky said.

"I don't think that's what experts would call my 'feelings.' "

"What did you find?" Dad got us back on track.

I looked at Pinky. "Tell my parents what was in the snow globe scene, the one from this morning."

Pinky lifted her hands and pointed at the air as she described it. "Some trees, like it was a park. Three kids playing; one was kicking a ball. Oh, and a cop was walking nearby."

"Okay, guess what I saw when I was in the park."

"Nooo." Pinky's eyes widened and she shook her head.

"Three kids kicking a ball around, and a Brooks Landing police officer by the name of Jake walking through on foot patrol. Just like in the snow globe."

Mom reached over and covered my hand with hers. Then Dad put both his hands on top of them.

"And you wouldn't make that up in front of your parents," Pinky said.

"Pinky, you know very well I wouldn't make that up, period."

Dad nodded. "We could always count on Cami to tell the truth, from the time she was a little girl." He withdrew his hands and moved the right one to a couple of feet from the floor, as the indicator of how tall I must have been.

"And she's not one to embellish the truth, either. Even with her sometimes overactive imagination," Mom added, and her lips tugged to the side in a sly smile.

I lifted my hands. "What do you think it means? Another baffling scene captured in a snow globe that shows up in real life."

"Way too weird for words and I don't want to think about it because it is honestly creeping me out." Pinky glanced over at her customers. "I gotta go. Refill time." She left our table and headed to the serving counter.

"There are such things as coincidences in the world," Dad said.

"I think that things happen for a reason, more often than not. But in this case, maybe the snow globe scenes that came to life really are just coincidences like your father says," Mom said.

I nodded. "I can accept that. What I have trouble with is

why they appear out of nowhere and then disappear into thin air."

"Cami, all you have to do is figure out who was in the shop earlier today and then came back some hours later. Or, like you mentioned, it could be that he—or she—was here sometime yesterday and set it on the shelf, forgot about it, then came back for it today," Mom said.

"Beth, the new snow globe could have been left by one person and taken by another," Dad said.

I'd thought of all three scenarios. I wondered about the lanky guy, and if he had come into either of the shops when I wasn't there. Had he been scoping the shop out to see if I was there the time he looked in the window and then turned tail and disappeared when he saw me looking at him? There was no reason I could think of to explain why he'd be avoiding me specifically.

Mom and Dad finished their afternoon snacks and stood to leave. "What a lovely break we had here, even with hearing about the strange snow globe mysteries that have been dropped in your lap," Mom said.

Dad wrapped an arm around my shoulder. "For the time being, I'd feel a lot better if you'd stay out of the park. Or at least don't go there alone until they find out who killed Jerrell Powers and have him locked up."

"Dad—"

Mom put her hand on my other shoulder. "Please, Cami."

"All right. Since it means that much to you, if I go back to Lakeside before the killer is found, I will take someone with me. Maybe even a police officer."

Mom and Dad smiled together when the last two words popped out. Then they headed for home. As I gathered the dishes, then carried them to the sink to wash and sanitize them, I considered my next course of action.

Pinky emerged from the back room. "Well, Cami, I'm going to shove off, unless there's something I forgot."

I glanced around. "Not that I know of. One thing I'd like you to think about when you're whipping up your baked delights: who was in your shop either yesterday or early this morning, before ten, and then came back this afternoon before the snow globe disappeared."

She stuck out her lips. "Cami, that's maybe too much to ask of my little brain."

"It is not. You are a people person. Out of everyone I know you are the one I can always count on to help me with any people-related question I have."

"You don't have to butter me up. I'll think about it and write down every name I can come up with."

"Thank you. I mean, don't you think it's curious?"

"I just want this whole business to disappear like the snow globes did. I can't stand how our lives have been turned upside down by someone who should never have come to Brooks Landing in the first place."

"I'm with you on that one, Pinky. The problem is that someone took the law into their own hands to get rid of him."

Pinky shrugged. "See you tomorrow. We have police who are investigating all of that, you know. Oh, did you tell Mark about the latest?"

"I haven't seen him yet today." I looked at the time. "If he doesn't stop in before quitting time, I'll give him a call."

"Later, then."

"All right."

Mark Weston saved me a phone call when he stopped by

a little after five. I heard the bell on Pinky's door ding and was happy to see it was him.

"Are you lonely? You act like you're glad I'm here," he said.

"I am. Not lonely, but glad you're here. There are a couple of things I need to tell you." I went behind Pinky's counter, poured him a cup of coffee, and set it in front of him.

Mark lowered himself slowly, duty belt and all, onto a stool. "Like what?"

"Okay. You know that guy I asked about the other night, the one I saw at Sherman's Bar and Grill?"

"The one with the beard and Buddy Holly glasses that nobody else saw?" He raised his eyebrows and his forehead wrinkled.

I put my hands on the counter and leaned toward him. "That's the one. And I'm sure someone else saw him since it was crowded in there. It's just that the others in our group missed him."

"Yeah, what about him?" He picked up his cup.

"It seems like I should know him, but can't place him. I even went through our yearbooks, thinking it might be someone from our school days." I straightened and poured myself a glass of water.

Mark took a drink of coffee. "I take it you didn't find him there."

"There are two men that could be possibilities. I'd appreciate if you'd check on them. See if they are still around. Some people change so much that if you don't see them from time to time, it's hard to recognize them."

"Are you looking to date the guy, or what?"

I laughed. "No, I am not currently in that market. I get

the feeling he may be keeping tabs on me, but I have no idea why."

"You are the biggest celebrity in town right now."

"You think that could be it?"

"Could be," Mark said.

"Here's the thing. I have seen someone a number of times who I'm convinced is the same guy as the one I saw at Sherman's."

"Buddy Holly?"

"Without the glasses. And maybe not the beard."

"So he also wears contacts and may have shaved?" He frowned slightly.

"That's entirely possible. I got a fairly good look at him the other day, but can't swear that he had the beard. He may have trimmed it. It was his eyes I noticed most."

"What about his eyes?"

"They're round, dark brown, with what I'd call an intense look."

Mark pulled a small memo pad from his breast pocket and wrote something on it. "Okay. You said you've seen him a number of times."

"Yes, and I only saw his face up close the one time, unfortunately. But then he was gone in a flash. I can tell you he's tall and thin, with broad shoulders. Sometimes he's riding by on a bike; sometimes he's walking. Last night he rode by my house and he looked in as he went by."

"Like he happened to look in as he rode by, or he made a point of looking in?" Mark glanced up from his memo pad.

"You know, it's hard to say, but he was on the other side of the street and maybe me being by the window caught his attention. I don't know."

Mark frowned. "Keep your curtains closed after dark."

First Clint, now Mark.

"I will. And you know the other night when that guy crashed in my alley and rode away?"

"Sure, Clint told me about it and I read the report. Why, you think it's the same guy?"

"I think it's very possible. Same long, lean body. But there again, it happened so fast, I barely caught a glimpse of him. Now that I've seen that guy a few times, I think it could be the same one."

"And keep your doors locked." *Yes, Clinton Junior.*

"I will." And I had, ever since Clint had lectured the heck out of me to do just that. And with the lanky guy hanging around I had to agree with him on that point. "Mark, have you seen a man around our age, maybe a little older, riding around town on a bike?"

"I see a lot of 'em. Not so many now that it's colder out, but still quite a few. What kind of bike does he have?"

I shrugged. "Not sure about that. I was always concentrating on the man himself."

"All right. Well, if you see him again, call me right away and I will respond ASAP, if I can. And I'll write up a 'be on the lookout' notice and post it for the other officers to see. Chances are he isn't on the prowl, but you can never be too careful. We don't need another Jerrell Powers on the loose. It would have been best if that guy had stayed away for good."

10

After Mark left I wandered around, watching the clock and checking the Curio Finds shelves for strange snow globes that were not part of our inventory. Thankfully, there were no new surprises sitting on the shelves among the regulars, or anywhere else in either of our shops, that I could spot. And the latest snow globe park scene had not reappeared to further confuse me.

I did a mental recap of the conversations I'd had over the past days. One thing was crystal clear: there certainly was no love lost between just about everyone I knew and Jerrell Powers. The only one who seemed to care for the man was Pamela Hemley, and it sounded like her love had waned to the point that she was ready to tell him the party was over. Thinking about her reminded me I needed to mention what I'd observed happening at her house. But how? Someone had been at her house without her knowledge and had not only let May Gregors in, but had also sent something in a paper bag along with her when she left.

I finally worked up enough courage to call Pam and had just picked up the phone when the bell on the door dinged and Archie Newberry walked in. I put the phone back in its holder and went into Brew Ha-Ha to help him. "Good to see you, Archie."

"Ah, Cami, you are here. I wasn't sure if you were off today. I didn't see you earlier when I stopped by"

"I was out for a while. So how have you been, Archie? I've hardly seen you all week."

"Fine, just fine. Busy tryin' to keep up with all the fall cleanup in the parks. You know, gettin' ready for winter, which'll be here before you know it. If a guy had more hours in the day, it'd help." He unzipped his canvas jacket.

"Archie, you already work long enough hours. And I have a feeling you don't even keep good track. You donate a lot of time to our fair city, don't you?"

Archie moved his head back and forth like he wasn't sure what to say. "Well, it's not like I need the money. I have everything I need."

"You could take a trip, maybe to see some other parks around the state, or anywhere in the nation."

"I don't much care for travel. My years in the service took care of that. Why go to other parks when we have more than enough around here?"

"We have some fine ones here, thanks to you."

Archie grinned. "Well, I can't think of anything I'd rather do."

I was going to tell him about the latest park scene snow

globe, but thought better of it. He was upset enough about what had happened to Jerrell Powers in his park and there was no reason to stir up more anxiety for him.

"Can I get you a cup of something?"

"No, no; thanks, though. I stopped by to talk to Pinky, but I can see she's not here."

"I can leave her a message for you."

"No, no, that's okay. It's sort of private."

What kind of a secret would Archie need to share with Pinky that he couldn't tell me about? If anyone in Brooks Landing, or at least in our group, could keep a secret, it was me. Pinky? If you swore her to secrecy, she'd probably remember, but it wasn't a guarantee. She was naturally gabby and sometimes forgot what bits of information were secrets she had sworn to keep.

Whatever it was my friends were talking about behind my back was wearing on me. What on earth could it possibly be if it wasn't concerning Jerrell Powers? The whole intrigue with them had started the day after his death. Every single one of them acted a little guilty. And now Archie seemed like he might be in on it, too.

"I'll tell her you were here, at least," I said.

"No need to bother. I'll stop by in the morning." Like he always did. Archie looked at his watch. "I guess it's about time for you to shove off, so I will, too."

"Can I give you a lift home?" Archie walked to the city shop each morning, drove one of its trucks to perform his park duties, then walked home again at the end of the day.

"No, the walking does me good. And I might stop by Erin's on the way." He would never come right out and say it, but out of all of us, Erin was his favorite. A few weeks back, he and another gentleman were sipping coffee at Pinky's counter. Erin had just left the shop, and I overheard Archie say, "There's a special place in my heart for that young'un." Archie had made it clear on more than one occasion that during his time in Vietnam, he'd had a lot of sympathy for the little ones who lived in the war-torn country.

"Archie, you're a good person to ask this question. Have you seen a tall man, late thirties or early forties, who bikes around town?"

Archie scratched at the whiskers on his cheek. "I guess I've seen a few guys like that. Don't think much about it when they speed by. There's the one who always wears those black pants the athletes wear, and goggles, too. With his helmet on, I can't tell you how old he'd be, but probably around forty. There's younger and older ones, too. Why is it that you ask?"

"I keep seeing this man and I can't place him."

"Well, if he's got you all curious, maybe you should wave him down and talk to the guy."

"Maybe I will." If someone else was with me, anyway. Hopefully Mark would spot him soon and find a way to talk to him.

"'Bye, Cami."

"Have a good night, Archie."

Archie was mumbling to himself before he reached the door, and I wasn't sure if he'd even heard me. He was one of the oddest ducks in the pond, but was very special to my friends and me. It was endearing how much he cared for us. The first time Erin, Pinky, and I met Archie was when we'd had a sleepover at Erin's house when we were eight, and had hiked to Lakeside Park the next day. It was a bright summer morning and Archie was there, tall and wiry, down on one knee, his long fingers working to fix a chain on a swing set.

We all giggled when we heard him talking, presumably to the swing. We stood and watched him work a minute until feisty little Erin interrupted his monologue. "Do you have an imaginary friend?" she asked. We knew what they were because Erin had had one when she was a very little girl.

Archie jumped up as though he'd heard someone yell "Fire!" and turned to us. "What are you young'uns up to on this fine day?" I remembered how his gray-blue eyes had fixed mostly on Erin, and how they'd twinkled.

"We came here to swing," Erin said.

"Well, then, it's a good thing I fixed this here chain so you won't fall and get hurt."

"Thank you, mister."

"You're welcome. I best be getting back to work. And you have a real good time, now."

"We will. Thanks, mister." Erin was doing all the talking for us that day.

"I'd be obliged if you'd call me Archie. I'm sure I'll be seeing you girls from time to time here, and then you'll know who I am. Are you allowed to tell me your names?"

At the time I wasn't sure why we shouldn't tell him. We'd all been cautioned about being wary of strangers, and Archie was as strange a person as I'd ever met, but not one of us was afraid of him.

Erin raised her hand and pointed as she talked. "That's Cami and Alice, and I'm Erin."

"It's a real pleasure meetin' all of you." He picked up his

tools and his long stride took him out of our sight in seconds.

"I don't think grown-ups have imaginary friends, Erin," Pinky said.

"How do you know?"

"Because when you got older, yours went away. And my mom told me you had grown out of it. So there."

I shook my head and smiled at the memory of meeting Archie, and Erin and Pinky having their little squabble. There had been many over the years, but that one stuck in my brain. Probably because my parents had often commented on my imagination, yet I didn't have an imaginary friend and was honestly a little jealous that Erin did.

After I'd closed up the shops, I walked to my car still debating what to tell Pamela Hemley, and whether I should call or have a face-to-face with her. By the time I pulled out of the parking lot, I'd decided to at least drive to her house and see what happened. When I pulled up in front, it appeared dark inside, like no one was home. I breathed a sigh of relief, telling myself maybe tonight was not the night to talk to her after all. I took out my cell phone and dialed her home number to double-check. There was no answer and I didn't leave a message. If she checked caller ID and wanted to call me back, that would be up to her.

I wasn't in much of a spying mood, but drove around the block and parked where I had a good view of Pam's house, in case she came home in the next ten minutes or so. As much as I dreaded having the conversation and was fine with putting it off as long as possible, she had to know the truth. I turned off the car and watched the western sky turn shades of pink and blue as the sun prepared to go down for the night. A gentle breeze rustled the colorful autumn leaves, shaking some loose from the trees and sending them floating to the ground. I would have been content to stay there for as long as I was warm, but something shook me out of my musings.

The lanky guy was riding toward me on his bike. The right side of his face was captured in the dimming sunlight. I picked up my cell phone out of instinct, I guess, and hit the camera button. But he'd ridden on by before I could snap his picture. Dang. I dialed Mark's number.

"Cami, what's up?"

"I saw the lone lanky bike rider again."

"Where are you?"

I'd forgotten I'd have to tell him that. "On East Ridge Drive."

"What are you doing in that part of town? Are you driving around looking for the guy or what?"

That was a better explanation than the real reason. "No, I happened to see him, that's all."

"I'm climbing into my personal vehicle and will head over to that part of town. Should be there in a few minutes."

"I'll cruise around, too, before I head home."

"Just to let you know, if the guy is riding around, minding his own business, I'm not about to stop him and harass him."

"Of course not. I just want to know who he is and why he seems to be just about everywhere I am."

"I don't think I'll be able to ask him that, either."

"I know. I'm mainly hoping you'll recognize him so you can put me out of my misery."

"I'll do my best."

I turned my car around in a driveway and drove where I hoped the rider had gone, but he had disappeared on me once again. Holy macaroni, he was fast. He had to have gone down a side street, but which direction? If I turned right, it was sure as shooting he had turned left. I took my fifty-fifty chance, turned left at the next block, and resisted a strong temptation to go faster than the speed limit. After a few blocks of no action, except a number of motion detection lights going on as I passed, I did a U-turn and headed the opposite way.

I met Mark at the next intersection. I waited as he pulled up beside me then we unrolled our windows to talk. "I lost him," I said.

"No luck on my end, either. Cami, you might as well give it up. One of these days he'll come in for a cup of coffee or a snow globe and you can talk to him face-to-face."

"Thanks for trying, Mark. We're bound to run into each other sooner or later. Get back to your evening and I'll catch you tomorrow."

"All right. And remember about your curtains and doors."

I gave him a military-like salute. "Aye, aye, Officer Mark."

He shook his head and closed his window. We drove off in different directions, and then I went back to Pam's for one final try for the night. The house was still dark so I went home in search of a light supper and a lighter show to watch on television.

I was dipping a grilled cheese sandwich into a bowl of tomato soup when the phone rang. It startled me and I missed my mouth and dripped soup on my chest. Not that

I was jumpy or anything. I grabbed a dish towel and wiped my face and patted my chest to sop up the liquid. I reached for the phone and saw it was Erin calling.

"Hey, Erin, you still have a visitor?"

It took her a few seconds to answer. "Oh, you mean Archie? No, he was only here a little while. You know how he likes to check in to be sure all is well. Ever since Jerrell Powers broke in a few years ago, he sort of feels it's his job to stop by on his way home."

"That's not all bad."

"I actually kind of like it. It gives him something to think about besides trees and playground equipment."

"He could use another hobby."

Erin chuckled. "Pinky told me you two may host another class once things settle down. You could ask Archie if there's anything he'd like to learn to make and invite him to participate."

"He seemed intrigued with the snow globe–making class. Now I feel kind of bad I told him and Mark to stay out of the way of the members who had paid for the class."

"Don't worry about it." Erin was quiet a moment. "The other thing Pinky told me is that you actually agreed to go to that Halloween party with a bunch of strangers and hosted by people you've barely met."

"I could ask Mark to be my escort if it'd make you feel any better."

"What would make me feel better is if you call them and tell them you can't make it."

"I don't want to disappoint them. Besides, what would I tell them?"

"It's not like you owe them anything, seeing as how you don't even know them. You could say you have other plans."

"When was the last time I actually had plans on a Friday night?"

"Try last Friday."

"Oh, yeah. That was a fluke, and we planned the class that night because we seldom go out. And I'm not going to lie to those women who are all excited I'm coming to their party."

"Tell them you forgot that was the same weekend you had Gophers tickets or something like that."

"Erin—"

"Or you are going out with your friend, and I will be that friend."

"I really don't get why you guys are being so silly about this."

"There you go, three against one."

"With all due respect, my friend, this is not coming up for a vote."

"Well, think about it some more and I'm sure you'll agree it would be a dumb idea to go."

*Dumb idea?* That got my temperature up. My friends were treating me like I was an adolescent on my way into the proverbial lion's den. I didn't want to say anything I'd later regret so I left it at a mild promise and quick good-bye. "I will think about it, Erin. Gotta go, I'll talk to you later."

I hung up and thought about the irony of the whole thing. I really had no interest in being the main entertainment at the party, sharing the gory details about Jerrell Powers, until my friends went over the top about it. I took a bite of cold soup then put it in the microwave to warm while I considered the best way to learn once and for all if Pinky, Erin, or Mark had any connection to Powers's death. Deep down inside of me, I didn't believe they did, but their behavior and the way they were treating me kept sending up red flags.

I finished eating and went to my bedroom to change out of my tomato-stained blouse. It was silly to put on another top at that time of night so I got my flannel nightgown, robe, and bunny slippers out of the closet. I changed out of my day clothes into my nightclothes then sighed. It wasn't even 7:30 p.m. and I was ready for bed. Way too young to be acting like an old fogy. Going to the Halloween party was probably the best thing for me to do so I didn't shrivel up before my time. It wasn't like my social calendar was full; I didn't even have one. How pitiful was that? All work and no play, as they say.

I moved hangers, searching in the back of the closet for the special costume I'd seldom worn. It was a replica of an ivory cocktail dress Marilyn Monroe wore in the movie *The Seven Year Itch*. I loved the style. I'd found it at an online costume site and ordered it, along with matching 1950s-style high-heel shoes that had open toes and straps that went around my ankles. Those extra few inches made my legs look longer and more shapely. The key was maintaining a graceful gait in them, which was a bit of a challenge.

The dress had a halter-style bodice with a pleated fabric that came together at the back of the neck and closed with little buttons. The neckline was a little on the revealing side so I'd had it altered, especially since the dress left my arms, shoulders, and back bare. It showed enough skin. The halter was attached to a band that fit snugly from beneath the bust down to the waist. A belt tied on the left front side. The skirt was pleated and hung just below my calves.

I lifted the dress to my face and sniffed it. I'd had it dry-cleaned, but it had been a couple of years since I'd worn it, and I wanted to be sure it was fresh. It had picked up a mild cedar scent from the closet, which was fine, and saved me a trip to the cleaners. I rehung the dress and dug through the stack of boxes where the shoes I wore for special occasions were stored. I found the ivory ones and pulled them from their box.

I almost never wore heels over an inch or two high anymore and decided it was best to practice so I didn't make a fool of myself clunking around on them the night of the party. Off with the bunny slippers, on with the sexy heels. A few seconds after I'd buckled the straps and had gotten to my feet, the doorbell rang. I made it as fast as I could to the door, thinking it might be Mark who had found the bicycler after all.

The door was made of solid oak with no side window to peek out. "Who is it?"

"Clint Lonsbury."

*You have got to be kidding me. It's too late to pretend you aren't home so open the door and act cool.* I opened it partway, half-hidden behind it. Clint was wearing jeans and a brown corduroy jacket. The light spilling from the living room cast a warm glow on his face and made his dark eyes sparkle.

"How can I help you?"

"I'd be obliged if you'd let me in, for starters." He looked at my bathrobe. "Unless you're entertaining someone."

I was once again rescued from thinking he was attractive by his assumptions and comments. I pushed the door wide open and Clint walked in. His eyes traveled down my body to my feet. "Quite the getup you've got on. The shoes are a nice touch. And explain the extra inches you've gained in height. Are you getting ready to go out somewhere?"

Where was that hole I could crawl into? "No, just playing dress-up."

He started to smile, but changed it to a frown instead.

"Not on your way to bed?"

"Not this early. I wanted to get out of my work clothes and put my pajamas on, that's all."

He gave a nod. "The reason I'm here is I need to talk to you about that character you've been seeing around town. Mark told me about it and was concerned because you're concerned."

*Thanks for siccing Clint on me, Mark.* "Want to go sit in the kitchen?"

He lifted his arm. "After you."

I'd forgotten I'd just finished supper until I saw the remains of my food on the table and cooking supplies on the stove and counter. I cleared off the table as fast as possible so Clint would have a clean spot.

"You must be feeling better."

*Where is he going with that?* "What do you mean?"

"Your kitchen is not as pristine as the last couple of times I've been here. You know, your cleaning therapy sessions."

"Right." I did a wide sweep with my arm and brushed some crumbs on the floor in a gesture of mild rebellion.

Clint raised his eyebrows and sat down. I joined him on

the other side of the table. He said, "Tell me what's going on between you and that bike rider."

"There is nothing going on. I'm curious about who he is; it's that simple. I've been back in Brooks Landing for a few months now and have never noticed him until this past week. Which I guess doesn't mean much. He could have just moved to town himself."

"Or lost his license so now he has to hoof it or bike to the places he needs to be."

A police officer would think of that scenario. "The part that makes me wonder is I get the impression that either he knows me or he's got me under some kind of watch." Another possibility popped into my brain. "He doesn't work for your police department, does he?"

"My police department? Why would you ask that?"

"Because I find a body in the park, I accidentally leave my fingerprints on the weapon, and suddenly I move to the status of a possible suspect."

Clint cleared his throat. "If by some wild chance it turns out the man in question is a Brooks Landing police officer, I can assure you he is not on any kind of an assignment to keep an eye on you."

"Oh. Well, I guess that makes me feel better on that front, anyway."

"Tell me why you think he knows you or is watching you."

"Two reasons. The first is more of an impression, but a strong one. When we made eye contact the two times, he looked at me like he knew me but at the same time didn't want me to know who he was. The second reason is he seems to be wherever I am. At least, on a bunch of occasions over the last week."

Clint laid his arm on the table and stared at me until I could no longer maintain eye contact. "It might be as simple as he is taken with your beauty and doesn't know how to approach you."

His words and scrutiny sent my entire body into an immediate burn from the inside out. How I was able to restrain myself from sticking my head in a pail of ice-cold water is a good question. Clint saying I was beautiful was the last thing I expected to hear sitting there in my bathrobe and Marilyn Monroe shoes.

He leaned in closer to me, resting his chest against his arm. "I didn't mean to embarrass you. I'm sure you've heard that a hundred times."

"Um, well, not in so many words. Mom likes to quote that old saying, Beauty is in the eye of the beholder." I tried secretly to kick off my shoes, but the ankle straps held them on tight.

Clint nodded and continued to stare at me, which fueled the burn. After what seemed like five or six hours, he reached into the back pocket of his jeans and pulled out a little memo pad and pen. He shifted, prepared to write. "Give me the best description of the man that you can. Mark had a general one."

My body finally started cooling off. It was a relief to focus on something besides myself and I didn't mind giving him every detail I could think of about the lanky guy. After some minutes of hearing me out, Clint closed his memo pad, stuck his pen in his pocket, and stood up. "Why don't you stop down at the PD and I'll show you our collection of mug shots. If this man you keep seeing is in there, we'll know who we're looking for. And it'll give us an indication whether we need to be concerned about his activities or not."

I rose to my full, new height. "I can do that. How about tomorrow morning, before I open my shop?"

"That'll work for me. I'll be in the office most of the day."

I nodded. "Good. I'll be there around nine o'clock or so."

11

On the drive to the Brooks Landing Police Station I again marveled over Clint's compliment the night before, and how we had made it through twenty whole minutes without arguing. He hadn't even left a parting wisecrack about what he'd called my "getup" when my ankle turned and I'd grabbed the table for support.

The police station was housed in the city administration building, a sturdy, one-story brick structure that had been constructed about twenty years before. They shared a common front entry then split into separate units. The city offices were on the north side, the police on the south. I went through the door and found an older woman sitting at the front desk. She wore her longish gray hair in a ponytail on top and had a name badge with *Margaret* written on it. Her eyebrows shot up when I approached her, as if I had surprised her. "Our assistant chief is expecting you, Miss Brooks." She half turned and flung her left arm behind her toward a row of offices that were partially visible above the partition that enclosed her area and went halfway to the ceiling. "Go right on back there."

"Thank you." *And good morning to you.*

I walked to the right and then down a short hallway that ended with a row of three offices. I found Clint's in the middle, almost directly behind where Margaret was stationed. I passed the vacant police chief's dark office. Word had it he was burning up some of his weeks of accumulated vacation time, and he and his wife were off on an extended trip abroad. Not even a murder in his town had coaxed him back from wherever he was.

Clint's door was open and I heard him talking on the phone. I stepped into the doorway, planning to wait there until he'd finished, but he waved me in and ended his conversation. "Will do. Thanks."

I slipped in and took a second to admire his office. There was a framed bachelor of arts degree and certificates from a variety of police courses on the wall behind his desk. Clint stood up and drew his eyebrows together, looking like he was ready to dig into some serious work.

"Morning, Cam . . . *ryn*, and thanks for coming in. Here's the book I was telling you about." He turned and picked up a binder that was about two inches thick from the bottom shelf of an open bookcase that rested against the wall behind his desk. "Have a seat." He set it on his desk and pushed it toward me as we both sat down. "The males are in the first section and are arranged in order of age, from youngest to oldest."

I pulled the book closer and opened to the first page with a mug shot of a man who looked like he was about sixteen, and then flipped through the subsequent pages. Under each photo there was a description that gave the person's name, date of birth, height, weight, eye and hair color, and distinguishing features such as scars, marks, or tattoos. Other notes had also been added. One read, *He walks with a limp due to a leg length discrepancy.* Another was, *He has a stuttering condition.*

I went through the first pages of the very young men quickly then slowed down when I got to the men who were in their thirties and forties. There was only one whose description was similar to the lanky guy, and it clearly was not him. I scanned the last of the men's section, and flipped back in case I'd missed something, and then closed the book. "He's not in here that I can see."

Clint reached over, picked up the mug shot book, and put it back on the case behind him. "It was worth a try anyway."

"The next time I spot him, I'll try to get a picture."

"I wouldn't do that if I were you. You're not a police officer or private investigator working on a case. At this point, we have no evidence he's done anything wrong, unless it turns out he was the one who stole that kid's bike."

"There's something about him. You might recognize him if you see his picture."

"Cami, people nowadays don't take kindly to having their pictures snapped without permission, and you have no idea how he may react, what he might do."

"I wasn't planning to do it if he was up close and personal, or anything."

"I'd put that idea to rest and call the PD if you see him again. Call me, call Mark, so we can get this settled and you can rest easy."

I nodded.

"I also wanted you to take a look at a photo of the knife the ME removed from our victim, Jerrell Powers."

I squirmed a little in the chair and hoped Clint didn't notice. "Um, well, I guess I can do that." The only reason he'd ask me such a thing had to be that he wanted to see how I reacted, how guilty I looked. Right?

Clint picked up a thick file from the side of his desk and opened it. I glanced down at the photos of the crime scene, but moved my eyes away before I saw much. Clint found what he was looking for and handed the shot of the knife over to me. My fingers trembled a little and I willed them to be steady as I accepted the eight-by-ten-inch color photo.

A shiver ran through me when I recognized the knife as one from Pinky's set. Or one that looked very much like it. It had a brown handle and a serrated cutting edge that came to a sharp point. I read the brand name on the blade and knew it was a popular one. There had to be countless people in Brooks Landing besides Pinky with the same set of knives.

Clint leaned in and I leaned back. I was pretty sure his intense stare was going to make the little makeup I wore melt right off my face.

"You've seen it before," Clint said.

Between his look and his words, it was not humanly possible to stop my face from flushing. "Um, if this is the murder weapon, yes, I saw it on that night, um, in Mr. Powers. But I would never have been able to identify it."

"So where else have you seen it? Your kitchen drawer, maybe?"

The man was infuriating. "No. As a matter of fact, I don't own any knives of that brand."

"Then where?"

"Well, I know Pinky has some like that at her shop, but I'm sure a lot of other people do, too. The company must be the biggest knife seller in the country."

"Where does she keep her knives at the shop?"

"Behind the counter. Pinky uses them to cut those giant muffins of hers for people. Or when she bakes bagels; she cuts them to spread on cream cheese or whatever."

"And just about anyone at the counter would have access?"

"Maybe. I guess."

"Hmm. Something to think about. But the first step is finding out if Pinky is missing a particular knife from her set."

I bit my tongue. I couldn't tell Clint that my three friends had been acting strangely all week and that I had a teeny tiny inkling of doubt over whether they had any involvement in Jerrell Powers's death. And I kicked myself every time I did. The truth had to bubble to the surface someday, and that day could not come soon enough.

I looked around for a clock. "Gosh, I wonder what time it is. I sort of lost track."

Clint turned his arm and looked down at his watch. "Nine forty-four."

I stood. "If there's nothing else, I should get to the shop."

"No, you go ahead. I'll be there in a few minutes myself. I'll talk to Pinky, have her check her knife supply."

"Okay." My voice was weak, but my knees were weaker.

Clint shuffled some papers from the Jerrell Powers file and was putting the knife photo in another folder as I slipped out the door. When I walked past Margaret's desk, I waved good-bye and she gave me a single curt nod in reply.

"Thank God it's Friday," she muttered under her breath as I pushed open the front door. Apparently there was something about me or my visit she didn't approve of. But that was the least of my worries. My biggest concern at the moment was ensuring that Pinky's knife set was intact.

I let myself in through the Curio Finds door instead of popping in through Brew Ha-Ha like I did most days. One look at my face and Pinky would know something was up. I hadn't had enough time to compose myself and I was in a near panic about what Clint's visit would turn up.

"I'm here," I called and lifted my hand in a wave that conveniently covered my face as I passed by the archway that connected our shops. Pinky was waiting on a few people at the counter and said, "Hey," as I sped through to the back storeroom. I hung my coat and purse on a hook and wondered how long it would be before Clint made his official appearance. I went back into the shop and busied myself with turning on the overhead lights and flipped the sign to Open.

Seconds after I'd finished, Pinky's door's bell dinged and I heard Clint greeting her. I braved my way over to the archway and watched as he took a seat at the counter next to a man who was paying Pinky for his order. When the man left, Pinky set a cup of coffee in front of Clint. Great, well, at least his slurping might take my mind off things when he questioned Pinky. Clint set the folder on the counter and pushed it away from the mug of hot brew.

"Cami, quit lurking in the archway. Come join Clint and me for a cup of something before the customers start piling in."

I was about to deny that I was lurking, but in fact, I was. "Sure." I looked up at the blackboard, where she had the menu listed, to see the featured daily special. I read out loud. "The loco cocoa: a hefty shot of espresso tamed with hot cocoa." I shook my head. "Pinky, where do you come up with those names?"

She shrugged. "Espresso makes me a little loco. How about you, Clint?"

Clint raised his hands, indicating he wasn't going to commit to an answer, then picked up his mug and took a healthy slurp. "Mmm. I'll give you two thumbs up for the loco cocoa and let you know how I feel in about ten minutes." He set his mug aside.

I sat down on a stool, leaving one place between Clint and me. "I'll try one, too, but I can make it."

Pinky waved her hand. "Nah, I'm here."

Clint waited until Pinky had made a drink for me and one for herself then opened the folder, withdrew the knife photo, and handed it to Pinky. "Does it look familiar to you?"

Pinky took a quick look. "Sure. Well, maybe not this one exactly, but I have knives like this." Her hand opened and she lost her grip on the photo. It dropped and landed on top of the file folder. She stared at it like she was in a trance. "Don't tell me this is the *one*, the one that was used . . ."

"It's the one."

"Holy moly, I've never seen a police photo of anything from a crime before. Holy moly."

"So your knife set is intact?"

Pinky looked like she had been caught with her hand in someone's cookie jar. "I actually seem to be missing the one that looks like that." She snuck another peek at the photo. "I didn't think much about it when I couldn't find it the other day. I wondered if maybe I accidentally threw it away. I have silverware disappear all the time around here." Most of us knew Pinky was absentminded and tended to lose things. "Or that I'd misplaced it, and it'd turn up in some odd spot."

"That might have been what happened, that it turned up in a very odd spot," Clint said.

Pinky's face paled. "I'll look again until I find my knife. It's gotta be around here somewhere." She pulled out the portable silverware sorter she had stored under the counter. There were butter knives, forks, spoons, and a number of cutting knives from the set that the knife was missing from. She looked at me. "Cami?"

I shook my head. "I honestly don't know when I've used that knife, Pinky."

She stepped back until she was resting against the wall counter for support.

"How often do you leave a cutting knife on the serving counter where others would have access to it?"

"Pretty often, I guess." She paused and grew even paler. "So a knife like mine was used in *the murder*?" Pinky was genuinely distressed, which I would be, too, if I were her. And it backed up my belief that she could not have been the one to do Jerrell Powers in. Had she been covering for someone else, and didn't realize her knife had been used, after all? "It's gotta be the most popular brand out there. A friend sold Erin and me a set eons ago."

Clint's eyebrows drew together. "You don't say. Erin owns the same set?"

Pinky's hand-in-the-cookie-jar look returned. "Yeah."

His head went up and down in an exaggerated nod then he looked at his watch. "School gets out at what time?" He asked the question like he knew the answer. When neither Pinky nor I responded, he said, "Two forty-five. All right." Even though his drink had had plenty of time to cool, he took a big loud slurping gulp of it. Pinky was likely accustomed to people with noisy drinking habits and didn't seem to notice.

"Good drink combo, Pinky." Clint reached in his back pocket, pulled out his wallet, found some bills, threw them on the counter, then held up his mug. "Can I get this in a cup to go?"

Pinky took the cup from him, poured the coffee in a disposable one, popped on a lid, and handed it back. "Put that money away. I can buy my friends a cuppa once in a while."

Clint stood, picked up the cup, and ignored Pinky's offer. "Thanks." He nodded and left.

"Cami, this is serious. My knife is missing and one just like it ended up in Jerrell Powers. Do you think someone really did steal it?"

"I have no idea, Pinky. How long do you think it's been missing?"

She shrugged. "I wish I knew. You know how scatterbrained I am at times. It could be a week, more or less."

Pinky's group of businessman regulars came in, followed by an older couple. I helped her until I saw a woman in my shop and went to attend to her.

The day dragged on as I kept thinking about the fact that Erin and Pinky each owned a knife like the one used to kill Jerrell Powers. And Pinky's was missing. Clint hadn't warned us not to contact Erin, but I presumed he wouldn't take kindly to me sending her a warning text. I wondered what Erin would have to say.

The lanky guy peeked in my shop window from behind his Buddy Holly glasses and put all thoughts of the murder weapon on hold for the time being. When our eyes met, he turned and headed north. I set the snow globe of an ancient castle sitting on the Rhine River bank I was dusting back on the shelf and hurried to the door. When I pushed it open a cold, damp breeze sent a chill through me, but didn't stop me from taking off at a jog after him. But he had once again disappeared. I figured he must have gone down the narrow walkway between our building and the next, so I took that route.

When I reached the parking lot, I saw the backside of him as he rode away on the bicycle. "Hey, I want to talk to you," I called out. He didn't hear me, or else he pretended he didn't, because he kept going. I was a little out of breath from nerves and the jog, short as it was. I reached into my pocket for my cell phone to call Mark then remembered I'd left it on the shop counter. Doggone it, anyway. The nippy air and the need to call the police propelled me to hurry back to the shop as fast as possible.

Pinky was standing in the archway when I got back in. "I didn't know where you'd gone to. Your phone was ringing, but by the time I realized you must not be able to answer it, they'd hung up. What's up? Your face is all flushed."

"That strange man looked in my window just now, and I tried to catch up to him, but he was faster. Which, of course, doesn't take much since most people are." I found my phone and dialed Mark's number. It went to voicemail, so I tried Clint's.

"Assistant Chief Lonsbury."

"It's Camryn. He was just here, looking in my window, but got away before I could talk to him."

"Are you talking about your alleged admirer?"

"Yes. Do you think you can track him down?"

"I'm in the office, but I'll have the two officers on patrol look for him. Was he on foot?"

"No, he was on his bicycle."

"Are you able to give a description of the bike now?"

"Not exactly. But I know for sure now that it was black."

"That works. Which way did he go?"

"Across the back parking lot toward First Avenue."

"Okay, hold on while I get on the radio and give the info to my officers." I heard Clint give his badge number and call for two other officers by their badge numbers. I recognized one as Mark's: 513. Clint relayed what I'd told him then I heard Mark and another male both say, "Ten-four."

"Are you there, Camryn?" Clint said.

"I am."

"You got a good look at the man in question?"

"I did, and he is definitely the same guy. No doubt in my

mind. If I could just figure out why he looks vaguely familiar."

"My point is, when he looked at you, did you feel threatened in any way?"

I thought about that a few seconds. "No. I got the impression he wanted to tell me something but lost his nerve when we made eye contact. It's just odd."

"Until we figure out what in the heck he is up to, watch your back. Now that you've had another encounter and another good look at the man, I'm going to talk to the county, see if we can schedule an appointment for you to work with their sketch artist. It'd help our officers to see what he looks like, or close to it. Might prevent them from stopping the wrong tall man riding a bike."

"All right. Thank you, Clint."

I went back to dusting the shelves of snow globes, burning with curiosity over the identity of the disappearing bicycler. My mind went back to our high school days. I'd looked through the yearbooks, but there were a few kids from each class who didn't have their photo included for one reason or another. Was there a boy who had maybe transferred at midyear, too late to make it into the book? That was a possibility. The problem was, I could not think of anyone, girl or boy, who had done that.

I wandered over to the archway holding a snow globe filled with ice-skating children. Pinky was washing some mugs. "Hey, Pink, do you remember any new boys coming to our school senior year?"

Pinky gave her head a shake and scrunched up her face. "What in the world brought that up?"

"I'm trying to place that guy who has been popping in and out of my life the past week. I don't think he's one of our classmates, unless he's changed a lot since high school."

"We didn't have any new kids come during the school year. Mary Ellen Davies moved here the summer before, but she was the only one. You are digging deep. Holler next time you see him. I'll run out and see if I can trip him."

I shook my head at her proposal then looked at the snow globe and gave it a shake. "I'm just plain old frustrated, that's all." I went back to my duties and returned the globe to its spot. For some reason I felt the need to look at each snow globe in the shop for assurance that no new ones had appeared. I had gotten paranoid, for sure.

Each globe was unique and held a story or dream or promise, it seemed. And if you were a purist about what constituted a good snowy scene, some of the scenes fit and some didn't. There were a number from places around the world, like the Eiffel Tower standing tall with green grass at its base, or the desert town of Bethlehem in Israel, where snow was very rare, or New Dehli, India, where I was pretty sure it never snowed. But I wasn't the official snow globe police who picked which cities were captured under snowy domes and which ones weren't.

And there were the other ones, like a single ballerina who spun to music on her tippy toes when the crank on her globe was wound and released, the one with a trio of youthful cherubs with their mouths open in apparent song, and the one with a carousel of horses. Whether the figurines technically fit in a snow globe or not, it didn't seem to matter. I liked each one of them, and so did my customers. I found the globe I went back to the most often: the lighthouse on the brown ceramic base. I turned on its light, picked it up, gave it a shake, then set it down and watched it for a while, appreciating what it represented.

"Are you dreaming about a trip to the North Shore, or what?" Pinky's voice startled me.

"Maybe next summer. No, this is one of my favorites. A port in the storm, a light at the end of the tunnel."

Pinky came up beside me and practically stuck her nose in my face. "You're not getting all deep on me, are you? Like, I don't think you're talking about lighthouses here, but what they might symbolize."

"Maybe."

Pinky put her arm around my shoulder. "Why don't you go home early today? I'll stay."

I reached up and gave her dangling hand a squeeze. "No, the deal is, you come in early, I stay late."

"All right, then, I'll take off. It's four o'clock, and no sign of Erin yet today. I was afraid to call her what with Clint about to question her and everything."

"Yeah, she almost always stops by on Fridays; she must have had something else to do. I've been waiting for her to call and tell us how it went when Clint talked to her. Which tells me it hasn't happened yet."

"Yeah, I'll drive by her place and let you know if there's a police car there."

"Okay."

"And I'll be on the lookout for a tall guy riding around on a bike."

"Be sure to call Mark or Clint or the PD first if you do. Then call me."

"Yes, ma'am. Toodle-oo." She turned and headed back to her shop. A minute later she called out a final good-bye. I finished dusting the last shelf and paused by a snow globe of two women sitting at a table with cups of coffee in front of them. For some reason, it reminded me that I needed to talk to Pamela Hemley about someone letting May Gregors into her house at a time Pam said she hadn't been there. Maybe I'd invite her over for a cup of coffee.

I went to the counter and used the shop phone to make the call. It was after 5:30, and Pam answered right away. "Hello?" She sounded hesitant.

"Hi, it's Camryn."

"Hi."

"Pam, I was wondering if you'd have time to stop by my shop. We could have a cup of something at Brew Ha-Ha."

"Why? Are you doing this because it's the one-week anniversary of, you know . . ."

"Well, no, that's not it, but we can sure talk about it if you want."

"When do you want me to come over?"

"As soon as you can make it, if that works. I usually close at six, but I'll wait for you."

She didn't say anything for a while. "Okay. I'll be there in a few minutes."

"Good. See you then."

I hung up and prayed I wouldn't totally mess up what I had to say. I straightened some items on my counter then headed into the coffee shop. As I grabbed two mugs, the bell on Pinky's door dinged and Pam came in. Her eyes were red and puffy. "Sorry, I sort of had a crying jag," she said.

"Understandable, given everything you've been through. Come and sit down and tell me what you want to drink."

She glanced up at the menu on the wall. "Maybe a hot chocolate. No offense, but nothing looks that good to me right now."

"That's all right. A hot chocolate coming right up. With or without marshmallows?"

"Without, thanks."

I served up two of the same and carried them to a table in the back. "Let's sit here."

I set the mugs down and Pam took one of the pink padded chairs and I sat across from her on a black one.

We each took a sip before I said, "Something has been bothering me and I need to tell you about it."

She raised her bloodshot eyes. "What?"

"I stopped by your house on Wednesday morning and I saw someone who really surprised me go in."

"Who?" Her eyebrows drew together.

"May Gregors."

*"May Gregors went into my house?"* I thought she was going to drop her mug, so I reached over and guided it to the table. "On Wednesday morning?"

"Yes, I tried to tell you before this, but I honestly didn't know the best way to do it."

Pam stared at me. "You're saying May Gregors went into my house. How? The doors were locked." Her surprise was genuine and confirmed she'd told me the truth about being at work.

"Someone let her in."

"Who?"

"I couldn't see who it was. I thought it was you, but then when you said you weren't home, I figured it was your sister, Lauren. But you said she had gone back to her home in St. Cloud, so I don't know."

"Lauren," Pam whispered. "Only four people have a key to my house. My two kids and Lauren and me. Lauren." She shook her head. "Why would she let Jerrell's ex-wife into my house?"

"If it was her, you'll have to ask. And there's something else. May left carrying a brown paper bag she didn't have when she went in. I thought maybe you had found her missing snow globe–making supplies."

Pam shook her head. "She took something from my house?"

"I don't know what it was. I'd be happy to be there with you when you talk to May, or even to your sister. You know, to verify what I saw."

Pam pulled out her cell phone. "I'm calling Lauren to ask her about it." She hit numbers and a few seconds later said, "Hi. . . . Really? I'm at Brew Ha-Ha. Meet me here instead. . . . Okay, 'bye." She pushed the end button. "Lauren's in Brooks Landing. She wanted to surprise me, take me out for a nice dinner."

Lauren arrived in no time, and when she walked through the door it struck me that it had only been a week since I'd met the two of them when they had attended May's fateful class. Lauren's eyebrows rose when she saw I was the one sharing a drink with her sister. She slid onto a chair between us and she and Pam locked eyes.

"Can I get you something to drink, Lauren?" I asked, mostly to break the tension.

She threw a glance my way. "No, thanks. What's going on here anyway?"

Pam seemed unable to speak as she and Lauren studied each other's expressions, so I butted in. "We're trying to solve a little mystery here."

Lauren turned to me. "Oh? What kind of mystery?"

"A Wednesday-morning-at-Pam's-house kind of mystery."

"Wednesday morning?" Lauren looked down and then sideways at Pam. "Did you talk to May, or what?"

Pam shook her head. "So it was you who let her into *my house*?"

"I was going to tell you when you were more up to it."

"Tell me what?"

"That box of pictures and letters Jerrell had from his daughter. The one he had hidden that you found when he was in the halfway house. You showed it to me last year and said you should find out where his daughter was. And now that Jerrell's dead, there was no reason not to get them back to her. Or her mother."

"So you went behind my back and had May pick those things up?"

Lauren reached over and put her hand on Pam's, but Pam pulled hers away and dropped both hands onto her lap. "I guess I was wrong, when you put it that way. I was trying to protect you from having to deal with that along with everything else. So I called May and she was happy to get her daughter's letters and pictures."

I supposed May wouldn't have felt comfortable confessing all that to me.

Tears formed in Pam's eyes and dropped onto her

cheekbones. "You don't have to protect me from everything, Lauren. I was planning to meet with Jerrell's daughter sometime. Tell her that he had problems, but that he really was a caring man, deep down."

Lauren didn't seem to want to argue with Pam about that because she said, "Old habits die hard and I am really sorry I interfered. I stuck my nose in your business again. I know you loved Jerrell, and you can still meet with his daughter sometime."

Pam's shoulders shrugged up and down then she nodded. "I wasn't going to tell you this, but I guess I could use some more of your help after all."

Lauren leaned in toward her. "What is it?"

"Jerrell's going to be buried tomorrow. I thought I'd be the only one there, but maybe his daughter should at least know about it, in case she'd want to be there to say a final good-bye."

Lauren lowered her chin and concentrated on Pam. "So you want me to tell May so she can tell her daughter."

"Yes."

"Where and when is it?"

"Hillside Cemetery, at two o'clock tomorrow afternoon."

Lauren's lips formed an "ooh." "It's late notice, but I'll call May right away and then the ball will be in her court." Lauren reached for Pam's hand and got a good grip on it that time. "And I'll be there with you."

"So will I. If it's okay with you, Pam?" Did I really say that? Pinky and Erin would kill me if they knew. Not to mention what Mark and Clint would have to say about it.

More tears spilled out of Pam's eyes and rolled down her cheeks. She pulled a paper napkin from the holder in the center of the table and blew her nose. "Lauren, I don't think I'm up to going anywhere tonight. I'm not hungry and I feel a mess."

Lauren stood and waited for Pam. "Not a problem. How about I come over to your house and we just hang out?"

Pam pushed herself up and nodded. She looked at me and her lips quivered. "Thank you."

I gave her my best smile. "See you tomorrow."

Before any of us had taken a step, the shop door's bell dinged and in walked Erin, who stopped short when she saw the three of us standing there. "What's going on?"

Erin and Pam exchanged dirty looks until Lauren grabbed her sister's hand and pulled her toward the door. "We were just leaving."

"What were they doing here, really?" Erin asked after the door closed behind them.

"It's a long story, but first Pam stopped by, then her sister joined her."

"Pam was crying."

"I think she's done that a lot this past week."

"I know you're about to close up, but I had a message from Clint, and when I called him back just now he asked if—since I was here—he could stop by to ask me about something."

That answered one of my burning questions: Clint had not yet spoken to Erin.

I nodded. "Did you go somewhere after school today, Erin?"

"Yeah, I kind of forgot about it, or I would have told you guys. We had a baby shower for one of the teachers. She won't be going on leave until sometime around Christmas, but we thought we'd do it now before things get crazy with the holidays."

Clint came in with his photo file. "Hi, Erin. Camryn." He glanced around the empty coffee shop. "Not overly wild in here."

"This is as busy as I like it at closing time. People feel pressured to leave when I turn the Open sign to the Closed side, and I don't like making them uncomfortable."

"I suppose."

"As long as we don't have another Friday night like the last one," Erin said.

We all agreed on that.

"Erin, I'll get straight to the point of why we're here. I understand you have a set of Sharpcut knives."

Erin gave her head a little shake and her shoulders a shrug. "As a matter of fact, I do. But what does—" She stopped when the "why" part of the question dawned on her. My own heart beat a little harder wondering how Erin was feeling and how she would react to Clint's questions.

Clint laid his folder on the counter and opened it, revealing the knife photo inside. He picked it up and handed it to Erin, who looked at it but didn't take it from him. She nodded. "It looks like mine, except mine had a little burn mark from my gas stove."

"You said 'had.' "

"I haven't seen it for a while. It just disappeared. I didn't have much use for that size knife with the little cooking I do for myself. I use the paring knife, mostly. Pinky was looking for it one time she was there and wanted to cut a muffin but she couldn't find it."

Clint studied her. "Any idea how long it's been missing?"

"I really don't. As far as I knew, it was in my drawer with the rest of the knives."

"Days, weeks, months?"

Erin shrugged. "It could be years. I have no clue. My mother left most of hers when she moved so I have tons I never use."

Clint reached over and picked a photo from the bottom of the pile. "That burn mark. Did it resemble this? It's the reverse side of the same knife." He held it up so we could both look at it. Erin teetered a bit and I put my arm around her waist to steady her.

"It looks just like my knife. But how? How . . ."

I guided Erin onto a counter stool and Clint picked up the folder, replaced the pictures, and closed it. He pulled out a small memo pad and pen and set them on the counter in front of Erin. "When was it that Pinky was looking for that knife?"

Erin shook her head. "Maybe three or four weeks ago."

"Then why don't you write down the names of everyone who's been in your house in the last month or so. We'll start from there."

Erin narrowed her eyes at Clint. "Really? Okay, well, give me a minute."

The thought that Erin's knife had disappeared at some point and ended up being used in a murder distressed me, to say the least. She couldn't have known it was her knife before she saw the picture of the little burn mark, could she?

"I'll go lock up my shop," I said.

"We're keeping you," Clint said.

I waved my hand. "Not at all. It takes a while to ring out the cash register and take care of all the little last-minute details." I left them to deal with their official business while

I went about my own, still thinking about how it could be that my friend was indirectly involved in Jerrell Powers's death. What a thing for her to deal with. The man who had broken into her house had ended up stabbed with her very own knife. A very strange coincidence, but things like that popped up in News of the Weird every day.

I dawdled, pretending to be doing any number of actual closing-up-shop activities, especially when Clint wandered away from Erin's side to peer into my shop. That was when I disappeared into the back room for a very long six minutes. I finished with everything I could think of to do then returned to the coffee shop. Erin was still hard at it, poking the pen into the paper as she thought, and then adding another name to the list. She looked like a student taking a complex test.

I checked the coffee and hot water machines then cleared and wiped off the tables as quietly as possible. It was evident Clint was a man used to waiting, and it occurred to me that was part of his job: hurry up and wait.

"That's all I can think of. My friends, work friends, family." Erin tapped the pen against the side of her head. "I'm trying to remember if there have been any repair people, but no, not in the last month. So I guess that's it." She slid the paper and pen to her right, toward Clint.

Clint read over the names. "Looks like I know most of the folks. Do you have phone numbers for your school friends?" He handed it back to Erin.

Erin pulled out her cell phone. "Give me a minute; they're in my contacts." She worked for a while, looking up numbers then jotting them under the names they belonged with. When she finished she handed the list back to Clint. "Anything else?" she asked.

Clint shook his head. "Not for right now. It looks like I got plenty to keep me busy." He headed to the door. "Call me if you think of anyone else, Erin."

"I will."

We said our good-byes and he left.

"Cami, I almost fainted when I realized my missing knife had ended up in Jerrell Powers's back. What are the chances?"

I had wondered the same thing myself. "Do you want to get a bite to eat?"

"Thanks, but it has been such a long week, I just want to go home, sit on the couch with a bowl of popcorn and a good book, and basically vegetate until bedtime."

"That sounds very tempting. I think I'll go home and do the same thing."

"So you're not going to tell me what Pamela and her sister were doing here."

"It was no big deal, really. Lauren had given some of Jerrell's things to May without Pam's knowledge and she was upset."

"So they came here to hash it out?"

I didn't want to tell Erin I was spying on Pamela's house. "Pam stopped by first, then Lauren came to town to surprise her and found out she was here. Everything's fine."

"If you say so. The less I have to do with Pamela, the less I will be reminded of Jerrell Powers and his evil ways."

**12**

There seemed to be no real rhyme or reason to retail sales, and Saturday was an unusually busy morning. People not only browsed, they bought. As morning turned into afternoon, I wondered if I'd be able to break away for Jerrell Powers's burial service. I considered asking Dad to cover for me, but would never be able to explain why I needed his help. Pinky's business was slower than mine, and at 1:50 I asked if it'd be all right with her if I ran an errand.

"You go right ahead. As long as you're not going to McDonald's for a cup of coffee."

I giggled. "I would never tell you if I did."

Pinky snapped her towel and told me to take off. I had worn a longish black tweed skirt and boots, and with my medium-weight black coat, and the hat and gloves I'd left in my car, I figured I'd be warm enough at the cemetery. I drove the half mile west of town and arrived with only a minute to spare. My car was the fourth one in line when I parked behind an SUV.

It felt unreal joining the small group—Pamela, Lauren, a man wearing a clerical collar and holding a Bible, and another man dressed in black from head to toe, who I presumed was from the funeral home. Missing were May and her daughter, which did not surprise me. Pam gave me a hug and told me how glad she was I had come. And in some ironic way, it seemed fitting, since I was the one who'd found his body, I should be there.

The minister was brief, giving Pam some words of encouragement. Then Pam said a few things before she broke down. The minister was reading the committal words, "Ashes to ashes, dust to dust," when I noticed something move from behind a tree forty or so feet away. First a hand reached around the side of the tree, and then a man's head poked out from behind it. He was tall and had on a black stocking cap and sunglasses. Were my eyes playing tricks on me or was it the lanky guy? I looked around for a bicycle, but didn't spot one.

The last thing I wanted to do was create a scene, so I tried to calculate how much longer the minister would be, and if the man behind the tree would take off before he'd finished. When he caught me looking at him, he jerked his head back behind the tree. What in the world was going on with that man? It was getting creepier by the day. It was one thing to be skulking around town, and another to be hiding behind a tree watching a few people gathered around a coffin at a cemetery on a breezy Saturday afternoon in October.

I missed what the minister said until I heard, "Amen."

Apparently the lanky guy heard it, too, and surmised it was his cue to take off. At the risk of being rude, I said, "Excuse me," and went jogging toward him, at a snail's pace compared to his sprint. My skirt and boots may have slowed me down a bit, but even if I had been wearing athletic wear, like he was, it wouldn't have made much difference.

"Hey, come back here! I need to talk to you." But he didn't slow down or even turn around to see who was yelling at him. He dipped behind another gigantic oak tree some fifty or sixty yards ahead then came out riding his bike and headed across the cemetery lawn until he hit the gravel drive that led to a larger gravel rural road.

I'd left my cell phone in the car and jogged back to get it to dial for help, then decided it was best to follow the guy to see where he went rather than call Brooks Landing PD. I looked over at the four burial attendees, who all had their mouths open with various looks of surprise on their faces. It would have been comical under different circumstances, and I wasn't sure how to explain what I was doing, or why, so I called out, "Sorry, I'll be back."

I climbed into my car and flew out of the graveyard as if I were being chased by ghosts. It was more like I was in search of someone who acted like a spy or some sort of secret agent. Maybe that was it. Was I being followed after all? As I drove down the county road, I realized that didn't make sense. I had arrived at the cemetery with only a minute before the service was to start. He would have had to be very close behind me to get to where he was standing a few minutes later. It was remotely possible he just happened to be at the rural cemetery. But why was he hiding behind a tree? That was one of the key questions in the whole matter.

It seemed he had disappeared again. Where in heaven's name had he gone to this time? I passed cornfields that still had crops and some pastures with hills and valleys and trees, but no obvious hiding places. The man may have lived in the immediate area, for all I knew, and happened to be riding by when he spotted the gathering in the cemetery and stopped to check it out. Was it all one big twist of fate? I didn't believe that for a minute, but couldn't imagine what was really going on with him and his random appearances. Golly.

I called the police department and relayed what had happened, and the woman on the other end told me she'd alert the on-duty officers. I thanked her then drove to the next driveway, turned around, and went back to the group who was waiting at Jerrell Powers's grave.

The whole thing was too crazy to share with the four of them, so I simply said, "I thought it was an old friend of mine, but it turns out it wasn't." Pam was the only one who nodded. It was clear from her grief-struck, tearstained face that she had other things on her mind than trying to process my wacky behavior.

When I got back to the shops, I managed to avoid telling Pinky where I'd been for over thirty minutes. I quietly made a phone call at three o'clock to the Brooks Landing Police Department and asked if they'd had any luck tracking down the tall man whose identity was unknown. It was

Mark's weekend off and I knew he had gone up north that morning for some end-of-season trout fishing with a buddy. I asked if Clint was available. The same woman I'd met, Margaret, said he was out on a call and she'd have him call me back. "That's all right. I can talk to him Monday," I told her.

My parents had invited me over for a light supper—just the three of us—and I was relieved when it was finally quitting time.

"Want to do something tonight?" Pinky asked.

"I'm Mom's and Dad's entertainment for the evening. At least that's the way Dad put it when he asked me over."

"You're lucky to have them. You know that, don't you?"

"Of course. How about you, what are your plans?"

"Nothing, really. I may stop by Erin's on the way home."

I slapped my side. "Dang, I meant to call her today. After her shock last night, I'm surprised she didn't stop in to talk about her knife being the you-know-what."

Pinky nodded. "Erin did call earlier. It must have been when you were shopping." I don't know how she had arrived at that conclusion, but I didn't correct her.

"How is she doing, anyhow?"

Pinky hitched a shoulder up and down. "You know Erin. Sometimes she sounds sort of flip about things when she doesn't really mean to be."

"Yeah, she gets defensive. Like if she admits to feeling bad about something, she might appear to be weak. We know that under that tough exterior lies a soft heart."

"Of gold," Pinky added. "So give me a call if you get done early at your parents' house and want to get together."

"Will do. Tell Erin to hang in there."

"Okeydokey."

It was a treat walking into my parents' house, the one I grew up in, and smelling the tantalizing aroma of the marinara sauce simmering on the stove. Their definition of "light supper" was not the same as mine. I'd say a salad was more on the light side, but I loved pasta and garlic bread, so who was I to argue?

It was good to share a meal with Mom and Dad. Just the three of us. Dad was less animated, and more influenced by Mom's calming presence.

"Cami, our friends have been calling us since that article Sandy wrote up about you and the whole murder case came out," Mom said.

I had avoided reading it, except what Clint had pointed out when he'd stopped me. "Sorry to bring you into all that. You've got enough going on."

Dad reached over and put his hand on mine. "Don't you worry your pretty little self about that. We get by just fine. Right, Mother?"

Mom gave him her sweet, loving smile, the one I loved best. "Right, Father."

Dad got up from the dining room table and walked into the living room. He came back a minute later with a copy of the local newspaper. "What concerns us most is how you're doing. According to this, it sounds like you're being looked at by the police." He set the paper on the table next to me. Both Jerrell Powers's and Benjamin Arnold's mug shots were included in the article.

I picked it up, and for the first time was able to study the image of the man I had found dead on a park bench. "That is uncanny."

"What is?" Mom asked.

I hadn't realized I'd said the words out loud. "Um, well, um . . . I've seen a man around town who looks a lot like Jerrell Powers, but I know for sure it can't be him."

"Not everyone looks like his picture, you know. If you'd take a look at my driver's license, you'd know what I'm talking about."

It broke the moment and I smiled. "Dad, ninety-nine percent of people do not look like their driver's license photo."

"Well, your mother is in the one percent who does." He ran his hand from her cheek to under her chin and held it. "How could this beauty look bad in any picture?"

He had a point. Mom grabbed his hand and squeezed. "Flattery will get you just about anywhere, as you well know, Ed, but let's not go overboard."

They held hands and snickered. I stood up and started clearing the dishes.

"We'll do that," Mom said.

"You cooked. Cleaning up is the least I can do." Plus it would give me some thinking time.

After I'd finished the dishes, I found the newspaper again, which Dad had moved back to the living room, and took another look at Jerrell Powers's photo. "Can I borrow your paper? I haven't read the article yet."

Dad's eyebrows drew together. "You haven't? Sure, go ahead and take it."

I hugged Dad first then Mom. "Thanks for the wonderful meal."

"Anytime, sweetie. Come again soon," Mom said.

It was early, but I wanted to go home more than I wanted to get together with my friends. I needed to process why the lanky guy looked so much like Jerrell Powers, and I was afraid I'd spill the beans about being at his burial and chasing after a mystery man who had been hiding behind a tree at the cemetery. I would tell Pinky and Erin eventually, of course, but Erin especially did not need to hear about it until things settled down.

I had taken to doing a visual search of all the side streets whenever I drove and probably looked like a big chicken or turkey with my head bobbing in and out as I did so. I couldn't help myself; I had become obsessed with a lanky guy who was almost as fast on foot as he was on a bicycle.

After I parked in my garage, I walked to the house still on guard. I'd started carrying Mace when I went on walks during my Washington, D.C., days. Since my park adventure, and not knowing who had killed Jerrell Powers, I'd kept it handy in my pocket in case I found myself in a situation with potential danger. Even though I saw no sign of anybody in the alley or by my house, I pulled it out of my pocket so I was armed and ready.

I let myself in the back door as the little bird in the clock cuckooed eight times. It struck me that that was what had happened to me: I'd gone completely cuckoo in one short—make that long—week. I took off my coat and hung it in the front closet then found the newspaper in my large handbag. I carried it to the kitchen table and turned on the swag light that hung low over the center of it.

I looked from Jerrell Powers's mug shot to Benjamin Arnold's. They shared similar-looking features, like the guys at the halfway house had said: long, straight nose and high cheekbones. Jerrell looked friendlier than Benjamin, whose eyes were somewhat squinted and lips were pursed. Jerrell's hair was dark and cut fairly short. Benjamin's was reddish auburn, long and scraggly. Jerrell had a lean face; Benjamin's was fuller. I stared at the photos for a minute then went in search of scissors and a fine-line Sharpie pen. I found them in my office desk drawer.

Back at the table, I cut out both pictures and laid them on the table. I took the Sharpie and drew a pair of Buddy Holly–style glasses on Jerrell Powers. "Oh, my gosh, he could be the lanky guy." I picked my cell phone out of my pocket, found Pamela Hemley's number in the contacts, and called her.

"Hello?" Pam sounded wary, but at least she'd answered.

"Pam, it's Camryn. How are you holding up?"

"I'll be okay. Lauren's staying overnight tonight, so that'll help."

"Good. It was a nice service today."

"It was small, but Jerrell didn't have many friends and only one daughter. Lauren invited May, but I don't know if she told her daughter or not."

"What about Jerrell's parents, or other family?"

"He was an only child. His parents adopted him when they were older, and they were both dead before I met him."

"No aunts, uncles, cousins?"

"Not that I know of. I guess I should have found that out so I could let them know about what happened—" Pam stopped talking when the sobs started.

"I'll let you go, but I wanted you to know that I thought it was a nice service today, and I hope my rushing off like that didn't cause too much commotion."

"That's okay. Lauren thought maybe it was a boyfriend you'd had a spat with and were trying to work things out."

"It was something like that. Good night, Pam."

"'Night."

I hung up with new information. Jerrell had been an only child and may or may not have had cousins. Say he'd had a cousin who looked just like him. Why would that person show up in Brooks Landing? To pick up where Jerrell left off, committing crimes and taking advantage of a woman like Pamela?

After another look at Jerrell sporting the Buddy Holly glasses, I focused on Benjamin Arnold's mug shot. I'd seen those few pictures of him when he was younger and a little thinner. The guy at the halfway house had said he'd lost weight because he didn't like the food there. I sat back down at the table and when I picked up Arnold's photo there was a penny underneath it. *Where did that come from?* I raised my eyes heavenward.

I'm not sure what gave me the idea, but I sat down with my Sharpie pen and started working. I drew a line down each of Arnold's cheeks to cut out some of the fullness. Then I shaded his hair, dotted in some facial hair, and added the Buddy Holly glasses. The likeness to the lanky guy was striking and had me out of my chair and on my feet in a flash. When my cell phone rang, I think my whole body lifted from the ground.

"Hello?"

"Cam—uh—ryn, it's Clint."

"Oh, Clint, where are you?"

"Why do you ask?"

I looked down at my sketch. "Do you mind stopping by my house, or are you tied up with something?"

"No, I can come over. Are you okay?" Clint sounded concerned.

"I'm okay, but hurry."

Good timing, Assistant Chief Lonsbury. What would he say when he saw the alterations I'd made to Arnold's picture? I considered brewing a small pot of coffee, but then I'd have to contend with loud drinking noises making it hard for me to concentrate. Clint arrived five or six minutes later.

I opened the door to a serious, almost brooding assistant chief in blue jeans and a quilted flannel jacket. "Thanks for coming. I have something to show you."

"You're sure you're okay?"

"Yes, come into the kitchen."

He followed me and watched when I pointed at the newspaper photos of Powers and Arnold. He picked up the one of Powers and stared at it.

"That's why the tall, lanky guy looks so familiar to me. He could be Jerrell Powers's twin," I said.

Clint frowned. "According to his records, he's an only child."

"Pamela Hemley just told me that." I picked up Arnold's photo and handed it to him. "Check this out."

"My God. He looks just like Jerrell Powers."

"I'd be willing to bet he is the elusive bike rider I keep seeing."

Clint turned to me. "Are you saying you think Benjamin

Arnold has been hiding right under our noses the whole time?"

"I don't know about the whole time. The first time I saw his face was Tuesday night at Sherman's Bar and Grill. If he was the one who crashed in the back alley here, then he's been here since at least Monday."

Clint nodded. "My prime suspect. The thing that doesn't wash is why he's still hanging around town now that the dirty work has been done. Or why he altered his appearance to look like the man he killed."

"It doesn't make sense to me, either. Part of it just happened when he lost weight. They have similar features. How tall is Benjamin Arnold?"

"Six-one."

"And Jerrell Powers?"

"Six-one."

"That fits. And I'd say that is about the height of the tall, lanky rider." I took a quick breath. "And something happened again today."

Clint narrowed his eyes on me. "Yes, that's why I called you in the first place. I was out on interviews all day and I'd just read the report from my staff when I got back to the office. So let me ask you, first, what in tarnation were you doing at Jerrell Powers's burial service? And second, why would you pursue someone who may be armed and dangerous?"

I hadn't considered the armed and dangerous part. "To answer your first question, I felt sorry for Pamela not having much support. I know Jerrell was a scoundrel, but she loved him anyway. And the second question . . . well, maybe I shouldn't have followed him, but I thought he might live in the area and we could find out who he was."

When Clint put his hands on my shoulders and held them firmly, I felt like I had as a little girl the few times I'd been really naughty and my dad had done the same thing. "Camryn, we've been through this before. Leave police business to the professionals who know what they are doing and are equipped to deal with all kinds of situations that may arise. You can't run willy-nilly after this unknown person. What if he had turned and come after you?"

"I didn't exactly run willy-nilly, whatever that means. I can't even run regularly very well, if you really must know. And if he'd come after me, and seemed threatening, I'd have given him a shot of Mace in his face."

He jerked his head. "Mace? You mean pepper spray?"

The friend in Washington who'd given it to me called it Mace. "Yes."

"Are you trained to use that?"

"What do you mean?"

"You know, have you taken a self-defense class?"

I shook my head. I didn't know there were classes that taught Mace-spraying techniques.

"Then have you at least given yourself a little shot to see what would happen, how you would react if you accidentally got a blast of it when you were aiming at someone else? Like if the nozzle got turned the other way, or if the wind blew it back in your face?"

"Um, well, no."

"I'd recommend it, if you've got someone around to help you in case you have a bad reaction. The next time we have defense training for our officers it might be a good idea for you to sit in. At the PD we use Freeze Plus P. Nasty stuff, but if you get a dose of it, you've got to be able to work through it with your skin burning, your eyes burning and impossible to keep open, and your nose running."

"Okay." Life was humbling at times.

"And don't be experimenting when you're all alone. Some people have a negative respiratory reaction and have trouble breathing."

Very humbling. Maybe I would consider using other self-defense methods instead. Brooks Landing Community Education offered karate classes.

"Getting back to the possibility that Ben Arnold may be in town, I'm going to issue an all-points bulletin alerting both the city and the county. Can I take your newspaper drawings?"

I nodded.

"If this is the way he looks, I'll ask Buffalo County to generate a computer sketch we can circulate. And this saves you a trip over there to work with their artist. Now that we know who we are most likely looking for, it shouldn't take long to flush him out."

"If I didn't scare him away this afternoon," I said.

"There is that possibility. Since he's usually traveling by bike, there's a strong chance he doesn't have a car. I'll contact the surrounding counties and ask them to be on the lookout for him. In the meantime, are you remembering to keep your doors locked?"

"Yes."

"Good." He glanced at his watch. "And if you see him again, what is the first thing you're going to do?"

"Call the police station?"

"Dial nine-one-one, and then call me pronto after that."

"Okay." I certainly planned to do as Clint ordered but would soon discover the true meaning behind that phrase regarding "the best-laid plans."

Two days later, on Monday morning, my three new party-planning friends came into the coffee shop, and then poked their heads in Curio Finds.

"Camryn, hi!" Tara's voice startled me.

I turned and smiled at the women. "Good morning."

"We can hardly wait for the party Friday night."

"Did you decide if you're wearing a costume? It's perfectly all right if you don't," Heather said.

"Yes, I think that would be fun. It's been a while."

"Oh, good. And do you need a ride?" Emily asked.

"No, that's not necessary, but I do need the address and a phone number."

Tara looked at Heather. "Oh, my gosh, did you forget to send her an invitation?"

"I'm so sorry. I thought you said you were going to drop it off for her here."

Tara hit her forehead with the heel of her hand. "I totally spaced out on that. I am sooo sorry, Camryn. I'll run right home and get you a copy."

"No, really, you don't have to make a special trip. Anytime before Friday is fine."

"Okay, we'll bring it by tomorrow after our workout. I'm so embarrassed we forgot to get that to you."

"Not to worry." My shop phone rang. "Excuse me. See you girls tomorrow."

They all waved and said thanks for the umpteenth time.

................

Erin stopped in at the coffee shop after school, then she and Pinky marched in to Curio Finds looking as stern as I'd ever seen either of them.

"What's going on?" I said.

"That's what we'd like to know," Erin said.

"What did I do this time?"

"You went to Jerrell Powers's burial service. I mean really, Cami," Pinky said.

"You have been doing the craziest things. Besides that, you accepted an invitation to a party with people you don't know, you go running after strange men—"

"Erin, that might not be so crazy after all. We keep hearing how we're not getting any younger," Pinky said.

Erin reached over and gave her a mild slap on the arm. "It's crazy behavior for Cami."

"That's true," Pinky said.

"Getting back to the burial. What were you thinking?" Erin was tenacious at times, probably a plus in her chosen career.

"I wish people would quit tattling about every little thing I do."

"*Little?*" Erin said.

"I didn't mean it like that. Okay, I went because I felt sorry for Pamela having no support from friends or family. I'm glad I went, for her. And her sister was there, too, and I know it took a lot for her to be there."

"Lauren was probably glad to be there so she could say 'good riddance,'" Erin said.

"Erin, I think you should be careful about what you say. The wrong person could get the wrong idea."

"What do you mean?"

"You know, about the knife."

"Cami Brooks, I cannot believe you just said that. Take it back." Erin took a step away from me and crossed her arms on her chest.

"Okay, that wasn't very sensitive, but it's true."

"Like who are you talking about?"

"Like Clint. He's investigating the murder. I think he's talking to everyone who you listed as being at your house, thinking one of them stole your knife, so he can clear you. I don't think it's smart to keep spouting off about how you—or someone else, like Lauren—is glad Jerrell Powers is dead."

Erin took in a loud breath through her nose then released it. She looked at Pinky. "What do you think, Pinky?"

Pinky shrugged. "Cami has a point. Why give anyone fuel for the fire? Until they find out who did it, it wouldn't hurt for any of us to keep kind of a low profile."

I raised my hands for their attention. "And what I wanted to tell you is there is a possibility that Benjamin Arnold is in town."

"The guy who threatened Jerrell Powers at the halfway house?" Erin said.

"He's the one. And the other possibility is that he's the tall dark stranger who hides behind Buddy Holly glasses and keeps turning up here and there, including at the cemetery on Saturday. I ran after him before I knew who he might be."

"Holy moly, Mark didn't tell me that part," Pinky said. I figured Mark had been her informant; he usually was. She took my hand and led me into her shop with Erin close behind. "We need to sit down and talk about this."

We took chairs at a table and each of us looked at the other for a minute or two before Erin broke the silence. "That's what I'm talking about, Cami. You have been doing the craziest things lately. No offense, but I think living in Washington did something to you."

"You're right, but let's not get into that right now, or my seemingly unusual behavior. The police are on the lookout for Benjamin Arnold. Clint has alerted area police departments. Arnold may have taken off for parts unknown after I followed him. But Clint thinks he'll turn up eventually."

Pinky looked at Erin. "Did you notice Cami said Clint's name twice in, like, three sentences?"

I rolled my eyes. "Oh, brother."

"This whole investigation can't be over fast enough. I just want to get back to the way things were in our old, simple lives," Erin said.

Pinky nodded. "I'm a little freaked out about Benjamin Arnold being in town. What would he be doing hanging around now, since Jerrell Powers is dead?"

We were quiet for a while, then Erin changed the subject. "Pinky tells me you insist on going to that Halloween party on Friday night."

I had dug myself in too deep to get out of it. "I'm not sure about 'insist.'"

"You know what I mean. Well, then, maybe you should take Clint with you."

"Clint? You think he'd like dressing up as Marilyn Monroe's leading man?"

"You're wearing your Marilyn costume?" Erin said.

"Holy moly, can you imagine how Clint would look in a tuxedo? Really *scrumptious* eye candy."

"Yes, I am going in costume, Erin. And Pinky, I was being a little sarcastic. I will not be asking Clinton Lonsbury to a Halloween costume party. You guys do not have to worry about me. I will muddle through somehow on my own, and I promise to keep my cell phone with me. If I feel uncomfortable in any way, I'll lock myself in the bathroom and call for help."

Pinky and Erin shook their heads at me. It seemed their silly arguments had dried up, a first for them.

13

My three new friends dropped the invitation off at the shop on Tuesday, which confirmed for me that I was committed to dress up as Marilyn Monroe, show up at the party, do my best to fit in, give my little presentation, and have fun, no matter what. I'd practiced walking around in the high heels in the evenings after work.

On Thursday, I had just gotten home when it struck me that I hadn't locked the shop door. At least I couldn't remember doing it. Pinky had left, and I knew I'd checked her machines, shut off her lights, and locked her door. I'd gone through all the normal closing-up procedures in Curio Finds, but whether I'd locked the door after I stepped outside was a blank. Too many things on my mind had distracted me, was all I could figure.

I drove back downtown and parked in my usual spot in

back of the store out of habit. It would have been smarter to stop at the curb in front of the store. Much smarter, as it turned out. I headed down the dark walkway between our building and the next and almost reached the sidewalk on Central Avenue when a man dressed in black, from his hooded sweatshirt on down, rounded the corner of the shop building and ran smack into me. He grabbed my arms and held on tight. There was enough light from a streetlamp a half block away for me to realize in a split second it was the lanky guy I'd been seeing from a distance for over a week.

My hand was near my pocket and I moved it inside, ready to pull out the canister of Mace, then remembered I'd left it on my dresser at home. Jiminy Cricket, why had I let Clint put the fear of God into me about using the stuff until I'd been properly trained to do so? So what if I accidentally took a small hit of the spray? My attacker was bound to be more incapacitated if he got a full blast to the face.

*"Help."* My voice sounded like it did in bad dreams when I was in trouble: a barely choked-out whisper.

The lanky guy slid one arm behind my back and clamped the other over my mouth. "I'm not going to hurt you; I just need to talk to you. If you scream, I'll have to go and won't be able to do that. Are you going to scream?"

It took me a minute to decide whether I was being gullible or stupid. The Mace wasn't in my pocket, but my keys were. If he tried anything funny, I'd jab him in the neck or face with them. I shook my head no. He slowly lifted his hand away, dropped his arm from my back, and took a step back. My legs had turned to mush and, rather than holding on to the lanky guy, I moved the two feet to the side of the building and leaned against it before I collapsed in a heap at his feet.

"I just stopped by your shop, but it was closed. I sure didn't expect to run into you. You scared me as much as I must have scared you."

"I don't think that's possible." My voice still hadn't gotten up to full volume.

He looked up and down the walkway. "Is there somewhere we can go to talk?"

"Right here is fine." Now that I'd figured out his identity, I was not about to go anywhere with him, never to be heard from again. At least standing where we were someone was bound to drive by and spot us eventually.

"You found Jerrell, and it looks to me like you've been doing some snooping around, trying to find out who killed him," he said.

How was I supposed to respond to that? "What are you talking about?"

"I've seen you at Pamela's house and when you followed your friends. You were even at the cemetery. After you ran after me, I knew it was time we talked."

"Oh."

"Do you have any idea who killed Jerrell?"

"No."

"You're looking at me like you've figured out who I am."

I nodded. There was no reason to tell him a bunch of police departments knew it, too.

"They think I did it. The police."

"Are you saying you didn't?" The longer I stalled, the more likely it was we'd be discovered.

"I'd never kill my brother, or anyone else, either."

Was that what halfway house residents called one another: "brother"? "Jerrell Powers was an only child. And from what I understand, so are you."

"I can't get into all that right now. I wanted to let one person know I'm not guilty of this crime. For once in my life. And I need to find out who killed Jerrell before I turn myself in. With my past, if they nab me, they'll quit looking for the real murderer." He turned his shadowed face and the streetlight gave the side of it a glow. "You seem pretty tight with a couple of the local police officers. They don't have any other suspects yet?"

I shook my head.

"Okay." With that, he turned and ran down the walkway toward where I'd parked. Maybe he'd left his bicycle there, or maybe he was staying at a rental property nearby and was on foot. I couldn't go after him for all kinds of reasons, but the two main ones were Clint would have my hide and I was too scared.

How could I tell Clint and Mark what had happened without them blowing a gasket? The fact that Arnold had not harmed me should count for something. When I trusted my legs to carry me, I walked the few feet to the front of my shop and stopped. I had come back for a reason, and after recovering from the shock of being in the death grip of the Brooks Landing Police Department's public enemy number one, it took me a full minute to remember what it was.

I checked the lock on my shop door. It was secure. I checked Pinky's. Also secure. I checked mine again. Still secure. I had risked life and limb for nothing. But one thing had come out of the whole ordeal. Benjamin Arnold had told me he hadn't killed Jerrell Powers and I believed him. I kept going back to the mysterious snow globes that had appeared and disappeared. One had depicted the murder scene; the other was a close match to what I'd seen on my stroll through the park when I met the police officer and saw the kids playing ball.

Pinky said she'd never seen the lanky guy in either shop. He would have had to have been in there at least four times to leave, then remove, the snow globes. With his criminal background, I had little doubt he could burgle his way in, but what would be the point?

The way he looked when he'd taken off, I didn't think he'd be waiting for me, but I didn't want to take any chances. I called Mark's number and it went straight to voicemail. Was he trying to avoid me? I phoned Clint and he answered right away.

"You're not going to like what just happened."

"How about you spit it out, and I'll decide."

After I'd spit it out for him, he decided he did not like what had happened. In fact, his voice was raised to a near yell when he said, "Where are you?"

"In front of my shop. My car is in the back lot."

"Go in the store, lock the door, and wait for me. I'll get there as quick as I can."

"Okay." I did as Clint had said and left the overhead store lights off. There was decent light with the security one on, and I felt vulnerable enough the way it was. I didn't want to make it any easier for someone to see me inside the store. I went to the back room and hung around there, looking at the boxes of extra merchandise and other things my parents were storing on the shelves.

Clint hadn't said where he was when we talked, but I knew he lived a couple of miles from downtown in a country home on a few acres. If he was there it wouldn't take long to get to the shop. I walked back to the main part of the shop with a box, set it down where I could see the front window from between the shelves, and sat on it. I thought about the fact that Benjamin Arnold had been watching me when I'd gone about my detective work. He'd seen me sitting in my car spying on Pam's house, and doing the same at Erin's.

He was right about being the police department's number one suspect. It still made the most sense to me that he turn himself in to the police and let them sort it all out. Even if he was innocent of the murder, he was guilty of leaving without telling his probation officer where he'd gone to. And if he hadn't come to Brooks Landing to kill Jerrell Powers as he had supposedly threatened to do, why had he come here?

I saw a Ford pickup pull up to the curb and park. Clint jumped out and was at my shop door by the time I stood up. He rapped loudly on the door like he was waking the dead. When I opened it, I had to admit I was relieved he was there. "I drove around the area, including your back parking lot, and there was no sign of him."

"He acts like a ghost the way he disappears, but I can tell you after having his arms wrapped around me that he really is flesh and blood and strong muscles."

Clint's eyes narrowed and he stared at me for a full minute before he spoke. "I'm going to contact all the rental property owners downtown and see if I can find out where in the hell he's hiding out. I'd run his picture in the local paper again, but it doesn't come out until Tuesday. The bad part about having a weekly, instead of a daily, newspaper is when we need to get information out now."

"I guess a lot of folks around here aren't into social media, but you have that computer image of the picture I altered from the Buffalo County Sheriff's Office. Maybe you could get more copies made and distribute them to local businesses and churches in the next couple of days. Someone is bound to have seen him and know where he's staying."

Clint came close to smiling. "You may have something there. I'll get on that first thing in the morning." His serious look returned. "Now tell me everything Arnold did and said to you, as close to word for word as you can remember."

Even though I'd been in a state of intense fear for those few minutes, it seemed like my senses had actually been more acute than normal, and I gave him the entire play-by-play. When Arnold had put his hand over my mouth, the funny detail that came back to me was that it had smelled like soap. More on the antiseptic side, rather than aloe or pine or lavender. At least he had cleaned up before the visit

Clint listened carefully, mostly maintaining a blank expression, but his eyebrows lifted and lowered a few times. "In any case, he hasn't got me convinced. Arnold says he had nothing to do with Jerrell Powers's murder, but he won't come forward, turn himself in. That alone speaks more of his guilt than his innocence."

There was no reason for me to defend Benjamin Arnold to Clint at that point. But there was an important thing Clint seemed to have put out of his mind: the murder weapon had come from Erin Vickerman's house. At least, one that looked like hers that had gone missing. Clint was planning to talk to everyone Erin remembered being at her home in the past month. Pinky had discovered it was missing three or four weeks before. Benjamin Arnold and Jerrell Powers had both been inmates in the halfway house at that time. There was a fairly long list of potential suspects, but unless Arnold was in cahoots with one of the locals, it eliminated him from consideration based on that one piece of evidence alone, as far as I was concerned.

"Let's get you to your car. I'll follow you home and make sure you get in safely."

C lint proved to be Johnny-on-the-spot running multiple copies of the cleaned-up version of the photo I had altered with the black Sharpie. When I got to work on Friday morning, a Brooks Landing police officer had already dropped two copies off and requested that Pinky and I hang them in our shops. Pinky was sitting on a chair behind her counter looking at it. "Morning, Cami. You know what? It's kind of creepy, but this picture of Benjamin Arnold makes him look a lot like Jerrell Powers."

"They do have a very similar look, that's for sure. I have no idea why he'd dye his hair to make himself look like Jerrell Powers, of all people, but maybe he didn't hate him as much as everyone thinks."

"What do you mean?"

"Stay sitting while I tell you what happened last night." But Pinky didn't stay sitting. She jumped up and was on the other side of the counter halfway through my story.

"Cami Brooks, first of all you didn't call when you found Jerrell Powers in the park. Okay, I can sort of get that because it was late at night. But then you get stopped and grabbed by the bad guy the police have been hunting for for two weeks, and you didn't call. And it was early."

"Pinky, as a matter of fact, I did call. First I phoned Mark, right after it happened. And then I tried both you and Erin when I got home. None of you answered. It seems like all three of you are avoiding me, and I can't figure out why."

Pinky's eyes darted to the left. "Nooo, really?" She pulled her cell phone out of her pants pocket and looked at it. "Sorry, Cami, I don't know how I missed the call."

I gave her biceps a squeeze. "It's okay, but now you know I tried to tell you last night. I'm sure Mark's heard all about it by now, and Erin will, too, when school lets out."

Pinky pulled on her headband and adjusted it. "Well, anyway, now that the police are circulating this picture, they'll find Mr. Arnold before long, and you can feel safe again."

I nodded and glanced up at Betty Boop. "Golly, it's time to turn on my lights and open the door."

Pinky handed me a copy of the picture. "They're asking us to hang this up, either in our front window or in some prominent place in our store." I didn't want it in the window and chose to hang it on the front counter.

Mark stopped by before noon. He stuck his thumbs in his service belt and shrugged. "I came by to apologize about last night. I had turned my personal cell off when I was on duty and forgot to turn it back on." He handed me a business card. "Here's my work number. I should have given it to you when this whole thing with Powers started. If you ever need me right away, call that number. I never turn that phone off."

I took the card. "Thanks. It turned out fine last night. And I could have called nine-one-one, too."

Archie Newberry came in a minute later. "Mornin'."

"Archie, long time, no see," I said.

"No, it seems like you've been off somewhere prit' near every day I've been by. And we've been mighty busy trying to get all the autumn tree trimmin' and everything done before the snow flies. Then it will be groomin' trails and clearin' the ice-skatin' rinks and fixin' equipment for the next season." He sat down at the counter and picked up the picture Pinky had been looking at earlier. "Who's this?"

"An updated image of Benjamin Arnold," I said.

Pinky waved the towel she was holding. "I was supposed to hang that up."

"He looks like somebody I've seen before," Archie said.

Mark's ears perked up and he leaned in closer to Archie. "You remember where?"

"Ah, well, let me think." He studied the picture. "He kinda looks like that no-goodnik—that Powers character."

"Is that right?" Mark took another look at the picture. "Yeah, there is some resemblance with the darker hair. Not so sure what the glasses do for him."

"They make him look like a rock-and-roll singer from when I was a kid. A guy named Buddy Holly," Archie said.

"Archie, even us younger people know all about Buddy Holly," I said.

"I suppose. Well, Pinky, if I can get a cup of today's special, I'll be movin' along."

We chatted until Archie left, and then Mark zeroed in on me. "I hear you've got that big party tonight."

Pinky's eyebrows shot up toward the ceiling.

"Don't even try to talk me out of going, Mark."

Mark lifted his hands with his palms toward me. "I wasn't going to. But if things get too wild, give me a call and I'll come rescue you. That's what friends are for."

It was best to be polite. "Thanks, friend, I will put your work cell phone number on speed dial."

As I zipped up the back of my Marilyn Monroe dress, I tried to think of a way to get out of going to the costume party. When my friends had all been so against it, I had dug my heels in, much as I would have done as a teenager. But the die was cast, and I was committed. Plus, it would be beyond rude to think of some excuse not to go. And I'd learned, in my years in the senate office, that the more elaborate the explanation, the more fake the excuse sounded. A man had called me one time to cancel an appointment, saying he'd just broken his ankle and would be laid up for a while. When I happened to run into him a few days later as he was rushing unimpeded down an office corridor, it was pretty obvious he had lied.

I turned my attention back to the costume. Someone had taught me a trick of turning panty hose into vintage-looking nylon stockings with a seam in the back by drawing a black line on them. I had a pair ready for the occasion, and after I'd put them on, I turned in front of the full-length mirror to be sure the lines were straight. Then I put on the shoes and buckled them. I took a final look at my hair and makeup and declared myself presentable.

My parents hadn't seen my costume and asked me to stop by their house on the way to the party. I told them I'd been invited by some new friends I'd met at the coffee shop, but left out that the evening's main attraction was me and my account of a spooky night's walk through Lakeside Park.

I put on a beige thigh-length rain-or-shine coat and dropped the canister of Mace in the pocket. Whether Clint thought I was properly trained in its use or not, it made me feel better. Before I left, I found a small flashlight in a kitchen drawer, turned on the back outside light, then the flashlight, and headed out to the garage, shining the beam around the darker areas. I had started carrying the garage door opener into my house after I'd parked in the garage so I didn't have to punch in the code manually when I needed access. As the door began to open I looked around to be sure the lanky Benjamin Arnold wasn't there to scare the living daylights out of me again.

When I climbed in the car and started the engine, I let out a big sigh of relief then drove to my parents' house wondering how the evening would turn out. I had not a clue I was in for one of the biggest surprises of my life.

"Cami, is that really you?" Tears formed in my mother's eyes as she took in the Marilyn Monroe package I presented.

"Beth, your daughter sure does clean up fine."

"Yes, she does. Turn around, sweetie, let me see how you look." When I did as she asked, Mom went on and on. "You even have seams in your stockings. Where did you ever find those in this day and age?"

. I swished the skirt of my dress for effect. "They actually still sell them, believe it or not. But they're a little too expensive for my taste, plus they seem to get runs pretty easily, so I drew these on a pair of panty hose with a fine-tipped permanent marker."

"How very creative of you." Mom smiled.

"Not me. I didn't come up with the idea. One of my D.C. friends gave me that helpful hint when I complained about ruining another pair of seamed stockings."

Mom moved her head back and forth. "Your hair, your new beauty mark, your dress, your shoes. They are all so authentic looking." She closed in from her admiring distance to an arm's length away from me. "Cami, your eyes, they're *blue*."

"I got a pair of colored contacts to match Marilyn's eyes, which I've read were called cornflower blue."

"Well, glory be, you thought of everything."

"As much as I like your natural emerald color, blue looks good on you, too," Dad said.

"The party is about to start, so I'd best get going." I gave each of my parents a hug. "Have a nice, quiet evening, you two."

Mom looked at Dad like that was the last thing she wanted. I was not about to pry. We said our good nights and I headed off.

Tara and her husband, Jack, lived in a nice development northwest of town. Out of the new habit I'd acquired, I glanced down each side street I crossed, convinced I would see a lanky guy named Benjamin, not Benedict, Arnold riding around like the Wicked Witch of the West in Doro-thy's dream in *The Wizard of Oz*. I smiled at that image.

There were a number of cars lining both sides of the street in front of my new friend's house and along the entire cul-de-sac. My heart started to pitter-patter in anticipation of telling a bunch of strangers about my experience two weeks before. I asked myself for the one-thousandth time how I had ever gotten into such a pickle, and then once again blamed my friends for pushing me into it, however inadvertently. In two or three hours, I would slip away and go back into my own comfort zone where I would get out of my costume and into my robe and bunny slippers.

The neighborhood was filled with strings of orange lights, pumpkins, black cats, skeletons, ghosts. *Starlight, moonlight, I hope to see a ghost tonight. . . .* That little ditty sprang into my mind as it had right before I'd found Jerrell Powers. *No, I really do not want to see a ghost or any other scary creature tonight, except maybe one decked out in a costume.*

Tara had lined her driveway with a number of carved pumpkins, each with a different expression, with candles burning inside. A few smiling ghosts attached to posts were dancing in the cool evening breeze. The house looked friendly enough and some of my anxiety faded.

The sound of voices, singing and laughing, spilled out of the house. As I lifted my hand and extended my finger to ring the bell, the door flew open and a fairy godmother with blue hair answered the door. She jumped up and down, flapping her magic wand, and then gave me a hug and pulled me inside. "Welcome, Camryn, I almost didn't recognize you walking down the driveway, but knew it had to be you because everyone else who RSVP'd is here. You look so beautiful."

"Thank you. So do you, Tara."

"She's here! Camryn Brooks is really here at *our* party." She took my hand and called out to her husband, Jack, and friends Emily and Heather by name. They were the first to join us, then at least thirty people formed a semicircle around us. Emily took my free hand. Heather moved so she was standing behind and between us and put her hand on my waist. I was officially trapped but gave what I hoped was a Monroe-like smile.

It must have worked because someone said, "She looks just like Marilyn Monroe," in a stage whisper. Jack came up to us and welcomed me then stood by his wife and encouraged everyone to go around the room and introduce themselves. Tara finally let go of my hand. It took a few minutes for everyone to tell me their names. And as hard as I tried to remember some of them, most of them were lost on me as soon as the next one was spoken.

Tara picked up my hand again and led me to a pair of decorated tables that were laden with food from every food group, and drinks, both alcoholic and not. "What would you like to drink? Jack loves to find new recipes for a festive, Halloween-themed drink."

"This year it's called a Black Cat, made with blackberry liqueur and juice," Jack said from behind us. "Do you want to try it? It's light on the liqueur and I think you'll like it."

"Okay. Sure, thanks."

Jack dipped a ladle into the punch bowl, poured the mixture into a glass cup, and handed it to me.

Tara gave me a black cocktail napkin. "Just in case." She had obviously noticed the way I walked in my high heels and had her doubts about whether the drink would make its way safely to my mouth.

I smiled and let her lead me around to small groups of people talking and laughing. After a half hour or so of socializing while sipping Jack's tasty concoction and then taking a couple of trips to the food table for shrimp, meatballs simmering in a spicy Korean sauce, pickle and ham and cream cheese roll-ups, meat and cheese pinwheels, a variety of salads, and sweets, Tara took my empty plate and told everyone it was time to hear my account of my nighttime discovery in Lakeside Park.

Tara led me to stand in front of the drinks table and the other guests arranged themselves; some stood while others sat down. I was tempted to begin with "It was a dark and stormy night," as so many scary stories did, but it had been a beautiful evening so that wouldn't have flown anyway. I felt a twinge of guilt sharing my experience because, bad guy or not, Jerrell Powers had been a human being. It struck me that so many people embraced spooky tales, and that they'd chosen me to narrate a real life one at their Halloween party.

I started the account of how I had left my shop late because we'd had a snow globe–making class there and I had forgotten I'd walked to work. It seemed as though the room temperature rose a degree every few minutes as the tension grew, and the bodies threw off more heat as the story progressed. When I reached the part where Jerrell had fallen off the bench and the reason for it was sticking out of his back, one woman let out a shriek and at least half the people in the room jumped—including me.

Tara waved her magic wand at the shrieking woman. "It's okay, Mindy."

There wasn't much to tell after that. I skimmed over the details of how the police and coroner conducted the investigation at the scene. And rather than confess I had stupidly grabbed the knife, I told them if they ever happened upon a crime scene, they should be careful not to touch anything because it would mess with the evidence the police needed to help solve the case.

People swarmed around me with all kinds of questions, most of which I couldn't answer. Some asked me to repeat details and wanted to know how I'd felt, what thoughts had gone through my brain, how I'd processed what had happened. I was about to excuse myself to go in search of a bottle of water when Tara tapped my shoulder. I turned to find a serious expression on her sparkly face.

"Camryn, someone is here to see you. It's Assistant Chief Clinton Lonsbury."

Before I could say "boo," Clint stepped in beside me, locked his arm through mine, and quietly said, "I need you to come with me."

I was mystified and mortified. And totally at a loss as to what was going on. If he was arresting me, he could have waited until there were thirty fewer people around. Then it occurred to me, what if something had happened to my parents? Or one of my friends?

"Tell everyone good night and we'll leave without making a scene."

I was too stunned to do anything else. "Thanks for having me, gotta go. 'Bye."

Clint kept his grip firm and escorted me to the door. Tara

came rushing up with my coat on her arm. "Here you go, Camryn." Clint took the coat from her and stepped back, releasing his hold. "Is it all right to give Camryn a hug?"

Clint must have nodded, because Tara threw her arms around me for a quick squeeze. "Thanks so much for coming. It was our best party ever." Emily and Heather joined us and each gave me a hug, then Clint helped me into my coat and we left with a roomful of people calling out their thanks and good-byes.

"Are you going to tell me what this is all about?"

"Yes, very soon."

"Why not now? Am I going to jail for a crime I didn't commit?"

"No."

"Well, that's a relief anyway. My car is right over there." The high heels made it tough for me to keep up with his pace, even with his arm around me, and I stumbled. He tightened his hold.

He leaned his head in closer to mine. "We'll worry about your car later. Do you need me to carry you?"

"No, I can walk just fine if you'd slow down." Amazingly, he did. "Clint, put me out of my misery and tell me what is going on."

"You'll know in a few minutes. No more talking until then."

He walked me to his pickup, opened the passenger door, and helped me in. At least it wasn't into the backseat of his police car. It must be something serious for him to drag me out of a party, and then not tell me what had happened. Maybe Benjamin Arnold had been found, dead or alive, and he needed me to identify him. What was it that couldn't wait until I'd gotten home in an hour or two? I was about to break the silence, despite his warning, when he pulled into Erin's driveway. It looked like there was a lamp on inside, but otherwise it was deserted.

"Did something happen to Erin?"

"Erin's fine. Let's go inside and she'll tell you why she asked me to pick you up and bring you here."

"Her mom—did something happen to her?"

Clint didn't answer as we got out of the car and walked up to the front door. I waited while he rang the doorbell. Erin opened it a second later, and then all hell broke loose. Lights came on in the large living room, revealing a big group of people. My friends and family. And they all started singing "Happy Birthday."

I'm sure I stood there with my mouth gaping open through the entire song. The place was decorated with streamers and balloons and made me feel like a kid again. When they'd finished singing, a few blew on noisemakers.

"You guys, I . . . I . . . don't know what to say." My birthday was the following week, on the twenty-eighth, and I'd never had a surprise party in my life, for any reason.

Pinky had the widest grin on her face of anyone. She wrapped an arm around me and handed me a glass of bubbly. "We never officially welcomed you back to Brooks Landing, and with your birthday coming up, we thought it was the perfect time to celebrate both special occasions."

Erin closed in on my other side and gave my back a few pats. "You are the hardest person in the world to keep a secret from."

"And then when you got asked to that other party on the same night as yours, we almost died," Pinky said.

Erin nodded. "The only thing we could do was tell those three girls what was happening on our end, and that you'd be leaving early."

"And we moved your party to an hour later," Pinky finished.

My parents came up next and each gave me a kiss. That explained the funny look Mom had given Dad earlier. "So you were in on it, too."

They both shrugged. "We didn't want to spoil the surprise," Mom said.

Pinky blew at the pink feathers of the boa scarf she had around her neck. "And then when Jerrell Powers turned up dead, we thought of postponing it until the case was settled; but then we decided that might take a long time and so we said, let's go for it and have one night of fun anyway."

There I was in my Marilyn Monroe getup, holding a champagne flute, surrounded by old friends from high school I hadn't seen in years, my brothers and sisters, my best friends, some of our closer clients, and Clint. And my friends' behavior the past couple of weeks made so much more sense. All the whispering, not including me in their activities, not returning my phone calls.

They weren't shutting me out; they were planning a big celebration for me. I was overcome with emotion, and my eyes filled with tears. Mom pulled out a clean tissue from somewhere on her person and handed it to me. "Thanks."

No one asked me to recap my scary adventure in the park, and I figured Erin and Pinky and Mark had warned the guests ahead of time not to broach the subject, which was more than fine by me. I'd thought Clint's duty had ended after he'd safely delivered me to Erin's, but he hung around and acted like he was enjoying himself, talking to people and eating some of the tasty Mexican cuisine treats they'd had catered by a local restaurant. He even raised his glass of champagne when Erin suggested they toast the "woman of the hour."

Being the center of attention at two parties in one night took a lot of energy, especially with all the things going on in the background with the investigation and Benjamin Arnold hanging around town.

Mark snuck up behind me and put his hands over my eyes as he'd done a hundred times through the years. "Guess who?"

"Superman?"

"Pretty darn close." He removed his hands and moved to face me. "Cami, the way you look tonight almost makes me forget our platonic friendship history." He wore a silly grin.

I gave him a peck on the cheek. "Thanks, Mark, but this Cinderella will be turning in her glass slippers soon, and when you see me tomorrow, I'll be back to small shop worker status."

"Ah, well, I suppose it's for the best. Remember when we kissed that time? How old were we anyway?"

"Seventeen, senior year. A gang of us had gone to the varsity football game, and then over to Pinky's for a party. Someone had the dumb idea of playing spin the bottle. You had to kiss me."

"Don't make it sound like it was a bad thing."

"Of course it wasn't bad. There was just no spark."

"Right. But I'm wondering what it would be like to kiss Marilyn Monroe tonight."

I bopped him on the chest. "You'll have to keep wondering, my friend."

"All right, if you say so."

Archie Newberry joined us. "You sure are spiffed up tonight, Cami. I almost didn't recognize you when you came in. Your ma was the one who told me it was you."

I smiled, hoping I didn't look as bad without my costume on as I was starting to believe. After we'd talked a while, I limped over to a chair by the dining room table and took my weight off my feet, which had likely swollen at least one size. And I didn't even have water retention issues. How women in the old days managed to work all day on their feet in heels at bank or clerk jobs, I would never begin to understand. My back—my whole body—was shouting protests after only a few hours.

Erin and Pinky pulled up chairs next to me. "Mark said we should play spin the bottle after Archie and your family leave," Erin said and laughed.

"Like we did in the old days, since most of our high school friends are here," Pinky added.

"I think Mark was kidding, but don't you dare get any ideas, or I'll go hide. And I'd hate to miss such a fun party." I crossed my leg and bent over to rub my foot.

"Those shoes are super cool, but I was wondering how you could stand wearing them," Pinky said.

"Speaking as one who is vertically challenged, I've been envying Cami all night," Erin said.

"The price we pay for authenticity," I said. I uncrossed and recrossed my legs so I could work on the other foot. "I really appreciate you guys throwing this party. When I walked in the door expecting some kind of bad news and saw everyone, I was touched more than I can ever tell you. It's been the best birthday party that I can remember."

"Sorry we acted so crazy about you going to that other party," Erin said.

"But can you imagine after setting the date for this party and inviting everyone, if we had to uninvite everyone?" Pinky said.

Mark had overheard us talking and walked over. He curled his hands, blew on the tips, and buffed them on his chest as if congratulating himself. "But I came up with a solution. With Clint's help, that is. I told the girls, 'Why can't we fix it so Cami can go to both parties?' So we had our people come an hour later and we told Tara what was going on so when Clint showed up to get you, she wouldn't make a big stink about you leaving."

"I was the only one who almost did that. But then I figured if I was under arrest, I would be in less trouble if I cooperated," I said.

Mark reached over and put his hand on mine. "That is true. Keep that in mind on the very slim chance that happens, Marilyn."

Pinky stood up. "Looks like your sisters are getting ready to take your parents home."

Erin and I got up with her and said our good-byes to my family and Archie and others as they left for home. As midnight rolled around, the only people still there were Pinky, Erin, Mark, Clint, and me. "I'll help you clean up," I said.

Pinky put her hands on my shoulders and steered me toward the door. "You'll do no such thing."

"Not much to do. People pretty much cleaned up them-selves. There's a little food to put away, and I'll throw the dishes in the sink to soak overnight. Not a big deal at all," Erin said as she got my coat out of her front closet.

I gave the three hosts bear hugs and thanked them. "You should not have done this, but I'm really glad you did. You are absolutely right: with all the bad stuff from the last couple of weeks, we needed a night of fun."

"Just what the doctor ordered, as my dad used to say." Erin smiled and raised her eyes to the picture of her father and mother that hung on the wall behind the couch.

Clint, who I'd hardly seen all night, joined us in the entry. "Ready, Marilyn?"

"As ready as I'll ever be."

Mark nudged Clint with his elbow. "Get her home safely, and no good-night kisses unless she says it's okay."

Clint was rendered speechless, as was I. I gave Mark the meanest-looking scowl I was able to muster. He was unre-pentant and grinned then broke into a belly laugh. I would get back at him as soon as was humanly possible. Clint reached for the doorknob, but I got there first and opened the door and stepped out. When my waddle gave me away, Clint slipped a hand around my waist and lifted me slightly. "Why don't you take those things off before you fall and break something?"

"I'll be fine . . . if you keep your arm where it is." Heaven help me, the words were out before I could stop myself. And I didn't even care. I was honestly worried I might fall, but was too stubborn to take my fancy shoes off and go stocking footed. Another bite out of the humble pie I'd been eating big portions of lately.

Clint helped me into his truck and before I fastened my seat belt, I leaned over, unbuckled my shoes, and eased them off. I was hoping to restore some feeling in my toes before I got behind the wheel of my car.

Clint got in the driver's seat and turned on the engine. "I'll give you a ride home and we'll pick up your car in the morning."

"Really, I'm fine to drive. I sipped on a weak drink at Tara's and only had the one glass of champagne at Erin's."

"I know you aren't impaired. It's late and it's dark, especially in your alley. Benjamin Arnold connected with you once, and I'd feel much better if I park in front of your house, where it's lighter, and make sure you get in safely."

Clint was starting to scare me about how dark my backyard was at night. Installing better, brighter security lights was something to check on. "Okay."

The drive home lasted a long four minutes with my solemn, silent chauffeur. He finally spoke when he pulled up to my house and turned off the engine. "Sit there a minute while I take a look around." He got out of his pickup and I undid my seat belt and craned my neck to see where he was going. He cut around the side of my house to the backyard then returned to the truck a few minutes later. He opened the passenger door and offered his hand to help me out. "No sign of anyone hiding out back there, which makes me feel better. I'll walk you in."

"I should be more stable on my feet now," I said and lifted my shoes up as the explanation.

"Good." Clint put his arm through mine anyway and delivered me to the front door. "If you have a few minutes, I'll give you an update on Benjamin Arnold."

"Sure, come on in." I slipped off my coat and hung it in the front closet, then we went into the kitchen. "Would you like anything to drink? Water, anything?"

"No, thanks. It's late so I'll be brief." I sat down at the kitchen table and Clint did the same. "First I stopped in at the hotel, which rents rooms out by the week. Then the two motels. And between two other officers and myself, we talked to just about every rental property owner in the downtown area. And got nothing. There are a few duplex owners who rent out their lower levels, but they are more particular who they rent to, generally speaking. At any rate, that's where we're at."

I nodded. "How about the list of people Erin gave you? The ones who had been at her house in the last month."

"Without going into details about the investigation, I can tell you we've talked to all but a couple. And no luck there, either. We've got to find Benjamin Arnold."

"What if he's not the one who did it?"

"Then we figure out who did. We can't eliminate Arnold until we interview him. If he's got a valid alibi—which I doubt or he would have come forward by now—we can release him to Cottonwood County, since they have a fugitive-from-justice hold on him."

"No word from his parents, either?"

"No, I called them today as well, to let them know their son had changed his appearance somewhat and has been spotted on a few occasions in Brooks Landing. His mother said she couldn't imagine what he'd be doing here, but I didn't get into any of what he'd told you." Clint stood up. "What time should I pick you up tomorrow?"

Something I'd forgotten about? "For what?"

"To get your car."

I put my hands on the table and pushed myself up. "Golly, I must be tired. Does nine forty work?"

He gave a single nod and said, "See you then," and started for the front door.

"Clint." When he turned I noticed the dark circles under his eyes and wondered when he'd last had a good night's sleep. "Thanks. For everything."

With another nod, he went out the door and headed to his truck. I glanced down at the floor and saw a penny lying there. I bent over and picked it up. "All right, there has been plenty of excitement around here lately, so I hope this means things are about to calm down." I carried the penny into the living room and dropped it into the blue and brown ceramic dish on the coffee table with the others I'd found lately.

I plopped down on the couch with hopes of relaxing after one of the most unpredictable evenings of my life. So the reason my friends hadn't wanted me to go to Tara and company's party was because they had planned one for me the same night. I grabbed a pillow, hugged it to my chest, and laughed. At least I wouldn't have to explain to my first hosts why the assistant chief of police had publicly dragged me off in the middle of their celebration. The fact that they knew about it ahead of time eased my embarrassment. And if they never invited me to another party, that was understandable and fine. I'd actually had more fun there than I'd thought I would. Almost everyone was attentive and appreciative and made me feel special. It'd be nice to have more friends, and although their initial interest was because of my park adventure, the three girls had treated me like they genuinely cared.

Of course, what my friends had done for me made me feel

like royalty. The whole time I'd thought they were ignoring me they were gearing up for a big celebration. I'd been wondering if they were covering up their possible involvement in Jerrell Powers's death, and instead it was a surprise for me. Deep in my soul I'd doubted any of them was capable of such a thing, but you heard the same thing from people on the news all the time. "I never would have believed So-and-So would be involved with something like this."

If it wasn't Mark or Erin or Pinky or Benjamin Arnold, did that mean the pendulum of potential guilt swung toward Pamela or Lauren or May? There were two things the killer had to have a connection to: the snow globe–making class and Erin Vickerman's knife. Archie? He hadn't taken the class, but he was at Erin's house on a fairly regular basis. Besides, why would he take one of her knives? He was protective of Erin and wouldn't do anything to implicate her in a crime, especially stealing her knife then using it to kill someone.

I couldn't imagine Pam would have been involved either. She was sincerely broken up by Jerrell's death, further evidenced by her need to give him a decent burial.

My top two suspects, then, were May and Lauren. How either one of them had pulled the whole thing off, then returned to plant and remove suspicious-looking snow globes, was a mystery I couldn't quite solve. I went into the bedroom and breathed a sigh of relief when I unzipped my dress, got out of my costume, and put on my pajamas. The little bird in the living room clock let out a lone "cuckoo," letting me know it was one o'clock in the morning.

I pulled on my pink bunny slippers and smiled. They were silly and not at all my style, but they were from one of my best friends in the world. One who'd thrown a big party in my honor. I cinched the robe's tie on my waist and went into the bathroom to wash off my makeup and brush my teeth, then went back to the couch. I pulled the fuzzy afghan from the back of the couch and tucked it around me as I slid into a reclining position and recapped the evening, thinking about each person I'd met at Tara's and each one who'd been at my birthday party. When I'd mentally gone through the whole group of high school friends, and all our conversations, my mind shifted to my encounter Thursday night and locked on a pressing question. "Where in Brooks Landing are you hiding, Mr. Benjamin Arnold?"

14

I woke up momentarily disoriented while the little cuckoo bird was chirping. When I glanced up at the clock, I saw it was nine o'clock. I had finally relaxed enough to get a good night's sleep and awoke full of energy, ready to tackle the day. I guessed it was because of the relief I'd experienced when I learned the reason for my friends' odd behavior. But had I known how the day's events were all going to shake out, I may have been tempted to lie back down, pull the covers over my head, and stay put.

I had just enough time to shower and dress before Clint was due to pick me up. I'd wait until I got to work to have coffee and a muffin, but drank a big glass of apple juice to quench my thirst and give my body some vitamins and minerals. When I went into the bathroom, I glanced at my Marilyn Monroe hairdo, which, surprisingly, was still in place.

Oh, well, time to wash away the last remnants of Marilyn. It had been fun while it lasted.

I climbed in the warm shower and let the water and shampoo wash away the hairspray. When I finished I wrapped a towel around my body and went to the bedroom closet to pick out an outfit. The days were getting cooler as Halloween approached so I decided on a pair of tan wool pants, a matching silk blouse, and a brown cable cardigan. I laid them on the bed and returned to the bathroom to dry my hair and put on my makeup. I was back to being Camryn Brooks, green eyes, freckles, and all.

I was watching out the front window when Clint pulled up in his police car four minutes early. When I walked out the door, I checked to be sure it was locked, convinced I had acquired an obsessive-compulsive disorder. Clint had gotten out of his car, but when he saw me, he climbed back in.

"Good morning," I said as I settled into the passenger seat.

"Morning," Clint said, as he picked up a coffee cup from the center console and took a loud, slurping sip. He had been fairly decent to me lately, and I did my best not to let the sound grate on my nerves. I could put up with almost anything for a few minutes.

"You know, you would have stolen the show last night, even if it wasn't your birthday party." He turned his head to me then back to the road.

"You mean because of my 'getup'?"

He smiled. "You bear a strong resemblance to Miss Monroe."

"At least I can make myself look like she did when she was all dolled up."

"You looked good last night, but you look better this morning."

My face warmed. "Oh. Thanks. I guess sleeping eight solid hours helps."

Clint looked over at me. "When we locate and apprehend Arnold, that's what I plan to do: hibernate for about twelve hours."

"That'd be good." I'd noticed Clint had been looking more haggard the past week. I should have figured he'd be losing sleep with the extra hours he was working and the stress of having an unsolved murder on his hands.

He pulled to a stop by my car. "Glad to see your car is intact since I was the one who made you leave it here last night."

I opened the door and climbed out. "Thanks for the ride."

"You know what to do if you have a Benjamin Arnold sighting."

"I do." I closed the door and got into my own vehicle. Clint waited until I started the engine before he left. We drove off in separate directions. I fell into what had become my customary procedure on the way to the store, looking down all side streets as I drove past. Maybe I was becoming compulsively obsessed after all.

Pinky was working away, grinding a batch of coffee beans when I arrived. "Hey, pal, all you do is work. And throw super-duper parties."

She stood up straight with her eyes wide open. "Cami, you gave me a start. I didn't hear the door dinger."

"That grinder is loud. Those beans smell really good and remind me I need a cup of coffee."

"Help yourself. Jamaican Blue Mountain on tap. Hey, you caused a stir with that sexy little outfit last night."

"Believe me, I would have changed had I known where Clint was taking me."

"You really were surprised, weren't you?"

I gave her a light hug. "I really was. The best birthday party of my life. But don't tell my parents I said that."

Pinky raised her right hand. "I'm glad it turned out so well, and I promise not to tell your folks."

"Can you keep another secret?"

"It depends." That was true. Pinky tried, but I knew she didn't always keep her lips sealed about confidential matters.

"Guess who wanted to kiss Marilyn Monroe last night?"

"Who?" A couple of her curls broke free from under her headband.

"Mark."

"*Our* Mark?"

"Our Mark."

"Ew. I mean, Mark's a great guy, good-looking, dependable, stable job. But—"

"You don't have to explain. We both love him like a brother, not a boyfriend."

"Exactly. Or else I would have nabbed him years ago."

"No spark."

"No spark."

"I've got a few minutes before I need to open up shop, so I'll take a cup of coffee to my back room to do a little organizing. Some new snow globes came in yesterday, and I need to get them marked and make room on the shelves for them."

"Have fun." She went back to her batch of beans.

I had twelve minutes, and that would give me a jump start on the project before any clients came in. At about five minutes to ten, I was on my way from the back room to use the bathroom when I saw Archie in my shop, setting something on a shelf. I held back and watched, wondering what he was doing. Was there a special snow globe he had his eye on that I could put aside and give him for Christmas? I could only see the back of it, but its shape alerted me that something was wrong. He stared at it for a few seconds, probably until the snow had settled, then picked it up again and put it in his jacket pocket.

I stepped out of the shadows. "Archie?"

His shoulders shot up a few inches and his eyes were wider than Pinky's had been when I'd startled her. His cheek moved back and forth rapidly in a nervous-looking twitch. "Uh—uh—uh—Cami. I didn't know you was here."

"What are you doing?" I spoke the words as casually as possible.

"I'm not stealin' nothin'."

It felt like arrows were shooting through my heart. "Why don't we go into Pinky's shop and get a cup of coffee, and we can talk about the fun party we had last night? I was just going to call Erin to thank her and see if she wanted to come down and join us."

Archie held his hand against his pocket as though he was protecting something precious as we walked side by side. Pinky looked from Archie to me when we came through the archway. "Archie, where'd you come from? Why do you guys have funny looks on your faces?"

I made a "shh" face at her and hoped Archie didn't notice.

"Pinky, can you get Archie a cup of coffee while I turn on my lights and unlock the door?"

Her eyebrows squeezed together. "Uh, sure."

Archie headed to a table and I had my shop open in about thirty seconds. My cell phone was in my pants pocket, but I picked up the shop phone also on the way back to Brew Ha-Ha. Pinky was still behind her counter putting cups and a plate of scones on a tray. I glanced over at Archie and saw him sitting at a table, moving the napkin holder around. I leaned in close to Pinky and whispered, "I'll take that tray. You call Mark and tell him to get over here right away. And Clint, too, but don't let Archie hear you. Go in my shop, if you need to."

Pinky knew me well enough to know I meant serious business and it was not the time to ask questions. She held my eyes with hers then nodded. I carried the treats to Archie's table, unloaded the drinks, and set the plate of scones in front of him. I'd lost my own appetite. I pulled a chair out from the table and sat down.

"I musta had too much to eat last night 'cause I'm not real hungry right about now."

"That's okay, you don't have to eat."

"It was a real nice party, all right. I sure do appreciate bein' with you kids." He fidgeted and kept his hand on his pocket.

"I'm glad you were there to help celebrate." I pointed to the hand that was stuck like glue to his jacket. "Archie, something is bothering you. And I'd say it has to do with whatever you've got in your pocket."

The side of his face twitched. "Well, now, why do you think that?"

I didn't answer right away and the longer I looked at him,

the more he squirmed. I wanted to reach over and touch his free hand, but I wasn't sure how he would react in his nervous state. "Archie, how about you show me what you've got? I know it's a snow globe, but I only saw the back of it, not the scene inside."

He shifted in his chair. "I didn't mean to interfere with your displays or nothin'. I only set it on the shelf for a minute to see how it looked with the others around it."

Was that what had happened the other two times homemade snow globes had appeared and disappeared? Pinky and our off-duty police friend Mark came in quietly and sat at the next table. Archie was looking down at his hand securing the pocket and didn't appear to notice them.

"Well, I was goin' to tell you all what happened, but I didn't know how to without lettin' you down."

My heart pounded so hard against my chest wall, I noticed my blouse was moving from its force. Before Archie said more, Clint walked in. I hadn't heard Pinky's door's bell ding and wondered if both Mark and Clint had come in through my shop door instead. Clint casually pulled out a chair between Archie and me and sat down. My stress level dropped about a hundred points. And then Erin came in. When we caught each other's eyes, I knew Pinky had called her, too, and she was as apprehensive as the rest of us were. Archie's face lifted to Erin, like it always did. She gave off some kind of radar or something that alerted Archie when she was near. He held his free hand out for her and she moved behind him and put her hands on his shoulders.

"I've been keeping a secret for a lotta years," Archie said. *A lot of years?*

Erin gave his shoulders a slight squeeze. "What's that, Archie?"

He reached up and patted one of her hands. "Well, it concerns you mostly, Erin. You see, when I was stationed in 'Nam, I got pretty involved with a special gal over there, and before long, she was in the family way. Then she disappeared. All I was ever able to find out was that her family sent her away, and she had a baby girl who was given up for adoption.

"When I first met you girls in the park all those years ago, and you told me where you were from, I couldn't help but think it was possible you were my daughter. 'Course, I couldn't prove it without a blood test, and didn't want to upset you or your folks, so I never said nothin'. But I always wondered."

Erin's naturally dark complexion paled. We were all looking at her with varying degrees of surprise registered on our faces. It was the very last thing in the world I would have guessed he'd say.

"Oh, Archie, you've always been one of my dearest friends, no matter what." Erin gave his shoulders a final pat and walked over to Pinky's and Mark's table. I think she needed to put a little distance between them to process the bombshell Archie had dropped.

I moved a hair toward Clint. "Clint, before you got here, I think Archie was about to show me the snow globe he's got in his pocket." I looked at Archie and I'm not sure how, but I managed to smile. A little.

Archie stuck his hand in his pocket. He was finally ready to give up the secret object he'd been guarding. Time had stopped and I wondered if it was still Saturday morning. When he pulled out the snow globe of a man appearing to be asleep on a park bench with trees and a streetlamp behind him and a full moon overhead, and set it on the table in front of me, a gasp left my mouth before I was able to stop it. I had suspected that was what he'd been hiding, but it still pulled the ground out from under me all the same. I heard the others make quiet, stunned sounds. Mark, Pinky, and Erin slid their chairs in for a better view. Clint leaned in for a close-up of the snow globe, but didn't touch it. When he leaned back I saw how glum he looked.

"Where'd you get this, Archie?" Clint said.

Archie cleared his throat and scratched his head. "I made it, and it sorta turned out to be a sign of things to come."

"In what way?"

"'Cause of what happened after."

"Why don't you start from the beginning, and walk us through it."

"It goes back to that class the girls had here; you know, the one where that May woman showed you how to make snow globes, snow and all."

None of us would ever forget it as long as we lived.

Archie took a minute before he went on. "Well, I wasn't signed up for the class, but when it got to the time when everyone was decidin' what to use for the inside scene, I started lookin' myself. When I seen that guy sittin' on the park bench among all those little figures, it made me want to make one of them globes for myself. I set the stuff I needed on an empty table in the back here in the coffee shop, and glued the little guy and some trees with the moon behind them in place, then helped myself to some of that magic water. That teacher was so busy she didn't even notice me do that, or when I borrowed one of those glue guns to seal it up."

She wasn't the only one.

"Then I wandered in to look at all the snow globes in Cami's shop, mostly because I'd never really had a good look at them. And to see how the one I'd made compared. I set mine down and started in looking at the others, and then the girls had that little ruckus so I went back to the coffee shop. I was kind of upset, what with that no-goodnik being back in town, and worrying about what he might be up to next. I didn't want nothin' bad to happen to any of you girls.

"So I walked down to the park. That helps me relax some when I get myself all tied up in knots. I was walkin' along the pathway when that no-goodnik himself stepped out in front of me. Of all the people who have no right to be in our fair city. He sorta came out of nowhere. I hardly had a second to wonder what in the heck he was up to when the turkey pulled out this knife and told me to give him my money.

"Well, if it wasn't bad enough that the girls after the class were all in a huff over the guy, but there he was, back to his criminal ways on his first day bein' free, in my park. I told him there was no way in hell I was going to give him nothin' but a black eye maybe.

"He lunged at me and I musta gone into combat mode because the next thing I knew he was on his belly with that knife of his sticking out of his own back. We were right next to a park bench and I hooked my arms under his and managed to pull him up and set him down on it. I backed up and looked at him, thinkin' I should tell somebody, but I didn't want to go to jail. As I stood there, it hit me that the snow globe I'd put together looked just like what I was lookin' at there in the park, for real. I reached in my pocket for it, to have a look for myself, but it wasn't there.

"That's when I remembered where I'd set it down. I high-tailed it back here, not really sure what I was going to do about it, but that's what I did. Then I saw Cami workin' on the computer, and I thought maybe I'd knock on the door. But I couldn't think of what to tell her, of why I was there. I was thinkin' maybe I'd have to stop by in the morning and sneak it out then, when no one was lookin'. About that same minute Cami got up and went back to the bathroom. I figured the front door was locked, but it wasn't so I went in quick. The key was in the lock and I locked the door behind me, out of force of habit, I guess."

"When you were going right out again?" Clint said.

"The only thing I could figure when I thought about it later was when it's dark out especially, I turn the lock, automatic-like."

Clint lifted his hand a little. "So you were in the shop. Then what happened?"

"I went to grab the globe, but I bumped it instead. And then I heard the bathroom door opening—it's got that squeak—so I dropped down and rolled under a shelf. I didn't want to scare Cami, having me standin' there when she thought she was alone. It seemed like I lay there a long time, real still, trying to hold my breath, or breathe real quiet. If she'da known I was there hiding, that would've really scared the daylights out of her. And then I'd have had to tell her why I was hiding, and she'd have had to call the police."

He was right, I would have been scared witless.

Archie went on. "I heard her walking around, and then she set something on a shelf above where I was and my heart was a-poundin' to beat the band. Finally, the lights went out and I heard the lock turn. I lay there a while longer, just to be sure the coast was clear, and then I got out from under the shelf, got my snow globe, and started up breathing regular again. But I had a little dilemma."

"What was that?"

"How to get out and lock the door from the outside when I didn't have a key. But it only took me a minute before I remembered the coffee shop lock was different. I went out that way instead."

"Where'd you go then?" Clint said.

"I headed straight for home. I heard sirens and wondered if they'd be for that no-goodnik, but I figured no one would be in the park 'til morning. I sorta thought I might go there myself and then call the police. I'da never thought Cami would be the one to find him. I wish I coulda saved her from that. I kinda thought since Powers was such a hoodlum it'd blow over pretty fast. But it didn't. It seemed like about everybody in the whole town was up in arms.

"And then I started feelin' more sorry for Cami with people not believin' she'd seen that first snow globe in her shop the night Powers died." Archie set his eyes on Clint. "You sorta thought she was making it all up, putting it there herself to back up her story, trying to convince everyone she'd really seen it after all."

Clint hitched up a shoulder. "Archie, in my job I deal with facts and evidence."

I had to ask. "Archie, what about the second one? The one with the police officer and the kids in the park? You left it here: Pinky and I both saw it. Then I went to the park and saw pretty much the same scene."

"Well, that's why I made that one. A policeman has been in the park a lot since that no-goodnik died there. And kids is always playin' there."

And I'd thought some kind of extrasensory or extraterrestrial thing was going on. "Why did you leave that one here on my shelf?"

"I'm gettin' mighty forgetful. Like the first one, I wanted to see what it looked like sittin' with all the others. Then by the time I'd gotten my coffee, I'd forgot about it 'til later."

"Why didn't you call us in the first place?" Clint said.

Archie moved a shoulder up and down. "I'd been blowing off steam about that character. Who'da believed I just happened to run into him in the park the same night he came back to town? And that I couldn't remember what happened right after he came at me until I saw him lying there on the ground?"

Clint looked around the coffee shop at all of us sitting at the tables. "All your friends would have, Archie."

We nodded and gathered around Archie in support.

# 15

Pinky, Erin, and I all waited until Clint and Mark left with Archie, en route to the police station, before we broke down like babies and cried. A few minutes later, when Pinky had some customers walk in, she did her best to dry her tears and pull herself together.

"When that Benjamin Arnold showed up I thought for sure he was the one who did it," Erin said.

"Except for the knife part, you mean. Arnold was still in the halfway house when you realized yours had disappeared."

"I know that now. I actually thought maybe someone else had one with similar damage. And either mine had gotten accidentally tossed or it would show up in some odd place in the house someday. That's what must have happened to Pinky's knife. We know she loses things a lot, but I still think it one weird coincidence she's missing the same one as I was."

"That is for sure. The mystery still remains of how Jerrell Powers got ahold of yours. Unless he stole it from your house a couple of years ago when he was helping himself to your clocks."

Erin nodded. "That must have been what happened. My knife could have been missing for two years. Like I said, I never use it."

"So you think Powers may have had it with his things somewhere."

"And must have hidden it before he got caught, yes."

Pinky had finished with her customers and came back to our table. "I cannot begin to believe this. Poor Archie. And Erin, all these years he thought you might have been his daughter."

Erin sniffled. "Archie's a very black-and-white kind of guy. And stubborn. When he gets something in his head, it's about impossible to get it out again. I can't believe he thought he might be my father—"

"Not going to get the blood tests done?" Pinky said.

"No. But I have been thinking for a long time about learning what I can about my biological mother and father. Where they are, if they're still alive."

"Yeah, I probably would, too, if I were you," Pinky said.

A middle-aged couple poked their heads through the archway. "Hi, we'd like to pay for our things," the man said.

I jumped up. "I am so sorry. I didn't hear you in there." I apologized again and asked if they needed help finding anything else. I wondered if anyone else had stopped by during our twenty-minute ordeal with Archie, and the ten or so minutes since.

Pinky had me cover for her at about one o'clock and went over to the police station to see if she could visit Archie. When she got back she told me Archie had been taken to the Buffalo County jail, where he'd stay until he made his first court appearance on Monday. He probably had about a million dollars stashed away after all his years working for the city, and living like a miser. And he had agreed with Clint and Mark that he'd best hire an attorney to represent him.

"And Clint asked if you'd stop over at the PD when you can break away."

"Since this has been about the quietest Saturday we've had for months, I'll go now, if it's okay with you."

"Sure, go. I'll call for help if it gets too crazy." She lifted her hands. "Bad choice of words because I have to believe we're done with crazy for, like, forever."

"Yeah." With a wave, I went to the back room for my coat and walked to the parking lot. It was only six blocks to the police station, but driving saved time. When I climbed into my car, something felt strange, but I wasn't sure what. There was a smell inside, like how a person smells if they've been outside in cool, crisp air. Maybe a window was open a crack. I checked and they were all shut up tight.

I pulled away and when I got to the edge of the parking lot to turn onto First Avenue, a voice spoke from the backseat. I slammed on the brakes and felt something heavy hit the back of my seat. I threw the car in park, opened the door, and jumped out. Benjamin Arnold sat up in the backseat and looked at me through the open door.

"Dang it, Benjamin, what in the world are you doing in my car?"

"I saw the police take that older guy away before. I needed to find out if he's the one."

"There are other ways, normal ways. Like walking into my shop and asking me."

"There always seem to be people around. Is he the one?" he persisted.

"Archie confessed to the crime, yes."

He sucked in a breath and his eyebrows rose above the frames of his glasses. "Then I'm ready to turn myself in to the police."

Clint would surely yell at me for not locking my car up, and he'd probably yell at me for giving his number one bad guy a ride to the station, but that was what I decided to do. "Get in the front seat." When Benjamin opened the backseat door and climbed out, I gave him a quick look-over. "You don't have any weapons on you, do you?"

He held his hands up. "No."

"Okay, let's go, then. And it's better if you wait to tell the police your story."

He walked around the car and got in, then I got back in the driver's seat, drove the short distance, and parked in front of the police station. When I walked in with Benjamin Arnold, Clint was by the front desk, handing some papers to the receptionist. He looked at us, blinked, opened his eyes wider, blinked again, and then straightened up to his full height, which seemed to be about seven feet tall at that moment.

"Benjamin Arnold?" Clint said and the receptionist stood

up, looking prepared to assist with whatever was about to happen.

"That's me."

Clint pointed to the wall a few feet away. "First thing, I need to pat-search you. Put your hands against the wall, and stand with your feet a few feet apart." Clint reached into Benjamin's pockets and pulled out a wallet and a pair of gloves then patted him down. "Let's go to my office." Clint looked at me. "You, too." He held his hand up, indicating that Benjamin was to take the lead. "Down the hall, take a left, and it's the second door on the right."

The three of us filed to the office. All I could think was, if someone had told me I'd been having the weirdest series of dreams in my life and it was time to wake up, I just might have believed him. Nothing since ten o'clock that morning had seemed real.

"Have a seat there." Clint pointed to the chair he wanted Benjamin to sit in. He moved another chair to his side and told me to sit there. When we were all settled, Clint opened the legal pad on his desk to a clean page. "Okay, Mr. Arnold, why don't you start from the time you were released from the halfway house and fill us in on what you've been doing, how you came to Brooks Landing, and where you've been staying the last couple of weeks."

Arnold folded his hands in his lap. "I guess I should go back about six months to when Jerrell and I began to suspect we were brothers."

Clint studied Benjamin. "Explain. I want to hear it from your mouth."

"From the time we met, and this is going to sound hokey, we had this love-hate thing going on between us."

"Love? Really? That's not the way I heard it described."

Benjamin nodded. "We got off on the wrong foot, no doubt about that. Then when we settled down after a while, and tried to get along better, we started noticing things about each other that were familiar. And I started losing weight and we saw more resemblance between us. One of the new guys who got admitted asked if we were brothers. Then we started to wonder if that was maybe true, or what."

"That you and Jerrell Powers were brothers? Why would you think that?"

"We both knew we had been adopted, and both of us were born at Clydesdale General in Clydesdale, Minnesota, one day apart. Okay, now I'll jump ahead. Jerrell knew he was born just before midnight on September eighth. My parents never told me the time I was born, and I never thought to ask. When I did, I found out I was born at three minutes *after* midnight on September ninth. Neither of our parents had been told by the adoption agency we had come from a set of twins. We're fraternal, not identical."

"Then how do you know you are?"

"When I got out, I headed straight to the agency and told them what I suspected. And I signed the form to let my biological parents, and my twin, contact me if they wanted. They wouldn't tell me who had adopted Jerrell, but I already knew that, and I knew from Jerrell that both his adoptive parents had died.

"So I hitchhiked to Brooks Landing to tell Jerrell what I'd found out, and when I got here I found out someone had killed him and you thought I was the one who'd done it."

"Where'd you hear that?"

"At Astrid's Café on Saturday afternoon. One of your police officers was telling the story to a few people. I heard about how Camryn had found Jerrell. I knew I hadn't done it and needed to find out who did. It was too late to tell Jerrell the truth about our birth, but I needed to know the truth about his death."

"According to one of the residents at the halfway house, you said you were going to hunt Jerrell Powers down and take care of him," Clint said.

Benjamin's eyes opened wider. "I didn't say anything like that. I said something to the effect of, 'I'll meet up with you, after I've settled things at the agency.'"

Clint jotted that down and nodded. "That's how rumors get started, and the main reason we were looking for you in the first place." He looked up at Benjamin. "Where have you been staying?"

Benjamin looked at his hands. "I didn't have much money, so I let myself into the Presbyterian church through the basement window at night and slept in the choir loft."

Clint frowned as he wrote that down.

"I slipped up a few times while I was out scouting, and Camryn saw me. And then when I finally decided to tell her who I was, and what I was doing, I went to her shop, but I was a few minutes late and she had already gone home for the day. Then we ran into each other in that alley and I found out my cover was blown anyway." Benjamin dug his hands into his thighs as if to push himself up.

"And you were the one who took that boy's bike and crashed it at Camryn's place?"

Benjamin nodded. "I was going to bring it back that night, but it was gone when I went back for it. I bought my own the next day."

"And the burglary tools that were hanging from the handlebar?"

"I used them to get in the church the first time. After that I left the window unlatched."

"I appreciate you being honest with me. I'm going to give you a piece of advice; whether you take it or not is up to you. It's too late for your brother, but it's not too late for you to start over. You've got parents who love you. It's time to do something positive with your life."

"I've been thinking that same thing the last months since I've been clean. I'm tired of going down the wrong path. It's not getting me anywhere I want to be."

"Your parents will be happy to hear that," I said.

Benjamin nodded. "I've put them through a lot."

Clint put his pen in his pocket. "I could charge you with misdemeanor theft, but you're in enough trouble and it's not worth the court time and fines since the boy got his bike back. I'm going to check with the Presbyterian church, see if they've noticed any damage caused by your visits, or if they want you charged with burglary. I'll leave that up to them. If they don't, you'll be heading back to Cottonwood County for the probation violation."

"I expected that."

"All right, stand up and turn around. You'll be in our county jail, either on burglary charges or until Cottonwood picks you up on their warrant." Clint put handcuffs on him.

Benjamin was cooperative, and Clint escorted him out to his police car with me in tow a minute later.

"Good luck and I hope you do change the course of your life," I said as Benjamin got in the backseat.

He looked at me and nodded. "I am going to try."

16

Pinky, Erin, Mark, and I sat together at a table in Brew Ha-Ha trying to convince ourselves that Archie, our friend since childhood, was really in jail for killing Jerrell Powers.

Mark cleared his throat. "Archie told Clint that he had Powers's wallet at his house, so that sort of sealed the deal."

"He's getting a good defense attorney, so we can be hopeful about that," Pinky said.

"It's really sad that all these years Archie thought of me as his long-lost daughter." Erin swirled a straw around in her drink.

"He was always the most protective of you. You know what I thought for a long time?" I said.

"What?"

"That he felt that way because of all the little children he'd seen in Vietnam, having to go through the war there. He told us that over the years."

"Yeah, that's close to what I thought, too," Erin said.

Mark grinned. "I thought it was because you're such a little pipsqueak."

Erin reached over and gave him a tap on the arm. "Wanna fight?"

Mark laughed, and the rest of us joined in, and then we got quiet again.

"Benjamin Arnold paid the little boy for the use of his bike. And the church didn't press charges so Benjamin Arnold will be on his way to Cottonwood County soon, and out of Brooks Landing for good, I hope," Mark said.

"Except now he found out he's got a niece and an ex-sister-in-law. May," I said.

"But they don't live here in Brooks Landing, so that won't bring Benjamin back to our town," Pinky said.

"True," I said.

Mark took a sip of his coffee then set down the cup. "Visiting hours at the jail are from one to three on Sundays. It'd be nice if we'd go see Archie."

We all agreed to do that.

I reached out and picked up Mark's hand on my left and Erin's hand on my right. "Let's make a pact." Erin and Mark locked their other hands with Pinky's. "We'll do what we can to help Archie get through this whole ordeal. Friends stick together and we all know he would never have hurt Powers unless he was in fear of his life. Each one of us can be a character witness and testify on his behalf. Agreed?"

"Agreed," the four of us said and dropped our joined hands on the table in a united tap to finalize our decision. It was comforting having my friends back like in the old days and I felt a surge of gratitude that left me smiling long after we said our good-byes and headed home.

# SNOW GLOBE–MAKING
# PROJECT AND TIPS

...............

## SUPPLIES

- Snow globe base and dome, or a jar and lid. These may be purchased at craft stores, or online at snow globe–making supply sites. Jars and lids are available at grocery or hardware stores.

- Benzoic acid, available at pharmacies, chemicals stores, or online.

- Scene figurines. There are figurines for sale at craft stores or online. A favorite photo can be laminated and used. A treasured trinket may be the scene of choice.

Select either a glass jar with a lid, or purchase a premade base and globe. Select the figurines of your choice to use in your scene.

Heat approximately five tablespoons of water in the microwave or on the stove top. Heat to just before boiling.

Stir in one gram of benzoic acid to the hot water and allow the acid to dissolve. Cool the mixture to room temperature.

Drop a bead of hot glue onto the lid of your jar, or globe base. Set the figure for the globe onto the glue. Hold the figure until the glue dries and it is secure.

Pour the room temperature benzoic acid solution into the clean jar or globe.

Fill the rest of the jar or globe with room temperature tap water from a measuring cup. This will help prevent over-filling the jar and ruining the benzoic acid solution.

Screw the lid or base, with the figurine glued in place, onto the jar or globe. Seal the jar if necessary with silicon adhesive or hot glue. Apply the adhesive around the lid before attaching it to the jar.

Flip the jar or globe over, so the lid or base is at the bottom. The benzoic acid should have separated from the water creating a snowflake effect.

# WELL-CRAFTED MYSTERIES
## FROM BERKLEY PRIME CRIME

- **Earlene Fowler** Don't miss these Agatha Award–winning quilting mysteries featuring Benni Harper.

- **Monica Ferris** These *USA Today* bestselling Needle-craft Mysteries include free knitting patterns.

- **Laura Childs** Her Scrapbooking Mysteries offer tips to satisfy the most die-hard crafters.

- **Maggie Sefton** These popular Knitting Mysteries come with knitting patterns and recipes.

- **Lucy Lawrence** These brilliant Decoupage Mysteries involve cutouts, glue, and varnish.

- **Elizabeth Lynn Casey** The Southern Sewing Circle Mysteries are filled with friends, southern charm—and murder.

**penguin.com**